Nest of Rakes

Justin Drake enters the world of executive coaching convinced that setting up a practice in his hometown of Bristol will bring riches as well as an opportunity to make the world the better place. But as he delves deeper into a world of corporate shenanigans, murky professional associations, zero hours work and encounters with shysters and radical activists, he discovers that his journey is mired in about-turns and betrayals. Thinking he is the only rake in town, he soon finds that is surrounded by a nest of them, all intent on finding a path to free them from the predations of life in contemporary Britain. Seeking a way out of this tangled web, he succeeds only in dragging his family deeper into the mess he has created. With the threat of destitution ever present, they grow to distrust empty offers of redemption, while there is no possible return to respectability. Luckily their sense of the absurd keeps them going, and comedy provides one way out.

Daniel Doherty: About the author

Daniel Doherty lives in Devon, England, having travelled the world in search of work and himself. This search continues through this novel. Always curious and ever restless, Daniel has written extensively for the sheer enjoyment of it, and also academically. The completion of this first novel is evidence of the fact that eventually – and probably for the first time – Daniel has done what his mother told him to: write a book.

Nest of Rakes:

The Better Bank

Joy and Justin Drake pause for a moment outside the Better Bank, its garish red and white logo emblazoned in three-foot-high letters above the ancient door.

'Aww, this takes me back,' sighs Justin. 'I remember as if it were yesterday, standing on this same spot as a young student, nervously opening my first bank account. It was exhilarating mind, paying in my first grant. Straight out of the bank I was, and into the old-fashioned tobacconist's next door for a tin of Golden Virginia and a pack of Rizla papers. Liquorish of course.'

'Justin, you mention that every time we pass here. Things have moved on. It is 2019, not 1999, when you first fell in love with the place.' Joy shrugs. 'And it is a perpetual tribute to the slavery that funded it. So much of this Bristol old money was earned on the back of black lives that didn't matter. Do you really think us coming here in person is going to increase your chances of getting a loan?'

'Yes, I do, actually,' says Justin, summoning hope in the face of a likely knock back. 'Surely at some level loyalty will be rewarded?'

'Well, we will soon put that theory to the test,' says Joy. 'I have taken the morning off work for this, so...'

'Joy, trust me. This blood-stained bank has seen me through...' Justin says, as he tries his best to ignore the homeless man squatted beneath the cash dispenser, holding out a battered coffee cup.

'Any change for a cup of tea, mate?' interrupts the begging man, holding out his Costa cup, while putting his foot on his skateboard to stop it rolling into the traffic. Justin fumbles in his pocket, spilling some coins into the outstretched cup. 'Sorry, that is all I have on me.'

'Cheers mate,' says the man, returning to fiddle with the wheels of his skateboard with an ancient penknife.

Leaving the sunshine behind to enter inside, they adjust their eyes to the artificial glow of an array of automatic telling machines blinking back at them, inviting them to transact without human contact. In the banking hall, a young man slouches behind a curved metallic podium, a plastic badge on his breast pocket announcing him as Hank Brewer, Customer Services Advisor. Hearing the creaking door, Hank takes his eyes off his smartphone for long enough to say, 'Good morning. You all right?'

'Good morning to you too,' says Justin, dusting fluff off the lapel of his best suit. 'We have an appointment? Justin Drake? For Mr Ted Fear?'

'Oh, I see. Bear with a second please.' Hank puts down his phone, reluctantly, to scroll through the screen perched on his podium. 'Problem with my password,' he tuts. 'Ah yes, there you are. I will need to see your bankcard, please.' Justin pulls out his wallet to retrieve his newly minted Best Bank plastic. Hank keeps his eyes on the screen. 'Okay, that checks,' he says, returning the card. 'I see you have an appointment with our temporary branch manager, Ted Fear? Let me ping him, I'm sure he will come out soon.'

Soon enough, Ted Fear shuffles into the banking hall, offering his hand. 'Welcome Mr and Mrs Drake. Just been looking at your file. Do you mind if I call you Justin and Joy?'

'That is fine, Mr Fear.'

'Oh no, Justin, just call me Ted. We are all on first name terms here nowadays. Very up to the minute. Though I am old school.'

'Which school is that?' asks Joy.

Ted's eyes mist over. 'Oh, you know, old school. That time when bank managers were up there with doctors, lawyers, clergy, professors.

Now we are lumped in with… God knows what. Double-glazing salesmen? But by all means, come into my booth.' They squeeze into a small, glass-fronted office at the rear of the banking hall, hardly large enough to contain all three or them. The Drake's do their best to make themselves comfortable, while Ted plays embarrassedly with his food-stained polythene tie. 'Please excuse me. You might have noticed I am sporting the old Singapore United Bank tie.'

Joy and Justin inspect the neckwear in question more closely, peering to detect the snake logo lurking behind the grime. 'I do have a Better Banking tie, but I am rather afraid that this is the one that jumped out of the wardrobe this morning. And between you and me, I rather like the oriental look.'

Justin squints at the tie. 'Isn't that the Singapore snake? I remember that logo coming in after the Bedminster Bank was taken over, when the snake replaced the old coat of arms? After the Great Crash of 2008, and the break-up of the banks?'

Ted brightens. 'Yes, it is. A snake. I love the Orient. In fact, I go on holiday to Thailand a lot. Have you been?'

'Yes,' says Joy, flatly, her face suggesting that she would rather save holiday conversations for her hairdresser, and not even then, if she can help it.

'Lovely people, the Thai,' says Ted, dreamily. 'Always smiling, not like us miserable Brits. Proper banks too. Real banknotes, very colourful, loads of tellers shifting little paper tickets. A good place for a widower. But enough about me. Though I could do with a holiday right now, come to think of it. Not feeling at all myself today. 'Oh, well,' he sighs, half-heartedly, 'let's get down to business.'

'Yes lets,' says Joy, playing with the Magic Carpet corporate lanyard swinging in front of her fleece. 'I need to be getting back to work as soon as I can.'

'Yes, I quite understand. Do excuse me rambling on. I hope you don't mind if I bring through Dominic Cross from Bournemouth head office? He is honouring us with a visit today. I feel sure he will introduce himself.'

Dominic duly bustles in, all brisk efficiency in a light blue suit that is rather too tight for him. He manoeuvres beside Ted into the last remaining seat, saying, 'good morning everyone. Bit of a squeeze in here. I'm Dominic Cross, Customer Relations Manager – Small Businesses Category – South West Division. You've done well to catch me today. I had a meeting with a major insurer here in Bristol this morning, so luckily I was able to respond to Ted's reach-out to meet you. Not that Ted can't handle such sales meetings himself, goodness no. He has been at the bank forever, haven't you Ted?'

Ted coughs again, his shoulders heaving involuntarily. 'Sorry, I must be going down with something.'

Dominic shuffles his chair, as far as space will permit, to distance himself from Ted's spasm. 'But, now you've met me face-to-face, then any other business that we might do can following this preliminary meeting will be handled on line or through our central call-centre.'

Joy's grimace at the mention of a call centre does not pass unnoticed by Dominic, whose raised eyebrows prompt her to explain herself.

'Oh, nothing,' says Joy, 'It's just that I work at an online distribution centre is all'. She waves her plastic ID on her lanyard at Dominic. 'Magic Carpet? You know? The online company striking fear into Amazon, or so they tell us. And we struggle with our call-centre a lot of the time, as do our customers. It drives them mad. Bot no doubt your call operation is super-efficient though, not like ours.'

Dominic seems irony-proof. 'Oh, we like to think so. But we prefer customers to come to us online nowadays, not voice-to-voice. And we have a chat facility online that can help guide our customers through any frequently asked questions they might have. But seeing as you are here in the flesh, let me continue, going forward. Ted, mind if I start?'

Ted shakes his head, stifling another bout of coughing.

Justin asks, 'but does this mean we cannot just come into the branch? Chat to a human being?'

'I suppose you can just walk in.' Dominic answers, begrudgingly. 'But look around at the empty banking hall. So few people in here, just up-to-the minute cashless transaction machines. Algorithms are really intelligent nowadays. No small talk to waste away your day, no queuing, just straight in. All chances of human room eliminated. And besides, this branch is scheduled into our closures programme this year. It is clicks not bricks nowadays,' Dominic looks pleased with his recital of this catchphrase borrowed from an online webinar, but delivered as though it were his spontaneous own. 'So, as a new customer…'

Justin interrupts, 'but I am not a new customer. I have been banking here at this branch for over twenty years...'

'I understand that, and thanks for the custom,' interrupts Dominic, dismissively. 'But as far as we at Better Bank are concerned, you are a new customer, since our recent rebrand. "Better Bank, Better Now". Better than ever. Isn't that right Ted?'

Ted coughs again, reddening in the face. 'Well yes, I hear from our market research people that customers like it. I was happy with the old title too, but I suppose I have to move with the times,' he says, folding his arms to conceal his Singapore tie,

Dominic scowls quietly at sight of the tail of the snake. 'The whole rebranding strategy is not simply cosmetic. We have re-set the company, zero-based it, and, given that we are starting afresh again, then we wish for all of our customers to feel new and fresh too, even those from the former legacy banks. So for all intents and purposes, we are treating you as a new customer. Hope that makes sense to you. Now, I understand you are looking for loan funding for your existing business?'

'Thank you, yes,' says Justin, trying to sound business-like, 'we are facing an important moment in our financial lives. A tipping point. We want to take our business to... to...'

Dominic helps him out. 'To the next level?'

'Precisely. Thank you. To the next level.'

'Which is?' Dominic prompts, his heavy eyebrows raised in questioning.

Justin scratches around for a response. 'Well, the level above the one we are at right now. Above our current level. Which is not a bad level at all, but we want to be at the next one. The better level. And to get there we need leverage, hopefully from the Better Bank. To tip us over...over... our tipping point.'

Dominic squints at his phone. 'I am looking now at the business plan and cash flow you emailed through to us...'

Justin interrupts. 'But did you not see my record of my banking history as well?'

Dominic looks at his watch, clearly wanting to move the conversation on. 'Yes, I think Ted took a look at that, but as he explained to you earlier, we are now starting with a blank sheet.'

Ted, catching Justin's eye, shakes his head by way of silent apology, allowing Dominic to continue. 'And as a new customer, going forward, we assess your loan worthiness on a credit rating, details of which we cannot disclose. I would say that your score looks barely adequate at the minute I am afraid, no better than that. But that does not preclude you from a loan. So, we have seen your plans going forward. Let us talk about this business you run .... Catalyst Consulting? Experts in executive coaching?

'That is correct,' says Justin, pushing over his cardboard business card, which Dominic places to one side, without sparing it a glance. 'So where do we fit in to the grand scheme of things, business category wise?' asks Justin, distracted by Joy, who is peering at her pulsating phone. Ignoring Justin's prod, she reads a text from her colleague Sharon from Magic Carpet.

'We need you back soon as you can. Where are you?'

Joy frowns, then turns her gaze once more to their interrogator. Dominic clears his throat, oblivious to this interruption. 'Okay, so let me explain the way we are set up. Within the small businesses space, we have a number of categories. These include those professions set up on well-grooved tramlines, such as accounting, or law, or medicine. Beyond the professions, our next category is recognisable small businesses or sole traders running cafés, retail outlets, taxi firms, pet shops, tanning salons, you get the drift. We know that terrain well.' His excitement rises. 'Then there is the more nebulous world of IT starts ups, where online whiz kids with their myriad apps and their disruptive technologies ply their trade. That is my speciality – and then we have....'

Justin looks hopeful. 'Yes? Our category? Consulting, perhaps?'

'No, sorry. It is in the category of "Other."'

'We fall into ... Other?' asks a miffed Joy, staring through the glass wall into the abyss of the banking hall.

'Correct. Other. Massage parlours, charity shops, spiritualist congregations, hypnotherapists, homeopathic doctors, that kind of thing. Believe you me, we have looked into this executive coaching sector extensively, and it is hard to place within any reliable existing category in terms of exposure or business risk. No barriers to entry, lots of different players, multiple conflicting offerings, together with a really high attrition rate in your trade.'

Justin feels the need to correct once more. 'But it is not a trade – it is a profession!'

'Possibly,' says Dominic, 'but an immature one - a relatively new market niche where the customer offer is hard to pin down.'

Justin's face falls. 'But it is a profession. To qualify for this work, I have done all the necessary training, collected the certificates, been assured that I have the necessary aptitude and resilience to see me through start-up. In fact, I have made it through start-up. For over two years now...'

'That may be so,' says Dominic, waving his phone towards his visitors, 'but we at Better Bank like to distinguish between starting up and staying up – two different things.' Once again, he is pleased that a slogan stolen from an online webinar is standing him good stead.

'And that is precisely why we are here – to float us sufficiently at Catalyst to ensure we stay up. Look, it says so in our plan.' Justin reaches for Dominic's screen. 'Can I show the part where..."

Dominic retrieves his phone. 'You say you are visible in the marketplace? But we have looked for you online and could not find you. Have you thought about Search Engine Optimisation?'

'We are not sure if we need or can afford optimisation at this point. Most of our work comes through reference and word of mouth.'

'So, your plan is nicely put together, but not, we are afraid, nicely enough at this point to justify including you as a promising start up going forward.'

Dominic mimics the closing signals that he learned on his "Dealing with Difficult Customers" workshop, folding his arms across his chest. 'Your personal banking is fine, buoyed by Joy's earnings, but you will need to prove that Catalyst is a goer before we invest. Shall we say a review point in nine months' time, to assess progress?'

'But I need the funds for...... training, marketing .... networking...'

Dominic places both hands on the table, palms down. 'Hmmm. From what we see of your accounts you have invested considerably in yourself already. And you are making a tax loss. What you need to do now is get out there and sell – in a crowded market.'

Ted tries hard to show an interest in all this, but then surrenders to a convulsive spasm. He slumps forward in his plastic bucket chair, his face losing all shape.

'Ted?' asks Joy, urgency in her voice.

'Something is wrong,' Ted gasps, grasping his left arm.

'Oh, for goodness sake, Ted, pull yourself together.' mutters Dominic, clearly ready to make his way back to head office.

'No, wait,' says Joy. 'I am a first aider. I think he is having a heart attack.'

'Really?' Dominic puts a hand on Ted's shoulder, willing the healing power of a senior manager's touch to percolate through to his stricken colleague.

'Yes, really.' Joy is all action. 'Call an ambulance. Someone. We need to get him out of this room. Lay him on the floor.' Justin and Joy push aside the desk, trapping Dominic in the corner of the booth, then between them gently steer Ted's shaking body into the empty banking hall.

Hank, alive to this commotion, leaves his podium to peer down at his boss and asks, 'you all right, Ted?'

'What does it look like!' Joy's scorn rocks Hank back on his heels. 'Get an ambulance - now.' Turning her attention back to Ted, she loosens the snake tie that is strangling him, and begins pummelling his chest. Hearing this kerfuffle, the homeless man comes in, clutching his cup, blanket and skateboard. He joins Joy on the floor. 'Here, let me help loosen his clothes. Don't worry! I was a trainee nurse once. Before. I'm Tom. Look, here comes his belt. Now we need to take off his shoes.'

Dominic, now free from the booth, looks in some horror at the sight of the homeless man. 'You cannot be here!' he shouts.

'I'm here to help, mate,' says Tom, scathingly, before returning to assist Joy. With Dom huffing and puffing, and Tom shaping up for a fight, the arrival of paramedics with full resuscitation kit prevents this confrontation escalating into a full-blown bust-up.

With calm precision the paramedics are on the case, alternating mouth to mouth with an application of their defibrillator. After several anxious minutes, the lead paramedic declares, 'I think we are out of danger, now,' as Ted's breathing assuming a semblance of normality. As he and his colleague ease Ted towards the door, Joy and Justin are left in the banking hall with Dominic, who shows Tom the door.

'Thanks for your help,' Dominic breathes at Tom, grudgingly, 'but you are not a customer. I am afraid you will have to leave.'

In the face of this summary dismissal, Tom makes his exit with all the dignity he can muster, saying to Dominic, 'you have no idea, mate. Simply no idea. See you on the outside.'

Joy finds it hard to conceal her disgust at this action. 'There was no need to do that,' she says to Dominic, 'Tom – and yes he does have a name - was really helpful there. He didn't need to help but he did. And knew exactly what to do in a crisis. Unlike you, waving your phone and acting as though you are in charge, while doing nothing. And all you can do by way of gratitude is to show him the door. You have no idea.'

Dominic exudes indignation. 'Maybe it is you that has no idea. We have to put up with his likes every day, begging, and it is no good for our business. No wonder we have so few walk-ins nowadays, with these jokers cluttering up our ATMs. Half of them have homes to go to. It is a scam. Playing on people's good nature. And at least I do not go as far as one of my colleagues, who says it is a shame we cannot put spikes on the pavement, like they do on park benches nowadays to keep the beggars away.'

Joy looks aghast, prompting Dominic to retreat towards the wall.

'Sorry, that was too much. I misspoke. Still in a bit of shock here.'

Dominic picks up Ted's encrusted tie, lying abandoned on the red and white carpet-tiled floor. 'Here – what's your name again?'

'Hank. Hank Brewer, Customer Service Advisor. Part of the Customer Experience Enhancement team.'

'That's right. Of course, I have seen you a few times. Could you get rid of this Singapore Bank tie please? I can't see Ted having much use of it anymore.'

As Hank moves to do his bidding, Joy intervenes. 'No Hank, thank you, but let me. I would like to keep this as a memento. Maybe even give it back to Ted when he is better.'

Dominic shrugs, his attention returning to his buzzing phone. 'Okay you two. Look, I am on this. I had best email HR, tell them about Ted. What a mess. Lucky I was here, with all of this going on, bringing some authority amid all this panic.' He taps on his phone for a minute, and then says, 'as I thought, best to leave this to HR. They know best how to deal with all of this sort of thing. Sickness benefits, arranging cover, all of that tricky stuff.'

Joy's eyebrows speak of disbelief. 'So glad you have so much confidence in HR to sort things out. They are the last people I would turn to in a crisis.'

Dominic shifts his attention from Joy, addressing Justin instead. 'Justin, you are the client here. Putting this drama to one side for a moment, life must go on. And I need to get going. Can I catch you online later about the nine-month review for the loan?'

'Justin, let's just leave this for now.' Joy takes Justin's arm, to steer him away from Dominic. 'This is going nowhere. Let's go outside, make sure Ted is okay.'

Standing by the open ambulance doors, they are comforted to see that Ted is safely stretchered within, and ready to leave for the hospital. Shutting the doors, the lead paramedic turns to thank Joy once more. 'You did a fine job in there. You and your homeless mate did all the right things, caught him just in time. He could easily have died. That doesn't happen too often, someone on site, able to act. You should be feeling really proud of yourselves. Now we need to get Ted to hospital, find out what is going on with this dickey ticker of his.' He gives them a big thumbs up, and they beam farewell in return.

Waving goodbye to the ambulance, they notice that a small crowd has gathered. Joy says, 'did you hear all of that, Tom? You were brilliant in there. Indispensable. And you did not need to help at all, given the way the bank treats you.'

'Thanks Joy,' says a bashful Tom. 'No worries. But this wasn't about banking or bankers. There was a human life at stake. Nothing comes before that. Look, not wishing to be rude, but gotta get back to my station on the pavement. See what this crowd might deliver. You never know.'

'No, don't go not just yet.' Joy raises her voice as she turns to the crowd. 'This man saved a life in there. Please give freely. Come on, get giving.'

Tom holds out his cup, while the crowd huddle around, wanting to hear more of the drama that has just ensued. As the bystanders reach for their change, Dominic charges through the door, but on seeing the crowd clustering around Tom, he draws upon his full authority to announce, 'I am in charge now. Crisis over. Nothing to see here. Please move along now, we have a business to run.'

Leaving lest they be provoked further, Justin steers Joy away to the Costa Coffee shop across the road, before she says anything more to Dominic that might kill their chance of funding forever. They settle by a seat in the cafe the window, still able to see the crowd, who are now beginning to disperse, while Tom returns to sit on the pavement once more, counting his takings.

Joy is the first to break the silence. 'Well, what a drama. I was not expecting all of that when I agreed to come on this financial wild goose chase. Never thought when we sallied forth that we should be saving the near extinct species of the lesser-tied bank manager.'

'Very funny. And no, nor did I. But it was you and Tom that did all the emergency work. I was a useless spare part.'

'Not entirely, assures Joy. 'You were there if we needed you.'

Justin looks doubtful. 'Maybe. But Joy, you were magnificent in there. So cool so in control. I have seen you like that with the kids, in a crisis, but this was different altogether. I was so impressed. You - and Tom, under your direction - saved a human life.'

'That is true. But you know, it is second nature to me. I am not unused to such dramas, back at the distribution centre. We endure many such incidents or near incidents in the course of a week. All those cases stacked high in our warehouse, and the forklift trucks flying around, chasing the clock. We have death on our minds a lot at Magic Carpet. I guess you coaches don't expect death to visit in your daily work.'

'That is true enough,' agrees Justin. 'And if we coaches were faced with such an emergency, then I doubt that we would have the slightest idea what to do. Active listening is not much use when someone is struggling for breath. Come to think of it, that is the nearest I have come to watching someone staring death in the face.'

'Well, at least you cared,' consoles Joy. 'Not sure Dominic was that bothered. It was just an unwanted interruption in his well-oiled day.'

'He was useless, wasn't he? Behind all that braggadocio, I would say he was really scared,' Justin stirred his cup, the froth spilling over the wide rim. 'This coffee is not bad for a coffee chain. I bet the Costa business hasn't been "othered" by the bank.'

'Definitely not. Though mine tastes quite bitter. You know, look at Tom over there, back to begging. It would have been nice to have brought him in here. Should I go get him? He has definitely been "othered" by respectable society, along with immigrants and asylum seekers.'

'That is a nice instinct, Joy. But I am not quite sure it would be the right thing. He has his patch to protect. Might see it as patronising. And you know, when the street people ask for money for coffee it is not really… that. Just a euphemism for other things.'

'I know all that,' sighs Joy, rolling her eyes. 'But he might have liked the gesture. Anyways, he is busy at his station again. Unlike Hank managing reception, back to looking terminally bored, as usual. Or at least looking bored with terminals, which is all he has to keep him company. That, and the rolling news.'

'You all right?' quotes Justin, mimicking Hank's up-speak perfectly. 'No not quite,' says Joy, taking his inquiry seriously. "I just need a moment to let the adrenalin flush from my system.'

Justin places his hand on hers. 'I fear that this might be the end for Ted, and for his beloved job. Sounds like it is all he has got. God, I do hope he gets a good package out of them, once he is discharged.'

'Me too. I fear for Mr Fear.'

'Yep, with his future in the hands of the robotic Dom. How are people like Dominic even allowed to exist? They crush the life out of the Ted's of this world who surely have much left to offer still. I think he might just head off to Thailand forever.'

'Talking of banking - after all of that excitement you still did not get your loan,' says Joy, watching through the window as Tom pulls closer to the wall of the bank, as the rain begins to fall.

'No, I didn't,' replies Justin. 'Dominic's refusal sounded final.'

'What an exercise in futility that was,' says Joy, removing her hand from his. 'Nothing personal, but I'm not sure why I took the morning off. Better things I could have been doing, beyond enduring Dominic and saving the life of his kindly but ineffectual granddad. It got us precisely nowhere, beyond the realisation that we will need to cut back on costs, and fund this white elephant of a consulting company ourselves.'

'Yep, and sorry again to waste your time.' Justin sighs. 'I was forever optimistic, trusting as always, but did not expect that treatment, after all this time. But at least we are not on the streets – literally.'

'Really disappointing. After being with them so long. Better now? They are not better now! Only worse now.' Joys eyes light up. 'I have an idea! We could vandalise that hideous Better Bank logo over the street, do a Banksy-style overnight disfigurement.'

'Loving the fantasy, but I don't think that would end well. Something has to change,' says Justin, shaking his head. 'I cannot continue bumping along the bottom in a saturated marketplace.'

'How come other coaches in your situation are doing okay then?' ask Joy.

'Oh, don't worry, they are struggling too,' says Justin, with a knowing smile. 'Sure, when we meet together at conferences or network meetings my counterparts put a brave face on it, boasting of buoyant current assignments, and of marketing pipelines packed with prospects to come. But my guess is that many of them are dying inside.'

'I see. And are you .... Justin? Are you dying inside?' She places her hand back on top of his.

Justin swallows hard. 'Good question. Yes, a part of me is dying. Maybe it seemed a good idea at the time to go independent. Then I ask myself, maybe it is not the path I have chosen that is at fault. It could well be that I am useless at standing on my own two feet.'

'But you are facing a brutal reality check, though. Maybe this could be the last roll of the dice.' Joy looks at her watch. 'I need to get back to work. And given this morning's abortive outcome, you need to find some work, pronto. Enough of all of this. You get home and prepare for your London trip tomorrow - and don't forget to pick up the kids.'

'Don't worry, I won't. Thanks again for the support – and the life saving. Mine as well as Ted's. I think I might mosey over and thank Tom again.'

'You could join him on the pavement.' Joy gathers up her things. 'Get down to his level. Get a closer sense of what being "othered" really means. Mind out for the spikes though. Dominic might have implanted them by now. Oh, and can you ask Tom for his number? There might be good reasons to keep in touch with him.'

Joy finds her car then heads north to the business park at Aztec West, on the outskirts of the city. As she parks up at her workplace, she is greeted by her friend Sharon, who is just finishing off her customary cigarette break in the Magic Carpet car park, just behind the bike sheds. After the rigours of the morning, Joy smiles at seeing a friendly face.

'Joy! Finally!' Sharon and Joy share a brief hug. 'Where have you been all morning? Spur of the moment spa treatment? I have been trying to reach you all day. Did you not see my text?'

'Yes, I did, and I know, I'm sorry. But I was busy saving a dying banker.'

'A dying bank?'

Joy grins. 'I doubt if too many banks are dying. Not just yet anyway. Too big to fail. But no, I was saving a dying banker. Just a small cog in capitalism's wheel.'

'Sounds unusual. Is this a voluntary pro bono thing, saving the patriarchy on behalf of Magic Carpet?'

'As if. Much more mundane than that,' sighs Joy, remembering the purpose of her futile morning. 'I was accompanying Justin on his endless search for funding for that business of his.'

'I see.' Sharon's eyes open wide, in mock surprise. 'So did Justin try to strangle the banker when he failed to cough up?'

'I kinda wish he had,' says Joy, giggling at the thought of Justin ever doing violence to anyone. 'But no, the dying elderly banker, the one wearing the old school tie, did not need strangling. The bank was throttling the life out of him anyway. He just keeled over with the inanity of it all. It was his young upwardly thrusting colleague who was inviting the tourniquet.'

'And you stepped into the breach?' Sharon asks. 'Not surprised. You're brill in these situations. That was why I was trying to get hold of you. We could have done with you this morning.'

'Why was that then?' asks Joy, feeling a small pang of guilt.

'All very messy. A new hire forklift driver crashed into a pile of windscreens. Glass everywhere.'

'Was he hurt?' asks Joy.

'He? No, it was a she. She was lucky, lot of scratches, but the lift-truck's safety bar saved her. So now she is to appear in front of disciplinary panel. To be chaired by – guess who?'

'Me?' asks Joy, while knowing the answer.

'Yes, you. The price you pay for taking the morning off to breathe life into an obsolete old man.'

'Quite a price to pay indeed,' muses Joy, 'and before you ask, Justin did not get the loan. It was a shitshow.'

'Gawd. You do get yourself in some right pickles, Joy. So there no hope of funding from the bank?'

Joy screws up her face. 'No, not really. The only form of hope they can offer is us being referred to a call centre.'

'On no,' says Sharon, shaking her head in commiseration. 'A fate worth than death. Your future in the hands of a caring sharing algorithm. Living the dream, the two of you. Talking of call centres, Glynis, one of the supervisors from our call-centre, was trying to get hold of you.'

'What did she want?'

'She wouldn't say,' Sharon replied. 'Just said she needed to talk to you, and you alone. She even came over in person.'

'I am sure that whatever it is can wait. After all, I hardly know this Glynis, and no doubt she wants the impossible, now. I have had enough already today. And now yet another disciplinary to organise.'

'It is tough on you,' says Sharon. 'So, what is your Justin going to do now?'

'Immediately? Tomorrow he goes to London for a coaching network conference. All fellow coaches selling to each other. Not a client in sight.'

'All spending, no getting?' asks Sharon. 'Makes me feel happy to have stayed single, since my divorce. These men do need a lot of supporting.'

'Yes, they sure do, Sharon. You don't know the half of it where supporting Justin is concerned. Sounds like you are enjoying your freedom?'

'Oh, yes.' Sharon smiles. 'Did I tell you that I have joined a choir?'

'Really? I didn't know you could sing.'

'Neither did I! But in the Wildfire Chorus – all women of course – the belief is that everyone can sing. And they are right, more or less. It is great fun. You should come along. You would love it.'

'I am sure I would. But right now, we need to get back inside. Lunch break over. Back on our heads.'

An Encounter in Cattle Class

On the London train back to Bristol the next day, marooned somewhere between Swindon and Bath, Justin reflects once more on the previous day's meeting at the Better Bank, painfully aware of a creeping sense of despair clawing at his gut, further aggravated by his dispiriting experience at the conference entitled, "Transforming Teamwork: what do you say after you say hello?" He discards the coaching "toolkit" gifted by the keynote speaker with a sigh of irritation. His fellow passenger surreptitiously glances at this toolkit, reading it upside down.

Suddenly aware that he has been caught in the act of snooping on a fellow passenger's reading materials – when all the unwritten rules of being British dictate that, "one must keep oneself to oneself," - he feels the need to strike up casual conversation, by way of hiding his embarrassment, while not sure what he might actually say after he says hello.

'We could be stuck here forever,' the impeccably dressed stranger offers as a conversational starter, while catching Justin's eye. 'Mind if I take a look at your flyer? I have read the Times twice over already, and there is not much in there of interest. Same old, same old.'

Justin is more than happy to have a fresh pair of eyes decipher what truth might lie beneath the deathless management-speak pervading the toolkit. 'No go ahead, take a look, I am done with it. I was actually at the conference so I can fill you in on the detail more, if you are interested.'

Finished scanning this highly colourful document, his fellow passenger says, 'oh, so you are in this line of work then? Coaching executives and their teams towards higher performance?'

'Yes, I am, for my sins,' replies Justin, glad for some respite from his doomy thoughts. Dimly aware that if introductions did not occur soon, that they would both be condemned to missing the moment where names are learned, he breaks the ice by saying, 'I am Justin Drake by the way, of Catalyst Consulting.'

These two strangers do not quite shake hands across the table, but at least they nod in recognition of each other's presence. 'Good to meet you, Justin. And I am Richard Finch, Finance Director of the Consignia Finance Group, working out of Bristol.'

'Oh, is that that highly modernistic building overlooking the Floating Harbour? Must be stimulating working with such an outlook,' asks Justin, feeling the need to move the conversation along.

'Well, it looks great from the outside, and it is pretty impressive inside, but we are not without our challenges, beyond the chrome and glass surfaces.'

'Well you would not be alone in that. In my line of work, we assume that even the best run companies have their internal frictions.'

Richard pauses, deciding to take the conversation below the casual level. 'We have a few problems of our own, that is for sure, a number of them in the team-working department. This brochure summarises them really quite nicely.'

Eager to seize on this invitational thread, Justin asks more of the challenges that Richard and his company was facing. Richard opens up some on the challenges posed by the volatile market conditions post the Great Crash of 2008, but keeps his description at a general level. 'Look, it would be good to talk this over with you more, Justin, especially from a teamwork point of view, but a public train is not quite the place. And besides this is my final destination, Bristol Temple Meads Station.'

'Oh yes, mine too. But perhaps I could drop by your office when convenient, to hear more as to what you are facing?'

'Justin, that could be helpful, and thanks for the offer. Why not give my PA a ring, and we will set something up?' With that, he passes over his impressive business card, embossed with an abstract logo, while Justin fumbles with his far less impressive cardboard effort.

'Thanks for that,' says Richard, scrutinising the card. 'Catalyst Consulting, eh? I look forward to hearing a lot more about what you might have to offer. Let us meet up next week.'

'I look forward to it. Oh, and Richard,' Justin says on impulse, picking up the conference booklet and offering it to his companion. 'Would this be of any use to you? You seemed interested, and I have a soft copy in the cloud.'

'Well, that is very kind of you,' replies Richard, shooting his cuffs through his impeccable pinstriped suit. 'I may even show it to some of my fellow executives, by way of priming them to the need for us to work as a team. Thank you.'

Justin's mood is buoyed by this brief encounter with Richard, the perfectly mannered executive. He is eager to hurry home and share this possible breakthrough with Joy, who should by now be returned home from yet another day fighting the good fight at Magic Carpet, at their online distribution centre on the outskirts of town. Finding her at the kitchen table, he kisses her on the cheek, then asks, 'how was your day, Joy?'

'Oh, same old rubbish,' Joy sighs. 'We're entering a period of 'mandatory overtime,' and it is my task to whip our staff into a state of frenzied excitement at the prospect. It has not been easy, but for them a job is a job. Not just for them, but I guess for me too. But that is the way it is in a twenty-first century sweatshop. And how about you, Justin? Nice time down in London, being sold yet more new web-based workbooks designed to dazzle any prospective clients that might turn up out of the blue at your front door?'

Ignoring this dig, Justin replies, 'well, the conference was business as usual. Or more precisely lack of business for Justin as usual, and yes you guessed right, it was stuffed full of coaches with all-singing, all-dancing products which they were gamely trying to sell to fellow coaches. And not a client prospect in sight.'

Joy is not happy to hear her pessimism confirmed. 'That is a shame. But then from what you tell me these get-togethers, they all seem to follow the same incestuous pattern, feeding a fantasy of hope when the reality is far grimmer.'

'That is true – but guess what?' says Justin, trying to build some suspense.

'No, don't tell me. You came face to face with Jesus at Paddington?'

'Well no, not quite. But something nearly as miraculous. On the train home I chatted to a bone fide executive, a hot-shot, who wants me to meet him at his glossy offices down by the Harbourside, to explore what I might do for his company. The light at the end of the tunnel may well be beckoning.'

Joy looks sceptical. 'Would that be the Box Tunnel, the one that the train always get stuck in just before you get into Bath?'

'Well, the invitation occurred just as we reached there, so yes, I suppose it was. The miracle out of the Box.'

'That sounds promising,' she says, though looking unconvinced, having heard enough stories of new commercial dawnings before to get too excited. 'Or maybe he was just bored and indulging you, wanting to pass the time?'

'Could be, but allow me to look on the bright side. I think he was for real.'

'Of course, sunny side up. Talking of which, we need to feed those children of ours. Any idea where they might be hiding this time?'

One week on from his auspicious train ride, Justin, resplendent in his one and only grey suit, offset by a blue patterned tie picked out from the back of the wardrobe, arrives expectantly at Consignia's shiny offices on the bank of the Floating Harbour, in the heart of the commercial district, overlooking the spire of St Mary Redcliff. Doing his best to suppress the fear that the whole train encounter was simply a dream, Justin is relieved to find that the well-coiffed receptionist has him on the visitor's list. She has him sign in, then hands him a pass that will get him through the electronic barrier and into the lift, where Richard's PA will greet him on the tenth floor, the C suite. Justin looks at the pass bearing his name, hoping that it will allow entry to the business as much as to the lift.

The lift doors open silently to reveal April, Richard's PA. With a welcoming smile, she leads Justin along the hushed corridor towards a glass- walled office, saying that Mr Finch is ready to see him now. Making an effort to put on his professional game-face, while shaking inside, Justin thanks her and enters. Richard leaves his desk to come forward in greeting, ushering Justin towards two art deco chairs, where, he assures Justin, 'we will feel more comfortable.'

Seated, and with a pot of coffee already sitting on the table, they navigate their way through the pleasantries easily enough, with Richard's habitual social skills to the fore.

'Good morning, Justin, and good to see you in some place other than that cattle-class carriage. Those trains, honestly. But I am happy that for once, our chance meeting might mean that some good might result from those infernal delays. And those seats are so uncomfortable. I feel sure they are making the seating narrower and narrower year by year, by stealth, to optimise passenger loading, while pushing up the prices without any sense of embarrassment. But that is the power of monopolies for you.'

'Yes, I have noticed that too,' replies Justin, happy to ease his nerves with this familiar small talk. 'Those rail companies have got us by … by the elbows.'

'Justin, no need for you to modify colloquialisms on my behalf. But I think I know what you are trying to say. Something about "short and curlies?" I would much prefer to travel first-class, get some work done. But then as Finance Director, I insist that all staff travel cattle-class, and I cannot make myself an exception to that ruling. The CEO exempts himself, of course, but then that is his prerogative, and no one dares comment.'

'I am sure he is a busy man, needs to stretch out and think,' Justin replies, cringing at the banalities issuing from his dry lips.

'So, let us get down to business,' says Richard, pushing his coffee cup to one side. 'I enjoyed going through your toolkit. It made a lot of sense and encourages me to take this team exercise further. We may even need to order some copies of the toolkit later on, for distribution to the team. I am sure you could organise that?'

'Yes, of course,' replies Justin, more than a little surprised that the toolkit had not immediately been assigned to executive shelf-ware, to sit alongside of the myriad other unread management books published by the University of Heathrow bookshop.

'Thank you, Justin. Now I assume you have done your homework, found out more about Consignia, our history and corporate mission?'

'Yes, I have researched Consignia as far as I can online, from your own year-end statements, your marketing materials and also from recent press coverage. It all makes for a most impressive read.'

'That's good to know,' says Richard, taking pause. 'Hmm, the press coverage. They seem to be on our case, do they not, questioning whether we are wise to be stepping out from our domestic client base to speculate in the Middle East, Africa and beyond?'

'Yes, I have read most of that material. They are suggesting you may be over-reaching your capacity to deliver? Not that I agree with that of course.' Justin wants to walk back this remark as quickly as he has spoken, for fear of being seen as one naive enough to believe all they read in the papers. "Not, of course, that I know enough yet, to agree with the medias' views, one way or another. Newspapers have to sell, of course, and they thrive on rumours and concocted dramas.'

'No need to apologise, Justin. In point of fact, someone from the inside is leaking to the press and our CEO, Philip Junior, is aghast at this happening. The unfortunate thing is, though, that the criticisms may have some substance.'

Justin leans forward at this offered morsel. 'That is interesting to hear. In what way might this suggestion that you are overreaching yourselves bear an element of truth?'

'Hmmm. I will tell you in due course. But first, for caution's sake, I must ask you to sign a confidentiality indemnity. Do not worry, it is a standard document that we have all of our agents and suppliers adhere to.' With that Richard goes to his desk to produce the document, which Justin reads over hurriedly, then duly signs, knowing that at that point he was ready to sign anything to move the conversation along. 'Thanks for that courtesy, Justin. So, let us get down to it. The Middle East expansion is very much a gleam in the CEO's eyes. He sees our competition moving in that geographical direction, and feels we must move too, before they steal first-mover advantage. And he is pushing through a whole raft of innovative products to meet his perception of that market's needs.'

'I see,' says Justin, deciding it is time to deploy his expensively acquired open questioning skills. 'So the CEO is impatient to move towards a tempting opportunity while others…?'

'Precisely. While others on the executive team are far more reluctant to fall in behind, feeling the step-out is premature, and may damage our asset base here at home.'

'I get the picture,' says Justin, pleased that his open question might progress him towards the early stages of closing the sale. After all, the marketing module of his coaching accreditation programme insisted that it is never too early to press the "close" button. 'So where might my services fit in to all of this?'

'I will get to where you might fit in good time, but first of all let me paint more of the picture for you. And besides, it would be helpful to talk it through, listen to my own summary as it comes out of my mouth.' Justin nods, respectfully, glad that the early sales seed is planted. Richard coughs, gathering his thoughts. 'Well, these differences across the team are becoming emotionally loaded, and are being more openly expressed around the executive suite, the C suite, where you now sit. The CEO is branding this questioning of the new strategy as little short of treacherous and undermining of him and his vision. I worry that these tensions, and associated leaks, are likely to cause imminent damage to the cohesion of our team unless some bridging is done soon. Your task, should we assign it, would be to come in as a neutral outsider, to get to the bottom of the breakdown in team dynamics, and suggest a way forward.'

Justin feels his heart rate rise at this invitation. 'I would be happy to accept such a brief. Such a role is familiar territory to me. It feels well within my skillset. I would suggest, if I may, that the way forward would be for me to interview each of the directors individually, then to prepare a summary report, to be discussed by all concerned, at a place detached from the distractions of everyday business.'

Richard recoils. 'An "awayday?" The CEO hates that term. He thinks that all awaydays are management jollies, achieve precious little, and are looked on cynically by the staff, who see them purely as talking shops.'

Justin feels the need to backtrack, not wanting to lose the ground he has gained so quickly. 'I squirm at the term awayday too. In fact, it is one that seldom use, unless the client prefers it. But we can find a different way of phrasing such an off-site meeting.'

Richard seems reassured. 'I am sure we can. You know, the longer we talk, the more comfortable I feel about you working with us. You listen well and seem to be your own man, not afraid to push back. I have alerted Philip of our meeting, and he is free this morning. I suggest we go along the corridor to run this initiative passed him, to see whether he may be amenable to our plan, and wish to engage your services?'

'Yes, of course,' Justin replies, following Richard down the deeply carpeted corridor.

The CEO's office is twice the size of Richard's, and more opulent. Philip ushers them both towards two leather sofas by the corner window overlooking the harbour, while Justin endeavours not to stare at the gigantic replica painting of Gainsborough's daughters that eclipses even the CEO's high winged leather chair. Philip Junior follows the direction of Justin's gaze. 'Gainsborough, don't you know? Fine looking lassies, eh? A copy, of course, but a perfect one. In fact, some experts say it is better than the original. Fresher. More up to the minute.' He barks a few staccato orders at his glamorous PA, before indicating that she must now leave and go about his bidding, before turning his attention to his audience.

'Look, as you can see, I have a lot on my plate,' Philip begins. 'I am meeting some Al Maktoum Royal Family members from Dubai later on, and these Sheiks do not like to be kept waiting. So, Richard, remind me what this meeting and this consultant are all about?' He waves airily in Justin's direction, his gold cufflinks flashing in the sunlight.

Richard adopts his most diplomatic tone, loaded with gravitas. 'Well, as you know there are differences of opinion around the executive team regarding our change of strategy.'

'Oh, for goodness sake, not this again!' puffs Philip. 'Doesn't my team know by now that is what strategies are for! To be changed when the market changes. They are never set in stone. And there are always differences in an executive team. I would worry if there were not. It is precisely that creative tension that keeps businesses from stagnating.'

Richard resolves not to be sidelined. 'Yes, I appreciate that we need to move with the market, but in this case these particular differences within the executive team are, in my view, building towards a crisis.'

Philip snorts at this. 'Are they? No one has told me it is that bad. All we need to do is to hunt down the source of these leaks to the press really soon. This whole thing is being talked up, and I want it crushed right now. I had the Financial Times on the phone again this morning, demanding to know what is going on. They are worried we might be unsettling the market. It is quite enough having the press talking up some trumped-up crisis, without my executive joining in this chorus too. That is the last thing we need.'

Richard sits impassively through this all too familiar rant, waiting for the spluttering to subside. 'Philip, I do hear your strength of feeling on this one.'

Philip, content for now that the strength of his vehemence has fully registered on his visitors, calms himself to ask of his colleague, 'so what exactly would this consultant be up to, should we choose to hire him? Calm some nerves around here, and steel our common resolve around the given strategy?'

'Well,' continues Richard, attempting to stay focused in the face of this attempt to circumscribe the intervention, 'I thought it best, at this point, if we hired someone from outside to take the temperature, assess the climate within the team, and flush out and work differences that are currently under the table, before they sabotage our position going forward. At that point, we can move towards a common strategic ground that we have all bought into, speaking to a positioning that we can confidently communicate to a sceptical world.'

Philip shifts in his chair. 'Well okay, if you put it that way, and if you think it will bring the executive team onside, then I do not see much harm in that, as long as this Justin is confidential, totally watertight, and not simply covertly supporting the agenda of some rogue voices that seek to undermine our vital mission.'

Growing anxious at being referred to in the third person, as if he were in the room but not actually present, or not real at all - silent like the Gainsborough daughters, but less visible - Justin decides it is time to speak up. 'Mr Junior, I must hasten to reassure you that I have already signed your confidentiality document, and that my whole business integrity revolves around trustworthiness and discretion.'

Once again, Justin's clunky delivery makes him squirm, but he proceeds in his best version of executive speak all the same. 'My task, should you agree it, is to sit with each of the directors in turn, including yourself, to assess where differences might sit. My intent is to work the issues, not the personalities. After these conversations, I would then produce a report for all to see, and to discuss together.'

'I see – but no awaydays, is that understood?' blurts Philip. 'I've no truck with cosmetic awaydays. What we need at this point is leadership, which I provide. In bucketsful. And at the end of the day this is not a democracy. But if Richard thinks this review necessary, and trusts you to do this, then so be it. I assume you have already discussed a contract and agreed the financials?'

Richard and Justin demonstrate vigorous synchronized nodding, even though their commercial conversation to date had been slight, to the point of non-existence. Philip seems mollified, for now, assured that he is in control of this situation, should it show the slightest sign of getting out of hand. He continues, 'Good. I do not need to see that contract now; but run it past me when it is ready please, Richard. Now

I really must go and find out more about Arab etiquette. I would not like us to lose face at this early stage with our distinguished delegates. I look forward to hearing the results of your report, Justin. Give it all you've got. And send Fiona in again. I need to make sure that she has been instructing the girls from marketing how to behave respectfully in front of foreign royalty.'

Justin has a vision of a cupboard full of burkas, ready to be donned, then inspected for Islamic rectitude by Philip himself. Back in the relative safety of Richard's office, Richard relaxes in one of his armchairs, exhaling contentedly. 'Well, I think that went really well, Justin. Well done you on making such an impression.'

Justin looks pleased but puzzled. 'You really think so? I said very little at all.'

'That is true enough,' reassured Richard, 'but whatever it is about you, Philip is prepared to give you a go. Believe me, behind all of the bluster, he is quite discerning. His bark is far worse than his bite. I would take this as a result, if I were you.'

'Oh, I will, don't worry,' agrees Justin. 'And thank you for all of your support and guidance. I just can't wait to get started. It feels as though there is real urgency behind this.'

'There is urgency, don't worry about that. We will not be dragging our heels. In fact, in a moment I will walk you down the corridor of this C suite. Introduce you to whomever executive is in and let them know what this survey is about. Then we can de-conflict diaries, sort out a schedule for you for the next week or so, and I will follow that up with an email to the team outlining our purpose and plan. Don't worry about running into resistance, we are pushing on an open door here.'

Justin fidgets for a moment, turning over the CEO's business card in his hand. 'Yes, I am already to go, and quite free for next week or so.

The CEO mentioned a contract? Perhaps we need to spend a moment or two on that, if you don't mind?'

'Yes, of course, agrees Richard. 'Look, we don't have the time to finesse this. Our usual rate for HR consulting and so forth is £800 a day. How does that sound?'

Justin tries - and fails - not to beam too broadly. 'That sounds just fine. Meets my usual day rate for such work,' he confirms, though in fact it is way ahead of his expectations. 'And he mentioned a contract? I just happen to have brought with me the standard contract format for coaching work drawn up by my professional body, the Coaching Fraternity, which covers most eventualities, including confidentiality and such like,' says Justin, laying the standardised document in front of Richard.

He scrutinises the four pages of small print briefly, before saying, 'this all looks like lawyerly boilerplate to me. I take no exception to any of this, and happy to have it playing in the background. But for the time being, let me draw up a head of agreement mentioning the fee-rate and duration, and we can take it from there. That will be enough to keep Philip happy, I feel sure.'

Richard's firmness of tone discourages Justin from pushing this contract issue further, even though he was a little disappointed to see the exhaustive professionalism of the Fraternity's template being discarded summarily. 'I feel sure that a shortened agreement will be more than adequate,' Justin agrees. 'Shall we take a walk down the corridor then, as you suggested earlier? It would be good for me to meet the executives before I begin my survey for real.'

Justin's interviewing of the executive team starts slowly enough, but through the week – as Justin learns more of the issues at hand, and points his questions more precisely – the layers of defence and denial among the executives gradually peel away, to reveal a shared discontent with the proposed future business strategy. Justin's report falls out fairly easily into plausible categories, and he is not displeased with the eventual business-like tone of it, which he is confident will elicit nods of recognition among the team. An unexpected breakthrough during the interview process occurs when the Marketing Director recalls him, post interview, to suggest that, 'instead of taking his word for it,' he talks to Joanna Cooke, one of his team leads, to explore the teamwork issues under discussion directly from a female perspective, for Justin to assess the extent to which there may be evidence of discrimination against women employees. Justin is delighted to be offered this opportunity for a direct line into an otherwise silent voice in his data collection exercise. Soon enough, Joanna and he are seated in the coffee shop in the airy Consignia atrium, where she is more than happy to open up on her experiences as a senior manager on the team; and indirectly on the treatment of the largely female members of her team.

Justin listens intently to all she has to say, whilst avoiding taking notes, as she had asked that they speak off-the-record. Reciting one account after another of gendered mistreatment, he gently encourages her to open up on the subject of the CEO's behaviour. Hesitant at first, she asks again for his trust, saying softly that this conversation must not go beyond these four walls. In fact, she says she would feel safer if they talk outside the building, by taking a walk around the harbour.

Justin is more than agreeable to this, and sure enough the level of disclosure ramped up a pace. 'If only the men were so expressive of the emotions that run at work as you,' he found himself saying, 'then my work would be so much easier. If only I didn't have to decode men's hidden feelings all of the time.'

Joanna looks directly at him at this point, stopping mid-stride to face him. 'Well, that was a very direct thing to say! You surprise me.'

'Oh, sorry if I was being unprofessional,' offers Justin. 'But given how open you have been with me, I feel I can do no less than be open with you.'

At this invitation, their conversation deepens still more. They sit on a vacant bench facing the river, moving their talk away for a while from the workplace setting to an exploration of their personal lives and dilemmas. She is more than curious to know more of Justin's work and of his world. Though knowing that boundaries were being transgressed here, he warms to theme, even to the extent of disclosing some of the tensions involved in being married to a hard-pressed manager, while attempting to maintain a semblance of family life.

'I guess you men think it is hard for you, 'she says, with a hint of a rebuke. 'My husband often says so. But I honestly feel it is far, far harder on women. Mind you,' she continues, 'I do wish my husband could be as expressive about his inner feelings as you are. That is not flattery, just the honest truth.'

Justin allows this remark to settle for a moment, unsure how to take the conversation further. He is aware of how closely they had moved together, on the bench. Or rather how closely he has moved towards her.

Sensing this proximity, Joanna declares, 'Justin, it has been really good to off-load on you like this, and thanks for the listening. I feel sure you will safeguard all I have disclosed to you. But the message must get out somehow about the way women are treated here. I doubt I will be involved in the follow-through to your report, but if there were any way for us to keep talking, informally, then I would very much value that opportunity.' With that, she presses her business card into Justin's hand.

He reciprocates the card-exchange ritual by reaching for his wallet to offer his card for her perusal. 'I would really appreciate more conversation with you too. It has been most illuminating, and beyond the survey agenda, I have really enjoyed your company. You can ring me at any time, I would be happy for that.'

'Oh? Because I am worth it?' she teased. 'Seriously speaking, that is generous of you, and I might well take you up on it. Now we had better get inside, before we are accused of eloping together.'

Justin returns to his desk to finalise his report in a small, confined office off the C suite, yet he cannot settle to it. His mind returns again and again to the shared walk with Joanna, and all that tumbled on for both of them on that impromptu excursion into each other's lives. While that conversation feels the most truthful, most human exchange he has experienced all week, he cannot paste in her exact words into the report without betraying her trust. He decides not to move away in his report from broad generalisations concerning gender issues; but now at least he knows in his heart that they run much deeper than the executives have suggested.

Putting these thoughts to one side, he smiles in quiet satisfaction at his inclusion of terms in his report that will cause the executives to know for sure that he understands their world and what they are facing: terms such as 'The preservation of the 'book'; 'maintaining the confidence of the customer base'; 'optimising harmonious co-working within the Customer Relations' team'; the need for 'new product development to reach beta stage.'

All of these lexical phrases, he feels, are zingers. He bites the end of his pencil as he chews over how to professionally describe what he had learned of the CEO's leadership style – characterised by bullying and a rampant sexism that was far from casual - – without upsetting too many sensibilities. He tries a few phrases for size, before settling for 'leadership has become increasingly directive, in the face of stress; and that there was mention of an undercurrent of feeling that levels of sexism and harassment were pushing to the surface in an increasingly unignorable way.'

'That should nail it,' he decides, giving himself a high-five. Through that week he had been feeling the frisson that comes from being taken into the confidence of a powerful people, of being offered a place at their confessional table. At long last, he felt that he was doing proper, grown-up executive coaching, and that his report was striking the right adult tone, without becoming overly strident or parental. He closes off his report on the screen, prints it out, then heads home for a good night's sleep prior to his big moment, the delivery of his report to the executive.

The success of his unexpected human connection with Joanna feeds a tailwind of burgeoning confidence that carries Justin into Consignia on the morning of the executive feedback meeting. He is bursting to share his forensically curated report and action plan with the executive team, whom he feels are going to recognise themselves in it. However, his enthusiasm is rudely interrupted by Philip Junior appearing in the corridor, seemingly out of nowhere, to bark at Justin, 'My office, right now.'

In the now forbidding office, Justin gazes out the window at the passing tourist ferry, while rather wishing he were on it. Philip blurts that he had seen Justin's preliminary invoice, issued at the end of his first week, and that it was way in excess of what he expected to pay. As Justin dithers, speechless, Philip reinforces his message. 'Bluntly, I am not going to pay it.'

He snorts at Justin's plaintiff reminder of the heads of agreement drafted with Richard, saying that he may be prepared to pay a global sum at the end of the assignment, but that Justin had better make the total realistic, and the work had better be good. He reminds Justin that, as CEO, he has other options, including going to an established consultancy, or simply pulling the plug on the whole intervention. He says he is suspicious that Justin has been 'talking up' problems with some maverick team members, that he has 'gone native.'

As Justin blusters in protest, Philips says, 'that, as the person with fullest responsibility for the wellbeing of this company, I am having trouble seeing any value-add from this intervention at this point. I need to get on, so I am afraid that this is all I have time for. In fact, I think we might be done here. Please see yourself out, unless you feel you have more to add.'

Justin exits the room in a state of shock, casting his eyes downwards in embarrassment as he walks past the glass-fronted offices of the other executives sharing the C suite. After two weeks of gaining their trust, of being allowed a voice within this inner sanctum, he is now cast out. As the lift doors open, he wishes only that they would swallow him up. Forever. On the descent he begins the process of beating himself up for failing to have made the financial contract more robust, a self-lacerating process that he knows will run for days.

He scurries across the lobby to gain the safety of the street, only to be called back by the security guard to return his visitors pass.

Staggering across the Millennium Bridge to seek the safety of his car parked in the station car park, he closes the car door then bangs his head against the steering wheel in frustration at his naivety. He tries without success to block out the anticipated mockery that will be ringing in his ears for weeks or even months to come. Derision that would be coming from his coaching network, indeed from anyone that he had boasted to about his great breakthrough. And he has no idea at all of how to break this news to Joy.

Realising that he is in no fit state to drive, he steps out of his car to spy the tourist boat, ready to depart the quay. Desperate for a temporary escape from his current predicament, he joins the queue of happy visitors now alighting the ferry. He pulls the cloak of anonymity around him, relieved that none of his fellow passengers know that he is a grim fugitive from the Consignia building that looms over the docking station.

He is lost in a deepening sense of remorse, hardly noticing the historical landmarks of Victorian Bristol as they glide by. He is brought back into the here-and-now only by a small boy playing a harmonica at the prow of the ferry, blowing the same two notes over and over, while his sister stares intently at the video game on her phone.

Their father is impatient that his children show some interest in the splendours unfolding all around them. 'Kids look up! See the Clifton Suspension Bridge above us, the one we drove over yesterday. It has been in operation for 150 years. Look at the cliffs and crags along the Avon Gorge, still the same as when Brunel built the bridge. Wow, a sail ship is just coming around the bend. A ship from the olden days, all its sails billowing in the breeze. Look!'

The children pause for a second of compliant observation, sighing "Yes Dad,' before their attentions return to the continued blowing of the same two notes on the harmonica, and the irresistible captivation of the video game.

Their father, giving up on the idea that his urgings will ever divert his children from their chosen preoccupations, turns to Justin for conversation. 'Hi mate, I see you looking at all this hero Brunel did. Singlehanded. The Temple Meads railway station, the Great Western Railway, the Box Tunnel; the Floating Harbour, the SS Great Britain, the first iron ship ever to steam across the Atlantic. Amazing, isn't it? Am I right?'

His questions could not be ignored. 'Oh yes,' said Justin, 'it is all quite remarkable.' Resigned to the fact that this conversation is likely to last for the duration of the boat trip, he decides to introduce himself. 'I am Justin, by the way,' he says, offering his hand.

'Good to meet you!' says his fellow traveller, clearly needing to discuss all that was unfolding before them. 'And I go by the name of Jim, aero-engineer of this parish. I was just thinking, all that we see before us are the products of Brunel's imagination, brought to life and still more or less functioning today. His original propeller design for the SS Great Britain is still the blueprint for all propellers since. How did he do it? Great Britain was great back then, Brunel knew that, and had the confidence to do whatever was necessary to make it greater still.' As he talks, Jim photos the passing tableau, indiscriminately, without breaking his flow.

Justin, taking the path of least resistance, responds in similar idiom. 'Things were really different back then. None of this talk of diversity, of Health and Safety at Work: of life balance, or of employees needing a wellness programme, or a safe place.' Justin feels sure that this sentiment would be fuel enough to spur his newly found companion onwards, while allowing him space to nurse his inner remorse.

'Yep. You got it,' says Jim, warming to his rant. 'Brunel would never have tolerated any of that snowflake stuff. All he needed was a team of engineers who knew that the completion of every project they worked mattered more than any other consideration, abetted by a workforce toiling away on zero hours, while risking death or injury each day, with no form of health insurance to fall back on. That is how you get things done in a hurry, great things, without fear of reprisal.'

'Yes, those were different times,' Justin lamely agrees, without any real enthusiasm for this polemic.

Oblivious to Justin's indifference, Jim continues with his drift. 'They were different times, and better times too in many ways. I work as an aerospace engineer and would love to junk all this modern managerial bullshit – excuse my language kids. What do you work at?'

Justin cringes, but knows he cannot really avoid the question. 'Well, I work as an executive coach – and before you say it, I am quite sure that Brunel did not need an executive coach to realise his ambitions. But for my sins that is what I do, though it may well not be for very much longer.'

'Oh, bad as that eh?' asks Jim. 'It does sound like a bit of flaky trade. Do you get heavily regulated, in your line of work? We are hamstrung by regulations, like Gulliver tied down by the little men with all their red tape, strapping us all down until we dare not think for ourselves.'

'I know what you mean,' says Justin, suddenly warming to this exchange. 'Believe it or not, we in coaching have lots of regulation and control. In fact, you have just reminded me – I have a professional supervision this afternoon.'

Jim surprises Justin by showing some compassionate interest. 'Is that some sort of inspection then? Do they come around and inspect your coaching work, measure you up? I know it is easy to physically measure what we engineers do. But I can't quite see how they can do that in your line of work.

Shame that though, when you could be out here for the rest of the day, enjoying the sun, instead of being cooped up in a dreary inspection meeting.'

'No, the supervision I am subject to is more of a ritual, with no real measurement involved. In fact, I recoil from the term 'supervision', when it not something that I willingly elect to go through.'

'But aren't you freelance?' asks Jim, struggling to understand Justin's work world. 'I would have thought the last thing you needed as a freelancer was reporting to someone who does not know your work directly.'

'Yes, exactly.' A passing swan pauses to blink at Justin, quite impervious to any thoughts of ever being trapped. 'In point of fact I chose to branch out on my own, away from a stultifying salaried existence, precisely to escape low-grade surveillance, only to walk into a more rigid version of it, imposed by amateurs.'

'Sounds awful.' Jim waves at the swan, which swims away. 'I would hate that. And who pays for this surveillance?'

'Ha! I do,' Justin replies. 'This supervisory inquisition is a requirement of keeping my professional licence to operate. So supervised to the death I must be. Mind you, it could be useful today, as I have one or two problems to sort out.'

'Really?' asks Jim. 'I thought your job was to solve others' problems. We do have executive coaches prowling the corridors at our place, hired at great expense, no doubt. Mind you, their help is not for the likes of us at the coalface. We get by simply by helping each other out. And of course by mercilessly taking the piss of each other. Banter between blokes works, a lot of the time, to relieve stress. But you said you were experiencing trouble in coaching paradise?'

'I cannot say too much, confidentiality and all of that. But I have just been shafted by a major player,' says Justin, just as the Consignia building hoves into view once more.

'Well, at least you have the contract to fall back on.'

'Hmm... That is the problem – I didn't contract properly. My bad.' Justin says, not welcoming this reminder of his self-inflicted omission.

'Oh, I see your problem. And good luck with it. Anyway, we are back on dry land,' says Jim. 'time to muster the troops. Been good to chat to you on this sunny day. Tell you what; let me take a selfie of you and me, with that shiny building reflecting in the water. That would be good to show the wife when we get home.'

'Can't you just take a picture of the building?' pleads Justin.

'Well, I could, but pictures need people in the foreground to bring it to life.'

Justin grudgingly assents to this, doing his best to fix a holiday grin while his Jim locks him in a sideways embrace that brings him closer than he would choose to the scent of Lynx Africa. Jim releases Justin from this unsolicited intimacy to show him the image of them grinning, heads together, framed in the shadow on the Consignia building.

'Thanks for being a sport, Justin. Tell you what, give me your phone and I will tap in my number, then send you the pic.'

Not at all sure why he would wish for such a reminder of this day, Justin nonetheless surrenders his phone, hoping this encounter might be reaching its death throws. With the photo transferred, Jim's attention turns to his children. 'Billy, stop playing that mouth organ for a second, would you? I am trying to say goodbye to this nice man who appreciates his city's history far more than you two Philistines. You are driving me and everyone else crazy. And Annie put that game away. It is time for us to go look at the ice cream shop.'

'Hurray!' the children chorus, visibly brightening, while their father lines them up for a selfie in front of the boat.

Grateful for the distraction that this conversation on the boat has provided, Justin is heading towards the car when he notices a woman in a summer's dress waving at him from across the Millennium Bridge. Not recognising her at all at first, Justin refocuses again to see that it is Joanna, now dressed in civvies, walking at pace over the bridge to greet him.

'Oh, hello Joanna,' says Justin, trying hard not to give the impression that he would rather not talk to another single soul that day, never mind someone from Consignia. 'Sorry if I did not recognise you at first. Always hard to place people out of a work context. And especially when you are not in your regulation marketing outfit. All the better for that, if I may say. Your dress is lovely.' Justin does not feel in control of any of words coming out of his mouth, but instead glad to be saying anything other than that he had been fired, ignominiously, from her firm.

'Well thank you, Justin, for the compliment. Means a lot, coming from you. I have the afternoon off, leaving my "Barbie goes Marketing" outfit behind me, to change into something more suitable for accompanying a friend to a flower show where her display with be featuring. And how liberating it feels, I must say, to be released for the day,' she says, looking over her shoulder at the Consignia building. 'Are you also free for the rest of the day? I saw you stepping off the boat. No doubt taking a celebratory trip after your report back to the executive?'

'Hmm, not quite.' Justin feels in his bones that he could not keep on a happy face for long, knowing that she would know soon enough from the office grapevine what a disaster his morning had been. 'Wish I had been celebrating, but in fact I was escaping disaster rather than a triumph. It went really badly. And I am afraid I am terrible company right this minute. Best to leave me alone to wallow in my misery.'

'Oh, I am so sorry to hear that,' she says, her carefree tone shifting to one of compassion. 'Another bruised consultant staggers out of Consignia, dazed and confused. I quite understand.' Her gaze shifts towards the Knights Templar pub, just a short walk across the plaza. 'Look, you gave me great listening last time we talked. Why not come for a quick coffee or a drink, I am happy to keep misery company for a while. I am not due at the flower show for a while.' Without waiting for an answer, she guides the reluctant Justin towards the pub's wide doors.

At the bar, she orders a large dry white wine, then turns to her captive to ask him, 'What's your poison?'

'The same for me please,' muttered Justin, 'unless they have cyanide on the drinks list.'

She makes a pretence of studying the list, before saying, 'sorry, cyanide not on offer.' She turns to the bartender to say, 'Another large dry white please. And no, I don't think we need to take a look at the meal-deal, thank you all the same.' She rolls her eyes at Justin. 'Typical Wetherspoons chain pub. The marketers always forcing the staff to on-sell. I feel sorry for them. In fact, I even feel a bit sorry for the marketers too, come to that.'

Sitting in a booth at the back of this unfeasibly large cut-price drinking emporium, she looks him in the eye, saying firmly, 'so tell me all about your meeting with the executive, as far as you can. I have the time. No need to hold back, you are among friends here.'

'I am not at all sure what to say at this point, Joanna, though it is kind of you to ask. The fact is that I never even got as far as delivering the report. The CEO cut me off at the pass, then summarily dismissed me. I doubt I will ever step inside the place again. Not sure if I ever want to. That is the ups and downs of it. And seeing you again makes matters worse. Beyond being kicked out when I was in full stride, I feel ashamed that I did not have the opportunity to do justice to the claims of the women encased in all that chrome and glass.'

'Don't worry about that,' soothes Joanna. 'We women are used to having to attend to our survival in the face of that hostile environment. As I have said before, you are not the first consultant who tries to speak the truth to be shown the door.'

Justin makes an unsuccessful attempt to suppress an involuntary sob, which grows to the release of a small tear in the corner of his eye. He turns in shame, hiding his face in a large white handkerchief. Finally collecting himself, he mutters, 'Sorry about that. But on top of everything else that is piling in, I have no idea how to break this news to my wife, Joy. She might not say it aloud, but she will think me such a pathetic loser. Again. And I am just so sick of this feeling. Sick to the stomach with it.'

He buries his face in his handkerchief again, while Joanna, not sure at all how to deal with this sudden outbreak of male vulnerability, gently places her hand on this free hand, thinking silence may be best at this point.

'Look, I am so sorry, Joanna,' he mutters, painfully, 'I am no use to anyone like this. And you looking so pretty, all geared up for a fun day out. I should probably just go and leave you to it.'

'Justin, it is quite okay. Take a moment. I am happy to be here for you. And I know it is a cliché, but I do feel your pain.' She pauses, 'In fact I know it matters little for me to say this right now, but it is a real privilege for me to be in the company of a man who can openly express his feelings, spontaneously, just as you are right now.'

Justin nods at this, his shame subsiding somewhat. 'Thanks for that. Do go on. I am lapping up your every word, even if it does not look like it.'

'Personal disclosure alert, 'Joanna continues, 'it is good to be with a man showing his feelings, because none of my colleagues ever show vulnerability, just bluff and bluster. And as for my husband, I kinda give up on that score. He leaves it to me to do all the feeling on our behalf, then accuses me of being over emotional.' She is aware that she has moved the conversation away from what Justin is facing, but she notices how good it feels to be vocalising her deeper truths to a man that she would normally confine to her woman friends alone.

'Oh really?' says Justin, his tears subsiding some at this conversational turn. 'Funny you should say that. I am the cry-baby at home,' he says, encouraged in this train of thought by the consoling warmth of her hand still resting on his. 'Joy is really good at expressing frustration, or exasperation. She can move to anger, but more often than not that comes out as sarcasm, which takes a lot of energy to break through. But hush my mouth, I am saying too much, being disloyal.'

Joanna shakes her head a little, to indicate it is quite permissible for him to speak in this way. 'Maybe a little too much information. But you are speaking your truth and I know well how couples distribute emotional expression unequally. They – sorry we – get caught in a pattern of it. And it is truly wearing, hard to break out of, when only one partner does the emotional labour. It just escalates.'

'Yes, you are right, it does. Helpful to know, but I still do not know what to say to her about getting fired. Or maybe about anything else that is really going on for me.' Justin says. 'Getting fired is just one more thing to add to my guilt list.'

Joanna moves her hand slowly, tenderly, away from his, lifting her glass to her lips. As she puts it down, he gazes at the smear of vivid fresh lipstick on her glass, the imprint of her lips glazed like satin in the light of the creamy wine. He turns towards her as she sweeps a lock of blond hair from her face, meeting his gaze.

'Go on,' she insists, 'what was that thought right now? Say it. Give it oxygen.' 'I just dunno. Feeling overwhelmed. Not sure what it is.'

'Yes, you do,' she says, taking his hand once more.

'Well, right now – beyond feeling hopelessly defeated and not knowing where to turn - I am feeling for the first time for a long time that I am in the company of someone who gets me. All of me. It is a wonderful feeling. And I have to confess that the sight of your lip imprint on your glass sent me somewhere altogether.' He gulps at this confession that spills out of nowhere.

'I see,' she says, noticing for the first time the smudge on her glass. 'Do you have any idea where it sent you, that random print of my lips?'

'Probably got me thinking about how it used to be on a first date, the excitement of that. Sorry, now I am saying too much. I really should go.'

'No, it is okay. That was a sweet thing to say. I do not take it personally. I don't think you were thinking about my lips. It could have been all the lips in the world, the universal lip's stain, maybe inviting a kiss. Could even have been the stain of original sin, the first temptation.'

He brightens visibly, a smile breaking out across his face for the first time that day. 'You are so right. That is exactly what it is. All the lips in the world, and the stain of temptation that they might freight. Now you have heard my secret thought. How about yours?

'Mine?'

'Yes, yours.'

'A bit like your lip's gaze,' she says, taking time to seek out her answer. 'I am not aware of anything much, beyond the exchange of our words, and of the feel of my hand on yours. Feels forbidden, somehow. But is also feels good. That deep need for that easy contact with a fellow human. I am not at all sure what brought us both to this place, at this time, but that feels right too. Something we both needed and never dared say, even to ourselves, especially to ourselves.'

'Say more,' invites Justin, inching closer.

'Most of all I am feeling something. Actually openly allowing a feeling in. I can feel my heart again, after so much shutting it off amid a world of busyness and distraction. Just thank you, Justin, for that.' She strokes his fingers, their eyes no longer shy, gazing deeply into each other, searching for a truth that is too intense to be uttered in words alone.

She moves her hand away, breaking the spell. 'But this feels really dangerous. I am not feeling in my normal control of things. I think we need to return to some kind of reality, maybe pick up on this some other time. And I have beautiful blossoms awaiting my admiration, and a friend eager to share all of that with me. She might even win a prize.'

'You must go,' declares Justin, pushing away his glass. 'And I have a supervision meeting to get to, though it is the last place I want to be. We need to get going... before.'

'Yes....before...'

'But we can't just go. This booth is still quite private. We have created our own cocoon. A hug?' he pleads, with no real idea of how to finish this.

They hug tenderly, and long, breathing in all they have shared. Eventually, she gently presses him away, saying, 'that is enough for now. This has been so real, so helpful, so releasing. I have your number; you gave it to me before. I will text you mine. No promises. What has happened here is a moment in time, one for us to hold between ourselves. We may never feel this again.'

'You are right. And now I must go for my professional reality check. And a review of my most recent failures and transgressions. I will never utter a word of this to anyone.'

Justin starts up the silent Prius to head up his supervisor's office, located on Clifton Down. He is feeling lifted by his encounter with Joanna, while not wanting to dwell for too long on that episode, lest it destabilise his already wavering sense of who he is in the world. His supervisor Brenda's home is set in a fine Georgian mansion overlooking the Avon Gorge and the piers of the Clifton Suspension Bridge, that popular suicide spot. As he climbs the stone stairs to the studded front door, Joy phones. He clings to the wrought-iron balcony for support, dreading having to impart his latest baleful news.

Joy inquires, urgently, 'how did it go? You know I am not allowed to make private calls from the sweatshop, but I need to know. Make it quick. I am sure you killed it. I bet you were a hero. I was thinking of you there, in the lions' den, dazzling them with your brilliant report.'

Justin stutters, 'It went really badly, I am afraid. The CEO kicked me out and I think I have lost the client. I feel so, so badly about it all. '

'Oh dear,' she says, not knowing how to take this conversation further.

Justin tries to help her out. 'I know. "Oh dear" indeed. No need to say anymore at this point. That sums it up perfectly. I will share all the gory details later. But right now, I am poised at Brenda's door, awaiting what I hope will prove, for once, to be a timely supervision conversation.'

'So sorry to hear this. That is the worst. Ring me later. But remember that I am pulling a late one this evening. Then I'm going for a works team dinner after, so be sure to be in time to pick up the kids from school.'

'Don't worry, I won't forget our precious cargo. That is, if there is anything left of me once Brenda is done. Bye for now, and thanks for taking the time to call.'

Brenda greets Justin warmly, but picks up immediately from the ending of the truncated call that something has gone badly awry in Justin's world.

'Come on in Justin,' says the beckoning Brenda, pulling her twinset around her. 'I shouldn't have been eavesdropping, but I could not help but hear you say that you have lost your client? Oh, my goodness. Tell me all about it, as far as you feel able.' She listens carefully as he talks her through the unfolding Consignia saga.

She commiserates, readying herself for a session that is going to draw upon all her powers to stay detached from her client's current emotional state. 'Sorry to hear of this turn of events. Can you speak to your underlying emotional state?'

Justin tries to gather himself, then says 'Hard to pin down an exact emotion. What it feels like, inside, is that I am torn between flight and fight in the face a charging rhino.' He surprises himself with this neat summary, the metaphor probably drawn from one of his coaching psychology classes.

'Tell me more about this flight or fight, take your time, you are in shock,' Brenda coaxes, leaning forward.

'Well, flight says walk away from this CEO and his games playing. Write this episode off as a lesson learned, before attempts at deeper engagement with Consignia starts to seriously undermine my sense of worth.'

'And the voice of fight?' She asks, leaning in more closely.

Taking breath before answering, his voice betrays a deeper strength of emotion. 'I want to hit out. Just hit out. All over the place. I want to use all of the information gathered from my interviews regarding the bullying nature of the CEO's approach against him, to confront him as a trickster. I am so tempted to whistle-blow, to expose the CEO. In fact, a really angry part of me just wishes to pull his whole plate-glassed edifice down, for preference right in front of his visiting Sheik, for purposes of maximum embarrassment and shaming.'

'Say more,' she says, softly.

'Well, fight also speaks to taking legal action. But it is clear to me that there would only be one winner in that legal scenario, and I know it would not be me, pitted as I would be against the company's deep pockets and an entire in-house legal department.'

Sitting back in her cushioned chair, Brenda mirrors his movements exactly, now with fingers joining in an attentive steeple, head resting against the cream doily. 'And more?'

He takes breath, fingers still together, his anger spent for now.

'Somewhere between flight and fight lies the option of just soldiering on, dropping my price, seeing this one through to the end if they will allow me, putting the whole of today's episode down to miserable experience. But I feel sure that this option will not be offered to me. Perhaps what I need to do is to brood alone in my metaphorical man-cave for a couple of days, until I am ready to face the world again.'

Breaking a long silence, Brenda asks, 'Would it be possible, at this early stage, for you to 'take a step backwards', to ask how this episode might cause you to approach such an occurrence differently in the future?'

Justin sighs. 'I really don't think I am ready for that. I really don't. I appreciate your efforts to help, but I am not there yet. In fact all I can think of is that even had I put in place tighter contracting processes; even if I had taken advantage of the comprehensive Coaching Fraternity guidelines, the much-lauded professional body contracting template; then I still doubt whether such guidelines would stop such a CEO sabotaging the intervention, if he were so minded.'

'Okay,' says Brenda. "Then let me ask: is there anything from your past that this episode reminds you of? Can you remember a time when you have been rejected, then felt all these feelings that are running through you now?'

'Nope.' Justin shakes his head. 'Nothing that I can put my finger on. This feels like a first-off.'

'Are you sure? Nothing from family life, from teachers, from the playground, from being pushed around in say, the swimming pool, or the football team?'

'Nope again.'

Brenda sits back, fingers still steepled. 'Justin, I sense very strongly your sense of shock, and of frustration. I think you need to allow the shock to subside; and only then can you consider your options. This healing will take time. Maybe we need to step up our sessions during this period? Just an idea? It could help you through?'

'That might prove helpful and thanks for the offer. But even if it were a good idea, I cannot afford it,' replies Justin, surprised by the boldness of this offer.

Brenda tries to sweeten the pill. 'I see. But we could come to some sort of agreement. Even deferred payments, until you find your feet.'

'I am sure we could, but I am deep enough in debt as it is,' says Justin, thinking that he cannot but compare this antiseptic, strangulated exchange with the easiness of his fluent sharing with Joanna.

Brenda backs off, knowing she has touched an unwelcome nerve. 'That is just fine. But do know I am here for you, to help you get back on track. That is my sole impulse here, not commercial gain. Right now, I would like to try the "does this rejection remind you of anything?" question again. I thought I saw a flicker of recognition the last time around.'

'Hmm. Rejection. That is quite a highly charged word to be playing with. But let me have a go. Well, I am reminded from my deep past of the number of times my dad, a jobbing musician who lived day to day, hand to mouth, was let down by agents and venue managers. When he felt --- yes, betrayed, when he felt betrayed. That stench of betrayal used to reverberate around the house for a day or two. We were all aware of that cloud. But he soon picked himself and got back to finding new work.'

His gaze, seeking distraction, moves to the uninspiring faded brown tapestry hanging behind her chair. It makes him wish for the relief of an extravagant Gainsborough print, something to remind him of the beauty of this world in all its splendour. But all he has to go on with for the time being, for visual relief, is this threadbare remnant, proudly picked up, perhaps, at a souk during a break at a Moroccan yoga retreat years ago, but now utterly disregarded.

'Good. We are making progress. You have unearthed a memory. But I have to say that was your father's memory, a proxy. It was a sense of his betrayal you coat- tailed on, not your own direct experience.'

Her default of radiating Zen-like calm is beginning to annoy Justin. He feels a flash of anger welling up from the wounded animal clawing away at his insides. 'Look, Brenda, I am getting so frustrated. I thought this session might prove helpful, but it has done nothing for me really. I even thought you might have some solutions, but I realise that was a stupid expectation. So, when were you last betrayed by a client? Let me put the betrayal question right back at you!'

Taken aback, her tone sharpens. 'This is not about me, it is about you.' She adopts a measured tone, while aware that she runs the risk of incensing him still further.

'Maybe it is about both of us,' retorts Justin. 'I know as much about you as I do about that unreadable tapestry hanging behind you.'

'Hmm. Could we get back to times when you felt betrayed?' She says, reminding herself to take a good look at her ancient tapestry sometime through a client's eyes, to discern how her neutral backdrop could arouse such ire.

'Well, as a matter of fact, I am feeling betrayed right now. Feeling strongly betrayed.'

'By me?' she asks, doing her best to maintain her mask of impassivity.

'Yes, by you.' He shifts his gaze directly onto her.

'I see. Well you know it is not unusual for clients to engage in transference, to project feelings of hostility onto their … their helper.'

'That might well be of some consolation to you to know that, but I am afraid that it is just another bullshit piece of defensiveness that your profession seems to revel in. Yes, I am feeling betrayed by you, and by all you represent. By this whole coaching charade, by this bogus circus.'

'Now come on Justin!'

'No, I won't come on. I thought when I began this work that coaching would be a force for the good in this world, but it is corrupted, all too easily subject to manipulation. I feel foolish here. Duped, naive, humiliated. Not just by this current benighted client, but by the marketers that sold me the coaching training as this latest bright shiny thing, assuring me it would make me a healthy return on my investment many times over. They sold me a pup. All of you are selling me a whole kennel-full of needy pups. And the incessant yapping is driving me crazy, to the point where I cannot think or feel freely anymore. I wish a mercy killing on the whole menagerie.'

'So, you feel betrayed by the marketers?' Brenda asks, looking for an out.

'Yes. And I also feel duped by the professional body that promises to offer protection and standards when in fact there is no evidence of a protective umbrella, just daunting standards to abide by. Standards that are more likely to be used in evidence against me rather than to be offered as a shield during the bad times.'

Brenda sits mutely, awaiting the next scrambled metaphor, while wishing this rant would end soon. But it doesn't. In fact, it seems to her as if Justin has hardly started venting his spleen. This level of vehemence was all new to her. She could hardly wait to get on FaceTime to her 'supervisor's supervisor,' to work through all the parallel processes at play here. There might even be a journal paper in this, she consoles herself.

'And another thing,' continues Justin, 'this is the self-same body that continues to insist that I spend money I have not got on my CPD, my precious continued professional development, and yes, also insists that I retain the likes of you, a supervisor, with funds that I have not got.'

'So, it is not me that you feel is betraying you, so much as the whole system?' Brenda asks.

'Well, it is the system, but it is you as well. You buy into the system and benefit greatly from it. You buy into all of this as much as the others.'

Other misgivings continue to fuel his outpourings. "I have invested all of my redundancy money on reinventing myself as a coach. I realise only now that I sit right at the bottom of a giant Ponzi scheme, and I see no way that I am going to realise a personal return from this strange dance.'

'A Ponzi scheme?'

'Yes, it is a business term. A bit like pyramid selling.'

'I see,' she nodded, not really seeing at all, but not wishing to expose her ignorance still further.

'Let me explain. The only real way to get rich out of coaching is through taking money off other entry-level coaches who sit way down at the bottom of the pyramid. The vulnerable, eager newbies that have drunk the Kool-Aid. That is where the real money is to be made, not through doing face-to-face coaching itself with real, actual, sweaty, difficult clients. And yes, I do include you, Brenda, in being complicit in this Ponzi scheme.'

He takes pause, but the feelings do not subside. 'Look, I know my costs in becoming a coach have been immense, but perhaps now it is time to consider jumping the good ship coaching. My every instinct says get out now, while you can, before this sense of disillusionment, of resentment consumes me, before it makes me bitter and twisted. In fact ... I have had enough of the lot of you, for now,'

A silence prevails, which Brenda eventually breaks. 'Justin – just a thought. Let me stick my neck out here. Amid all of this understandable anger – do you at any point take agency for the crisis you have come to me with?' She knew in her heart that she was rolling the final dice here, but a degree of desperation was creeping in.

'I knew, I just knew, that at some point you would pull that self-responsibility rabbit out of the hat,' says Justin, clenching his fists on the arms of the chair. 'You are so predictable, so robotic. I do not sense an ounce of humanity in your entire being. I had a chance encounter with a stranger today, just before I came here, who showed

61

more empathic connection in her little finger than you have in your entire body. Look, before I say something I really regret, I am off. And I do not imagine me wanting to come back here again. Ever.'

Post-mortem on Toast.

As the sun creeps through the blinds, Justin awakens alone, disturbed only by the sound of breakfast being prepared downstairs. Seeking to remember what might lie in front of him this day, his half-dreaming state is interrupted by an unwelcome remnant of memory from the day before. Slowly details began to trickle through until the full picture develops of the train crash that was his storming out of yesterday's meeting with his coaching supervisor; to be quickly followed by the memory of his losing the Consignia client work.

As he slowly opens his eyes, he realises, with the heaviest of hearts, that he is going to have to explain the previous day's dramas to his wife. Well, nearly all of the dramas, with the exception of course, of his encounter with Joanna, which he was doing his best, even as he stirred, to bury as an aberration that may never be told. To anyone. Dressing in the nearest thing to hand, Justin finds his way downstairs, where the good mornings are perfunctory. He messes around with the coffee pot and the toaster, half-heartedly commenting on the trivia spewing from the radio, while trying to forestall Joy's inevitable questions regarding his evening's supervision. After all, for reasons he did not quite understand, Joy was more than a little obsessive regarding his supervision sessions.

'Oh, I forgot to ask, how did it go with the Brenda?' Joy asks as if on cue, 'I couldn't ask you last night. It turned out to be a late night with the team, and I did not want to disturb your sleep. Did she help sort out your head about the bust up at Consignia? Such bad luck about you losing your ungrateful posh client. But tell me the whole dreary story of that debacle when I have had something to eat, and have the stomach to hear of your ejection. But first of all, your psychological séance in the Brenda cave. Tell all.'

'Look, you know the rules,' Justin mutters into his toast, 'I am not allowed to disclose what occurs at those supervisory sessions. They are private. But, seeing as you ask, it went okay, same old same old, her asking lots of questions and saying "ummm" a lot.'

'Ummm,' Joy intones, unerringly parroting Brenda. 'By your defensive tone, I take it that it went anything but okay. Come on, cough up. After all, it is our family finances that are funding these intimate tete-a-tete with Brenda up on the Downs, in the Admiral's mansion. How did you explain away being fired by your client? Did you get run out of the Brownies for that?'

'You know those supervision sessions are my 'safe place', where I work stuff out. They are my place to deal with unwelcome feelings, to process my underlying developmental issues, to identify impasses and parallel processes, to calibrate my response to the emergent....' Justin allows his voice to tail off, realising that the empty phrases are most likely to be heard as bullshit.

Joy is scornful. 'Safe place? What is it that you say to her that you cannot say to me? I wish I had the luxury of such a safe place, must say, to talk away my stresses. All I get at work is problems: then more problems.'

'No, of course I do not take her into details of our home life. These sessions are about work only. And they are a professional requirement after all. They are not for personal catharsis.' Fully aware that he is digging the hole ever deeper, Justin is for all of that unable to stop himself stuttering on. 'I have explained to you before that there are all sorts of rules about professional conversations with supervisors. There are boundaries, red lines, you know the score.'

'Well, you have mansplained often enough before about these various coaching equivalents of the off-side rule that we-women-are-too-stupid-to-understand,' Joy sighs, 'but our family money is funding these sessions, on top of all the rest of your continuous personal – what was it again? Your CP whatever?'

'Development?'

Hands on hips, Joy turns to confront Justin directly. 'Development? Continuous Personal Development? CPD? Ceepeedeepio? Feels more like continuous family impoverishment to me. Look, sorry to dump on you, when you got a kicking yesterday, but we both know that we are struggling to get by, and it is hard to bear when we waste this money on this surrogate work-wife, when it might be just as easy for you to talk to your real wife about what is on your mind.'

'Well, I hope I do talk to you about what is going on. Just as you talk to me about your work stuff. Neither of us is in a good place right now. And I hear your anger and frustration….'

'Uh oh, here we go,' she says, barely able to suppress her exasperation, 'I have asked you before you to keep that coaching lingo for your clients – and not to bring it home to use on me. You know it drives me crazy – it is so artificial, some kind of verbal dance, meaning nothing, talking about feelings with fancy words while avoiding feeling anything.'

Justin recoils in the face of this volley, stammering, 'no, that is not how it is, though I know it upsets you when I use such phrasing. Sorry, it has become a habit. But besides anything else, I am required to have regular supervision if I want to stay in business, whether you or I like it or not.'

Noticing Justin slump forward over the kitchen counter, Joy eases back some. 'I know it is not easy for you. But I just want to register that I am seriously unimpressed at what you have gotten into here with all this coaching stuff, and what it is doing to you. You just seem like a different person from the one I knew before you took up this coaching malarkey. And I really think I liked the previous, less complicated, less tortured you.'

'I don't think I have changed that much,' Justin protests, while in reality having little true grip on who he was anymore.

'I am not sure if you are the best judge of that,' challenges Joy. 'But I hope at least that something practical does come out of all this time and money you spend on her. For example, did she fix your latest work crisis that you 'took' to her? God! That is what you all say, isn't it? "Took to her". And now I have started to use this stupid hippy jargon as well, despite fighting the urge. I am catching the virus too, and I don't like it. This is how this brainwashing you have been subject to happens, without you even realising. And it transfers to me. It insidiously spreads to your family life, even to the way you talk to the kids.'

Justin senses - amid this conversational wreckage - an opening that might show his reckless actions of the previous evening in some sort of favourable light. 'Well, just so you know – I lied to you about how my session with Brenda went last night. Sorry but I did.'

'That is okay. Couples lie to each other all the time, sometimes with the best of intentions. And?'

'And no, actually, she didn't fix it. Far from it. In fact, it might relieve you to know that she was so far from fixing it that I sacked her there and then - on the spot - then stomped out. I think we are due the last invoice from her, then that is the last you will ever hear of her. We will be post-Brenda. You may not know it, but I do share your frustrations with her, and also share some of your misgivings about the whole process.'

She closes the dishwasher door slowly, allowing a small smile of surprise to spread across her face. 'Oh, well, that is good to know. So, you do have some spine after all. And I am glad that that over-inquisitive mother superior is gone from our lives; stopped snooping on your private life, your work disasters, and possibly even getting off on details of our marriage. It feels like there is something quite vampiric in this supervising role.'

'I think you might well be right. And there might well be something vampiric in the coaching work we do with clients also. Slyly sucking out their lifeblood, their natural vitality, in the name of helping along. Feeding off the hollowed-out human carcasses that these corporations leave strewn on the workplace floor, disregarding the cost. Anyway, she is gone.'

'Yes, she is. I hope forever and a day. Good riddance. But wait a minute. Don't you need her for - what do you call it – your professional license to operate? Doesn't your Coaching Fraternity check out whether you engage such a parasite, to ensure that you are spilling your guts to on a regular basis, while paying through the nose for the privilege?'

'Yes, it does.' Justin recoils yet again at Joy's grasp of the coaching requirements that hog-tie him, a knowledge that he surmises is borne of disdain as much as of wifely interest.

She ploughs on, remorselessly. 'So, you will need a Brenda replacement, for your snooper's charter mark 2? I thought the surveillance culture was bad enough at my distribution centre, but this beats it into a cocked hidden CCTV camera. Somehow, I can't imagine that the coaching cult will allow you just to sack her then walk away, without some kind of reaction?'

'Perhaps there will be consequences,' says Justin, for the first time considering this possibility. 'And yes, I will need to find a replacement.'

'Okay, then go for it,' encourages Joy. 'But next time around, could you let your wife see the catalogue before you choose another Brenda – pretty please? And .... just a question… are there any men that do this supervisory nappy-changing thing, or is this the sole preserve of women with higher consciousness and expanded mindfulness, seasoned with a large dollop of sanctimonious virtue- signalling?'

Trying to ignore the snark, Justin says, 'it's not the gender of the supervisor but the personal 'fit' that matters. But yes, you are right. There are more women than men doing this.'

Joy jumps on this reply. 'Ah yes the 'fit', I remember that term' she says, ratcheting up the sarcasm one more notch. 'I well remember that last time around it took... what … about three 'chemistry meetings' with four different debutants before you compared the various test tube specimens, to finally materialise ballistic Brenda. Who has proved to be as much use as an ashtray on a motorbike, and an expensive one at that. Excuse the spluttering of mixed metaphors, but honestly…'

'Well. I hope I have learned, from this first toe-in-the-water, not to make the same mistakes again.'

'I hope so too. So okay, but do we really have to go through all of that runners and rider's business again, before you get down to some serious – what do you call it, "psychological contracting" with the next lucky candidate?' Joy sits back, awaiting as simple and uncomplicated an answer as might ever be possible from this rule-bound coaching universe.

'Well, I just hope it will not be as tortuous next time around,' Justin replies, 'and anyway, this conversation is a little academic right now, as I need to find some work to get supervised before I seek out my next Brendster. My first priority today is to try to recover something from my lost coaching assignment, or find replacement work, before I even have to think about my personal support needs.'

'While you sort out your work front, could you not get a mate to do the supervising thing? Or even me? Anyway, before you become too suicidal, get the kids downstairs and off to school, please? I need to get to work, to keep the robots in the call-centre roboting. Sorry, but I will listen to your story of your being fired later on. I have been remiss. It must have been awful, after all the work you did, and those great expectations.'

'Thanks, the drama was of Dickensian proportions. But there is no real need to chew over the entrails of that saga once more. It will just make me depressed. Right now, I need to channel the spirit of my dad in his younger days. I need to pick myself up, dust myself off, and get back on the pony once more.' He is at some level pleased to be able to kill this Consignia post-mortem at birth, while aware that his time with Joanna had been entirely instrumental in putting the whole debacle behind him for the time being. He had no idea how that conversation had achieved that miracle. But it just had.

In the car and heading for school, the children are quick to pick up on the stressful vibe generated by their parent's kitchen squabble. Their low-level discomfort is communicated through little signs, like kicking the back of his driver's seat; or pointing out random children walking to school, with Amelia declaring these kids to be, 'normal children from normal families. It must be nice, being in a normal family. Why can't we be a normal family, Daddy?'

Justin sighs. "Our family is normal too, in its own way. This morning was just Mummy and Daddy having one of their moments, something that all couples do to let off steam. It is all blown over now.'

'Daddy?' asks Adam's unconvinced voice from the back seat.

'What is it?' asks a distracted Justin, trying vainly to keep his eyes on the traffic. 'I told you not to worry about our squabbles.'

Adam persists with his line of questioning. 'No, it is not about you bickering at each other. That is normal. It is just that we thought we heard Mummy saying that you had left your proper job and had gone to work in a Ponzi. What is a Ponzi Daddy? Is it a Pizza place? Cos we hope it is.'

Amelia decides this conversation thread was too good to miss.

'Daddy, if you are working in a pizza shop, why don't you bring pizza's home? We don't mind eating the funny shaped ones other customers don't want. Just feed us the bad stuff. Lots of fat and cheese and added sugar. Yum.'

'Sorry to disappoint, kids, but I am afraid my work does not involve pizza crust stuffing. Not yet anyway. My job now is to sit and listen to people's problems,' Justin explains, while realising that this description of his work feels lamely improbable, even as he utters it.

Undeterred, Adam continues with his well-intentioned career counselling. 'Why do that, Daddy? That is so boring. Why not get them to tell you nice stories instead? And you can't bring their problems home like you can a pizza.' Adam leans on his elbows, smugly satisfied with the logic of this.

'Well, that is true enough,' agrees their bemused father, 'though sometimes I do bring their problems home with me. It is just that you cannot see them.' His mind is drawn to the extent to which images of client's dilemmas habitually float in front of his eyes during dinner, distracting him from being present for the kids.

'Well you could bring home some photos of your clients, Daddy,' piped up Amelia, helpfully, 'and then we could see your work! I am sure they would not mind having their pictures up on the kitchen wall, like they do on a white-board in those murder series on telly. Then we would know who you were talking about. We're sure they wouldn't mind. Bring home, like, selfies of these people looking troubled, so we, your beloved children, can have a peek at what you do, and who you do it to.'

Adam feels sure this pictorial invitation needs development. 'You know what Daddy? You could ask them to draw pictures of their problems. Then we could show these drawings to our friends, to explain what their father does. Jeremy's dad is a fireman and he is really proud of his dad. Jeremy does not have to explain to us about climbing up ladders and stuff. We all know what his dad does already, and his dad is a hero. And Jeremy shows us some real pictures of his all-action dad saving cats, and picking drowning people off beaches when they get stuck in the mud, and flying in helicopters to rescue them from cliffs. Our teacher even had Jeremy do his dad's job as a project. We love Jeremy's dad.'

'Daddy, help us do a project on you!' insists Amelia. 'Even if you have to change your job. It would make us feel so proud of you. You never get stuck in mud then have to get out of it, like Jeremy's dad does.'

Justin feels he needs to admit defeat on this 'best dad' competition before it really ramps up. 'Well if there is one thing I know for certain, that is that you are both a couple of stick-in-the-muds. But I do love the mud you get stuck in, though I have no idea where it gurgles up from. Probably on your mother's side, that mud sticking talent.'

Adam was not going to be deflected from his mission to pin down his father's trade to his classmates in a way that might make sense. 'So, Daddy, can I say to my friends that you work in a problem factory? That you make up problems there?'

'Yes, you can say that. And sometimes I think I do manufacture problems, now you put it that way. Now, look, we have been outside school for ten minutes and people are staring at us, blocking everyone's way. Out you get and don't forget your backpacks and your lunches. Enjoy your day and try not to get into too much trouble. Just be aware that if you drop your concentration for just one second, you might just allow some learning to creep in. Just saying.'

Sitting in the silence of his car, Justin quietly admits to himself that his children have a point. It is not just their lack of understanding of a grown-up world. His work really is muddy. Indeterminate. A swamp. In no mood to return home to his so-called office with only his pot plant and his futile coaching certificates for company, he heads instead into a nearby layby to check the emails that have been vibrating on his phone in his top pocket. He sees the regular email notification from his phone provider offering upgrades on last week's upgrade, and a reminder from his professional coaching body that his fees are due. Amid this unwelcome spam, two mails non-standard emails attract his immediate attention.

One is from his spurned supervisor Brenda, inviting him to a 'review meeting' as a matter of some urgency, in order 'to resolve the underlying and unresolved issues' which had 'left her shaken' after his abrupt exit. If he knew the coach-speak for, 'It is not you, it is me,' then he would readily have used it. Instead, he invokes an oblique wording that might just deflect her for a while. His fingers tap out,

'Dear Brenda,

'I understand your disquiet, but please bear with me for a while, as I am reviewing my supervisory needs. Be assured that I will let you know once my thinking has progressed. Sorry for any inconvenience but this is going to take some deep processing.'

The second email is from Richard, the Consignia Finance Director responsible for his introduction to his nemesis, the CEO Philip Junior. Justin recoils, thinking this email must be signalling the final nail in the coffin of his assignment with his company – and perhaps the death knell in his already faltering career. in the coffin of his assignment with his company – and perhaps the death knell in his already faltering career.

'Dear Justin,

I am probably the last person you want to be hearing from right now, but I am just writing to say that I feel really bad about the way things went yesterday, and of course I take some responsibility for that, given I brought you along in the first place. But if you are still up for rescuing something from the wreckage– and I would fully understand if you were not – then I would very much like to take you for lunch to see if anything can be done to re-set this whole project. Talking of which, I wanted to say that I found your survey feedback results that you left behind for our perusal more than useful. In point of fact, they were really insightful. And another colleague on the team told me that your analysis "captured the team's problems to a tee".'

Please let me know if you are disposed for lunch.

Best regards

Richard.'

Justin sits bolt upright on reading this, feeling his self-esteem rise up through his leatherette seat, when only seconds before it had been seeping all the way through to the sump. Trying not to sound too over-keen, he replies politely, thanking Richard for his kind words and his luncheon invitation, which he is more than happy to accept. Richard's response is instantaneous, saying he is relieved that Justin is not discouraged, and suggesting that they make lunch date this week or next.

Deciding to play a little hard to get, Justin replies, 'regarding this week, I am only free today, due to a cancellation - which I know would be a stretch - or failing that Friday.'

A lie of course, as his calendar was yawningly free. However, Richard bites on that gambit, writing, 'I am, as chance would have it, free today, and that it would be good to get what was on my mind off my mind and into your mind, while it is still fresh. I like the way you listen. Helps me to hear what I am thinking. Let us meet in the Lebanese Restaurant on Queens Road, 12.30. They know me there.'

Given that he has time to spare – and bearing in mind the life-coaching injunction that no idle moment must ever be wasted – Justin decides to put to the test the visualisation skills picked up on his 'reflective practice for advanced coaches workshop' - only £457 plus VAT – guaranteed to 'illumine your inner magician'. Hovering above himself in a magic metaphoric helicopter – ignoring for a moment the confines of his car seat – he is no less than amazed to register the mood shift materialising within his inner chakras.

Slowing his heartbeat through tantric breathing exercises, he pays attention to the affirmative dialogue replacing the earlier swamp of self-doubt. 'You are still in the game after all,' whispers an exhalant voice, the voice of the top dog,

'In fact, you were never really out of the game at all! All those rumours of your professional demise are grossly exaggerated by your negative self-construct. Hell, you are more than still in the game. You are totally on it, nearing the top of your highest powers. You have gone into a commercial war zone, have spoken truth to power, even at the price of being shown the door, and lived to tell the tale. Just look at you! Here you are, poised to kick open the saloon's swing-doors once more, the comeback kid returned to clean up the town. You are not suffering from Imposter Syndrome. You are the real thing.'

This wave of self-affirmation materialises another email, this time from The Parallelogram Practice, responding to his application to become an associate of theirs. And he smiles at the realisation that this manifestation could be a dream come true, as this coaching intermediary has promised to solve all of his difficulties with marketing and cash-flow management, leaving him free to stick to his core business, which is to 'radiate your own brand of awesome.' He reads on with highest expectation.

'Dear Justin

We delighted to say that, following your recent application to join our team, and your performance at your 'chemistry' interview, you greatly impressed us all. In fact, so much so that we would very much like you to commence our associate on-boarding process forthwith, subject to references.

Please let us know if you are happy for us to contact your references as soon as we can, going forward. We so look forward to your name burnishing the sidebar of our website.'

Justin exhales a deep tantric breath, hearing his top dog growl delightedly, 'Bingo. Another bull's-eye. Two bull's-eyes in a row, all in one morning. Justin, baby, you are on a roll.' Time for more guided visualisation; time to channel his inner greatness. 'Justin, I see you sailing through this opportunity. I see you happily, proudly, practising your coaching behind the shield of an established entity. You will delegate all invoices and lawyerly matters while you stride the coaching universe unencumbered by administrivia.'

Even as he rides high on this wave of affirmation, Justin cannot suppress a voice of doubt, nagging away in the background, even while he is so deeply immersed in the flow. What is this unwelcome voice of hesitation threatening to unseat his seemingly irrepressible momentum? Was he not doing the guided meditation right? Had he forgotten a necessary step? Ah, there is no crack in the universe, no flaw in the method. There is just one unignorable blot on the landscape clouding his euphoria. The requirement for references. And one of the references he had given to Parallelogram was none other than that of Brenda, the supervisor. Whoops. However, there was no time to deal with that bump in the road right now. Not now that he had a vital, make or break, life-defining, watershed lunch meeting with Richard Finch to prepare for.

Joy sits at her "hot desk" in the open-plan office, blankly staring at her screen. Just too many emails, and her phone has been ringing off the hook all morning. She pushes back from her desk, wishing in vain that she had enough headspace to prepare for the disciplinary meeting that was coming her way. After all this time convening such inquisitions, she was now to be the one in the dock. Seeing her friend Sharon heading out from their open-plan office to the smoking area, she decides to follow her out the door before she starts shouting at her screen.

'Hi, Sharon. I need a break. I am suffocating in there. Just too much coming at me.'

'Oh, hello Joy, nice to see you out here. I could do with some company. A bit tired of feeling furtive, out here all alone, pursuing my filthy habit.' She opens a pack of cigarettes and fumbles for her lighter. 'Want one?'

I really shouldn't....' Joy shakes her head. 'I told Justin I have given up. Well actually, I have given up. Please don't tempt me.'

'You sure?' asks Sharon, pulling deeply on her first draw. 'I have seen your giving up before.'

'Sharon, you are the worst. Oh well, maybe just a puff. Things really are piling in on top of me right now. Thick and fast.' Joy accepts the proffered cigarette, turning it over between her fingers, before drawing deeply.

'I know what you mean.' Sharon looks up to the sky. 'All of us in the office are feeling the strain. Anything in particular? Do say.'

'Well, I a whole mix of things really, layering on top of each other.' Joy sighs. 'I am feeling more and more that I am being made to do things to staff, bad things, things that run against all that I stand for, but the pressure is there to do them. And sometimes I just don't. And I get into trouble, then I worry that I am under more scrutiny than ever. It is a vicious circle. Are we safe out here, by the way?' Her eyes scan the warehouse walls, looking for surveillance devices.

'Oh, I think so. No hidden cameras that I know of, out here, by the bike sheds. This is probably the last place at work where we can speak freely. How are things working out for Justin, after the dying bank loan drama?'

'Don't! Fact is, that husband of mine is getting himself into deeper and deeper water with this coaching lark. He was banished from a new client the other day, and has not much else on the horizon. Our family fortunes may soon rest on what I bring in here, and that feels under threat.'

Sharon offers her a sisterly pat on the arm. 'As if you didn't have enough to deal with, given all that is coming your way here at work.'

'Tell me about it,' mutters Joy, finishing off her friend's cigarette. 'It is not just him losing work. His professional licence may be under threat, too, due to his own stupidity. Picking a fight with his supervisor, Brenda, whom I don't trust an inch. I really have no idea what her agenda is with him, but I am suspicious.'

'Uh ho.' Sharon's waxed eyebrows rise in inquiry. 'The jealousy antennae twitching then?'

'Could be. A little. And I am not usually the jealous type. But he shares so much with Brenda. And after spilling his guts to that cursed witch, he now picks a fight with her, pissing her off royally. Dunno why, but I am obsessing a little about her.'

'Sounds like it. A bit. But then a woman's instinct is a powerful laser beam. You might want to trust that suspicion.'

'Thanks,' says Joy. 'You could be right. I have never met her face to face.... yeh, that's it. I want to sniff her out. Make my own mind up as to whether she is a threat to him, or to me?'

'Why not just do that? Set up a meet? On some pretext or another?'

'I would like that. But I can't just show up at her door. There are probably triple padlocks on that secure installation. And there are all sorts of less visible firewalls around her sacred professional relationship with Justin. She would not allow me to talk to her directly about any of that.'

'I get it. But hang on; she is for hire, is she not? Can't you just book an appointment? You coach enough folk around here to qualify for supervision from the outside. Make out you need her support. Be bold!'

'That is true enough.' Joy brightens at this prospect. 'Great idea! But hang on. She would recognise my name.'

'Well use another name. Get smart. Go undercover!'

'What a mate you are, Sharon. And I am so tempted.'

'So, go for it. Pick up the gauntlet! Accept my dare.'

'But this is an outrageous plan, Sharon. So duplicitous. Justin would go bonkers if he got to know of such a thing happening behind his back.'

'Well don't tell him!' Sharon lights another cigarette, puffs, then offers it to Joy. 'You need to scratch that itch, girl. You never know what you might find out. Trust your instinct that something is going on there with that woman that you need to know. Do not be the last one in the loop.'

'You are making a strong case here, Sharon. Tell you what I'll do. I might just take the first step, ring her, she how far I can go. Undercover. Use my maiden name.'

'A maiden once again. He he. Just do it.'

'I will. Use my maiden name, Highbury, just as I do at work. No need to mention the Drake name. Might just mix up the name further though, to ensure that she cannot trace me anywhere. And thanks for the push. Anyway, enough about me. How is your life outside this place? The choir full of women who can't sing still going strong?'

'Yep, getting more tuneful by the week. And the yoga is going great too. Amazing what you have time for when single.'

'How could yoga be fun? Sounds like torture.'

'It is more action-packed than you might think,' giggles Sharon. 'This week the fire alarm went off, just when we had all adopted the deep-dog.'

'Too much information. But go on.'

'We were so busy deep dogging, we just assumed it was a fire drill. But it was an actual real fire, lapping at the door of our studio.'

'And?'

'Our instructor opened the door…'

'Silly girl.' surmised Joy. 'I know what happened next. In came the flames and there you were untangling yourselves from deep dogging to do your fire walking act. The smell of smouldering Lycra everywhere?'

'You have the scene perfectly Joy! Then the bodybuilders from the gym caught wind of our plight and came to manhandle us out. That was the good bit. Can't wait for next week. Might just bring a can of petrol and some matches.'

'You lucky, lucky woman. We had best go back inside,' says Joy, stubbing out the cigarette, 'before the disciplinary flames begin to singe our asses too.'

'Yep, the guards in the goon towers have spotted us.'

A Taste of Beirut

The Lebanese restaurant on Queens Road is somewhat hushed in ambience. Richard has booked a cubicle far from the main action, in a space that allows them to talk in confidence. Justin decided not to dress up for this meeting, but then feels immediately mismatched, as the place exudes understated opulence. Richard rises to shake his hand warmly, their eye contact strong. Perched on the table beside Richard's elegantly folded linen napkin sits a large glass of frosted white wine. Sensing the direction of Justin's gaze, he confides that he did not usually drink at lunchtime, but that today does not feel like a normal day by any stretch of the imagination. 'Perhaps, Justin, you would wish to join me in a glass?' Hardly waiting for a reply, Richard indicates to the waiter that 'we may as well order the bottle.'

Over their mezze starter plates, Richard first of all apologises for the rough treatment dished out to Justin from the CEO, but says, 'Don't take this personally. Philip treats everyone in this way – including his own team, and such rudeness is frankly inexcusable.' He reveals that, post Justin's untimely exit, Philip had called the executive team together, berating them one and all for allowing such a troubling and biased report ever to see the light of day. This rebuke was not much of a surprise to any of the executive team, given that they have witnessed their leader's erratic behaviour deteriorating by the day. Indeed, it steels Richard's view that Justin's abrupt removal was a further symptom that Philip was a rogue elephant that needed stopping in his tracks, before more damage was done. Post their communal reprimand, Richard said that the team retreated in secret conclave to mull over what to do next, given that none of them felt that they could carry on like this much longer, without the whole company blowing apart.

Richard reassures Justin that - in his role as Finance Director - he had already authorised his recent invoice for the survey work, and that this would be paid immediately, in part to honour what they had all agreed was a solid and insightful piece of work. Secondly, given the mutinous groundswell among the team, he wants Justin to know that he has needed to take the lead in dealing with Philip's worst excesses, given that no one else was stepping up to the plate. He said that in plotting a way forward, he would much value some of Justin's time to help him sort out his thinking.

'So, you want me to give you a right good listening to?' Justin asks. They push the plates back, ready to get down to some serious coaching work, amid the remains of the humus and the stuffed olives. Snapping into "flow" mode, Justin is aware that in exploring the history and the possible futures that lie ahead of Richard and Consignia, he is losing all sense of time. His sequence of questions come effortlessly, evoking from Richard deeper and sometimes painfully honest answers. The bulk of the conversational excavation done, Justin pulls out a pen and pad to sketch out some of the issues they have covered, and the options open to Richard; this process of summarising on paper yielding a further generation of insight and clarity. Done for now, they both settle into contemplative silence. Eventually, Richard pushes his napkin to one side, breaking the silence to say that he has gained a new level of understanding and resolve regarding the many challenges ahead. Justin seizes on this moment to say, 'It has been good to help you see things more clearly, and to know better what options are open to you. But this time around I am sure you will understand that - before I get in more deeply – that I need to properly secure the scope of any further engagement, before I drift into a situation where I am overly exposed again.'

'Oh yes, absolutely, I get that,' Richard replies, 'and for my part I want a clearly contracted way forward for your engagement too. No guarantees at this point, but I feel confident that I can get my fellow executive team players to sign off to an independent audit of management performance - including my performance - with you as a key player in that process.'

'That sounds good, but what about Philip's reaction?' In his question, Justin notices how much his fear of Philip's wrath haunts him still.

'Well, If the whole team is behind such a review, then the CEO can hardly resist, lest he seems unnecessarily worried as to what him showing outright resistance would say about his own fears of what might he be exposed to in the process. We will appeal to his vanity – once more – and that should help to seal things.'

Justin mulls over these reassurances, saying, 'on that basis, this arrangement seems good to me, especially as you will honour the outstanding invoice. But we need to have my contract properly defined this time around, including some protection in case of premature cancellation.'

'Yes, of course we must do that,' agrees Richard, firmly. 'In fact, I wish I had done that first time around. Oh, speaking of which, if we need to do this properly, I will need your CV again, just to remind my colleagues that you are fully credentialed, including some references and testimonials.'

Justin does his best to conceal his second outbreak of reference-induced anxiety of the day. 'Of course, that is fair enough. Let me draft some terms of reference right away, then get that to you. I will chase up the references directly.'

With that, Richard settles the bill, allowing them to proceed, blinking, from the stygian Lebanese darkness into the Clifton sunshine, to go about their separate but somehow indivisible ways.

Justin trips down the hill from the restaurant, feeling nothing less than euphoric at the way things are left with Richard. The sweet buzz of a successful sale is compounded by a light-headedness traceable to the unaccustomed lunchtime wine. Justin absently pauses by the noble Victoria Rooms, deciding to rest awhile by the shimmering fountain, iridescent in the summer's sun. A throng of students mill on the broad stone steps under the faux Gothic portico, probably taking a break between their exams, for it is that time of year. Overhearing their post-mortems on the last exam – 'they never said that would come up! Bah!' - Justin is jolted back, in a flash, to his own student days at Bristol, over twenty years ago, when he uttered the self-same protests. Watching the students triggers a memory of a fine summer's evening in 1991, when he and his friends' final exams had just finished.

Back then, a lifetime ago, Justin's` nickname was 'Rake', based on a corruption of his family name Drake. 'De Rake,' they called him, with their worst Rasta accents. The reasons for selecting this name were lost in history, but nevertheless, Rake sticks to this day among those remaining friends, and it was a tag that Justin really enjoys. That summer's evening in 1991, his sadistic chums selected him to be the first victim to be thrown into these self-same fountains. 'Dunk the Rake, Dunk the Rake!' they cried as one. The drunken, half-drowned Rake hopelessly splashed about, soon enough joined by his friends in this watery release from student life. They bonded, perhaps for the last time, that evening.

Shortly after that epic goodbye, Joy came into his life for the first time. Jolted by that early memory of her, he is seized by a wish to ring her, to let her know that the meeting with Richard went well, and that he would spill (as well as burn) the beans over dinner, kids allowing. But he knows he is not allowed to ring her, given the stringent prohibition on making or receiving calls at her Magic Carpet distribution centre. Instead, he sends a simple text saying, 'it went well', while hoping it gets through. He pauses after sending, impulsively adding another text. He contemplates sending a witty, self- deprecating piece: but instead finds his thumbs punching in 'I am at the fountain where we first met. I simply love you, my Joy, my life, more than ever. X x x.'

The Set Up.

'Hello, Brenda Seagate here.'

'Oh, hello Brenda. Pardon me for ringing out of the blue, but my name is Joy Highbury -Harcross.' Even as she says it aloud for the first time, reading from her prompt sheet, Joy realises that she is already enjoying her newly confected identity. 'I was searching for a coaching supervisor on Google, and your profile looks excellent. Probably just what I was looking for. I was wondering if we might have an exploratory conversation?'

Brenda purrs down the line, 'yes, that is my occupation, and glad to hear that you are interested in my services. Tell me a little about your practice, please, before we proceed.'

'Well, I work for a large company here in Bristol, on the HR side.' Joy peers at her prompt sheet once more. 'I seem to spend most of my working day coaching staff with problems and difficulties. My colleagues help as a sounding board, but I feel I need right now is some help from the outside, an objective view. Someone who knows what I am facing, can reflect back where I might be going wrong.'

'I see,' replies Brenda. 'Well, from what I have heard so far, I think you have come to the right place. Let me tell you about my supervisory practice. It has three pillars. These are to support: to educate: and to ensure that professional standards are being maintained. I presume that you are a member of a professional coaching body?'

'Not as yet,' says Joy, glad that she anticipated this question, 'but I am shopping around, so to speak, for a suitable professional body. The front-runner so far is the Coaching Fraternity.'

'That would be a good choice. Many of my clients belong there, and I am a member myself. I would strongly advise that you join up soon.

Apart from your own protection and education, the Fraternity's standards would give a robust framework around which to build our developmental conversation.'

'Good, I will get right on it,' says Joy, enthusiastically, while feeling no appetite whatsoever for pursuing this path. 'So how might we proceed?'

'The first step would be to have what we call a chemistry meeting,' says Brenda, quite unaware of the face Joy is pulling at the mention of this benighted term. 'By that I mean that we meet, on an exploratory basis, where each of us assess whether the fit is right. And at that chemistry meeting, I will outline my terms and conditions, which you will know doubt be curious about. But this first meeting is free of charge.'

'That is generous. And I am keen to get started,' says Joy, pressing for closure.

'I am glad to hear such enthusiasm from a new client,' says Brenda. 'If the fit is right, then we can devise a contract that will run for the duration of the first year. Please be aware that this is no light undertaking. You need to be fully committed.'

'Oh, I will be. So, Brenda, when would you be free for this meeting?'

'Well in fact I have a few slots today or tomorrow, or else early next week. Today's slots are only late afternoon I am afraid, four or five o'clock.'

'Oh, five o'clock would be perfect. I can drop in after work, encourage me to leave early for a change. I see you are on Clifton Down? It is on my way home.'

'That is fine, Joy. See you five o'clock this evening then. I am looking forward to it.'

The Vanity of Small Differences.

Still captive to the free-wheeling dream state induced by his Lebanese lunch with Richard, Justin's feet lead him, as if on a piece of string, towards the thronging Clifton Triangle, replete with its many branded, hyper-competitive casual dining emporia. Time-scarce customers queue impatiently outside various doors, tapping on their phones, some absently gossiping about their work and their colleagues, especially about the unbearable ones, while they wait to finally flourish their contactless credit cards, the payment method where it feels as if no money has exchanged hands at all.

Drifting away at speed from this feeding frenzy, Justin pauses outside Bristol Museum, his eyes are caught by a large, garishly tinted banner, loudly proclaiming that Grayson Perry's 'Vanity of Small Differences' exhibition is now showing. This happenstance delights him, as he avidly followed the TV series 'All in the Best Possible Taste,' where Grayson walked viewers through his process of conceiving these monumental tapestries that seek to uncover the hidden mysteries of our contemporary class system. Justin is thrilled to have coincidentally stumbled upon this showing, and to find it out here in the provinces too, not trapped in some effete Islington gallery. While the TV series gave him some sense of the themes this show was freighting, he is delighted to have the opportunity to encounter the real thing.

He duly purchases his electronic exhibition ticket in the hallway - only to find that the RF code does nothing to raise the rail-station type barrier placed at the gallery entry. He tentatively beckons a passing curator who curses the barrier, then magics her ID card, leaving him free to enter within. He enjoys witnessing her contempt for this apparently labour-saving yet faulty technology. Catching her eye, he says, 'I doubt if us Luddites can do much to hold back the march of these robots, even when they fail to do their job. Perhaps your automatic barrier should shout – "disturbing artwork in the bagging area."'

'Oh yes' she chuckles, evidently enjoying this invitation to conspiracy, 'Grayson would have liked that announcement. Perhaps I should tip him off.'

Moving into the gallery, Justin notices that, despite his small screen acquaintance with these tapestries under the televisual guidance of the artist himself, he finds himself wholly unprepared for the scale of these six spectacular tapestries, when hung together in the same vaulted room. He muses that no amount of two-dimensional representation, especially on a small screen, can ever truly capture the immediacy and ambition of the tangible artwork. Each tapestry bears an adjoining legend, but he finds that the real joy lies in trying to make sense of the many artefacts contained within each of the pieces, and their juxtaposition one with another. Embedded within the tapestries are tales of middle-class angst, of the survival of 'old money' snobbery, and of a northern community shattered by job losses and industrial decline.

The theme of the barriers to social mobility – or the sheer pain of making a move through the class structure – reminds him of his and so many others' struggles with the perils of moving between social classes, though he fears that his current trajectory is socially downwards, perhaps to the bottom.

His attempts at exploring the minute details of each piece - as well as standing back to enjoy the totality of each tapestry - is now obscured by an incoming party of grey-haired, probably retired suburbanites. This tribe, fresh or not so fresh off a tourist coach, listlessly assemble around their highly articulate guide, whose sparkling enthusiasm for the exhibits is entirely undimmed by the shuffling passivity of her audience.

Justin grudgingly moves ahead of these pilgrims towards the final tapestry, which depicts the death of Perry's protagonist Thomas Rakewell. This sad, vainglorious depiction of upper-class shabbiness touches him deeply, for reasons he cannot easily put my finger on. A sidewall of the gallery displays two set of prints, one of Hogarth's Rakes progress, a highly moralistic eighteenth-century tale of a rich young man's downfall; the other a modern rendering on the same theme by David Hockney of his encounter with the underside of New York City in the Sixties, when, as a young artist, he struggled to make sense of previously unimagined hedonistic sub-culture with all of its temptations and pitfalls.

Culturally saturated enough for one day by all of this contrasting richness, Justin tags behind the crocodile of the grey ones as they shuffle out towards the gift shop, still sullen and expressionless. He asks himself - are they mute, stupefied, in the face of great art, or are they just mute? Were they offended by the various representations of middle-class anxiety, or did they just fail to identify with any of it? Justin muses that it is little wonder that the Bristol-based artist Banksy entitled his recent London show 'Exit through the Gift Shop,' speculating that Banksy's point was that unless a commercial transaction has taken place, then a poetic moment has not occurred. If this group were seeking a memento along the lines of a set of 'Vanity' fridge magnets, then they would have been disappointed, as there was no evidence of such kitsch. Justin espouses two possible reasons for this omission. The first would be that such items were never considered – on the grounds of taste. Or secondly, that Banksy has anonymously bought all such items, then systematically destroyed them.

Walking out of the museum, Justin picks up a flyer for an upcoming show at the revamped St Georges Chapel. Entitled 'Human Cargo', it looks intriguing indeed, a two-man show capturing the story of human migration through Bristol during the peak of the slavery years. Determined more than ever - after the impact of the Vanities - to enjoy his culture live rather than mediated through a screen, Justin makes a commitment to go and see this show when it opens in several weeks time.

Out again in the sparkling sunshine, his phone alarm buzzing in his pocket reminds him to pick up his car before the parking meter runs out. He heads past the imposing gothic tower that is the University's pride and joy, the Wills Memorial Building, to cross the busy road towards Berkeley Square, tucked in behind the main thoroughfare. He realises with a start that time has flown since his career-defining lunch, and that he needs to get a shift on, to pick up the kids, then to head to his coaching network meeting in Clifton, perhaps the last thing he wants to do, but then attendance is a requirement of his CPD. He returns to his pious Prius parked outside the Whole Health Hub, an impressive Georgian edifice set at the highest point of Berkeley Square. This terrace is overlooked only by the Cabot Tower, one of the few remaining symbols of faded mercantilism in the city, which at the time of its construction in 1897 was the highest edifice in town. Justin remembers reading somewhere that a primary motivator for the Wills family – of tobacco trading fame – in building the university's

Wills Tower in 1915 was for its industrialist funded height to eclipse that of the mercantile Cabot tower. Who knows whether such claims are true, he thinks, but they do have a certain ring to them.

Justin is a part-time associate of the Whole Health Hub, hiring rooms as required for his coaching assignations, even if the allocation of rooms is somewhat random. The WHH centre is hired out on a timeshare basis by an array of alternative health practitioners of every hue. His business coaching practice is right at the conventional end of the Whole Health and Wellness practitioner spectrum, but as the Hub brochure says, all of its practitioners share a focus on growth and renewal, rather than fixing problems or pathologies. 'We are the one-stop-shop for wellness, not illness', the brochure boldly claims, though there is little doubt that many who come through the doors could be defined as the well-heeled 'worried well.'

Justin's time-sharing of rooms means that beggars can't be choosers, especially if the need is immediate. As a result, he often finds himself coaching in a room replete with a massage table or a full-size skeleton, each of which can set a disquieting tone. His preference is for one of the smaller, more intimate rooms located far up the imposing Georgian staircase, and beyond earshot of the shouty spinning classes on the first floor.

The only trouble with the rooms up in the loft is that one of the adjacent rooms is block-booked by a voice coach, who puts his clients through an entire repertoire of vocal release, by way of refinement and catharsis. While Justin can see the benefits of this treatment for the voice coach's impressive client list of broadcasters, politicians, and shy executives, he notices that his clients can find it difficult to sustain reflective contemplation when the backdrop is Mongolian throat singing.

Justin consoles himself with the thought that nothing is perfect in this world, especially if you are trying to impress his executive clients with a prestigious address such as Berkeley Square affords, while doing it on the cheap. He muses that perhaps he should ask his clients whether they would prefer the 'groans or the bones' as an accompaniment to their self-actualization. Entering the lobby, the white-coated receptionist glances up to say she has no messages for him. But then she rarely has. In fact, Justin is surprised she deigns to talk to him at all, so lowly is he in the Hub's hierarchy. However, she does remember to say has that she asked the voice coach to dial it down a touch if Justin is coaching in the room next door. Grateful for small mercies – but entirely unconvinced that the muscular voice coach will take any notice – Justin heads for his car and home, just as his time on the parking meter runs out.

Sitting in the kitchen at home, while building up the strength to pick up his children, Justin is still suffused with the mood induced by his reminiscences at the fountains, and further inspired by Grayson Perry's indelible take on the social world they all inhabit. Wishing to capture the moment, Justin feels impulsed to open up his laptop and commit his free-flowing thoughts to his sporadically visited personal journal, a prerequisite of his CPD. But then he enjoys free-writing anyway, once he gets down to it. His fingers move to the keyboard, as he witnesses his thoughts appearing on the screen.

I settle to a state of contentedly celebrating my recent breakthrough with Richard, and all of the associations stimulated by my meandering waltz through Clifton memory sites, and the provocation of the Vanity

of Small Differences. I felt an impulse to ring my wife Joy, but know
that I cannot, as personal calls are strictly frowned up during working
hours, though all are expected to have their phones on when away
from there. All staff at that futuristic workplace, whether management
or shop floor, are required to be 'always on', including the zero-hours
supposedly self-employed, staff who can be called in for shifts at
really short notice. Or obversely have their shift planned for that day
cancelled for little given reason. Joy is trapped within a really tight
regime, and even if the pay for management is good, the price one
pays is high.

I do feel for her, experiencing a twang of guilt when I think of the
freedom I currently enjoy, compared to the restrictions and pressures
that perpetually box her in. I recoil when I inwardly admit that I do not
say often enough to her how compassionate I feel for her, caught up
as she is in her iron monkey cage, putting up with all this stress and
pressure at work to keep the family ship from sinking, while I build my
business. The sad truth is that I simply do not tell her often enough
how much I truly love her for who she is, and for her sense of
responsibility that keeps us all going.

Joy graduated with a highly lauded first-class honours degree in
English from Cambridge, and would be well suited for a quieter, more
cloistered academic life. But then we both met at the Business School
just down the road, immediately after our bachelor's degrees were
done – like me she drifted towards the business school, believing it
might prove somehow useful - and then we were both inexorably
caught up in corporate life shortly thereafter. When I say corporate
life, I do infer anything high-flying or glamorous. After several years
working in Human Resources in a chocolate factory, I then drifted into
an HR role in local government. In both environments my listening

skills proved comfortably in advance of my rudimentary attempts at imposing bureaucratic control upon the staff: while my empathic tendencies eclipsed my forlorn attempts to treat employees as human capital.

The initial excitement of our shared early accession to the hard-nosed commercial world, with all of its seductions, led inevitably to the trappings of the house, the mortgage, the car loans, then the blessing of family. She returned back to work at the headquarters of a major insurer after our first child, Adam, perhaps too soon. She felt driven to place herself back on the treadmill, only to find that the mill wheel was not quite where it was when she stepped off, as her career trajectory had been surpassed by her male colleagues, whose unbroken career progression was unencumbered by maternity breaks and child-care distractions. When the local authority offered me redundancy terms sufficient to fund my launching a career in coaching, it felt like a merciful release, a release that Joy was highly supportive of.

Perhaps it is the sheer tumult of our early forties lives that causes me to consistently hold back on spontaneous expressions of the love I feel towards her, in some ways more deeply than ever. More likely my reticence is borne of a deeply grooved defensiveness around my breaking out of the golden handcuffs, while she labours on in the monkey cage. I am not quite sure how or when we got locked into this pattern of jokey banter at each other's expense – and of course some of the ironising has an underlying tenderness to it – but the pattern seems by now to be our default position when discussing or comparing our lives.

Justin's phone pings in his pocket, dragging him away from the keyboard.

'Hello, who is this?' asks Justin, not recognising the number. He fears it might be the long arm of the law, reaching to punish him for his Consignia sins. The ringing of his phone, once a happy distraction, has now become a source of trepidation. And he is rather irritated by this break to the flow at his fingertips, while rather wondering how his supposedly professional free writing had suddenly taken such a personal turn. Not recognising the number, he asks, 'hello, who is this?' thinking it is his phone provider offering yet another upgrade that he doesn't need and can't afford.

'Oh, sorry to startle you – it is Joanna from Consignia Marketing Department – remember me? You interviewed me? We had a drink in the Merchant Venturers? Exchanged numbers? But maybe this is not a good time?'

Noting the hesitation in her upwardly inflected voice, Justin moves to reassure her that this call from out of the blue is most welcome. 'Oh no, hello Joanna, of course I remember you. I am fine to talk now, and good to hear a friendly voice. How are you?'

'Doing just fine thanks – same old same old. And I really enjoyed our conversation the other day?'

Again, the rising tone at the end of the sentence. He finds himself wanting to mimic it. 'Yes, me too? In fact, I more than enjoyed that moment. Can't imagine you would have thought otherwise? It was more than good to meet you. Our chance chat in the Merchant Venturers pub.'

She smiles down her phone. 'Yes, that was quite a coincidence.'

'And you were really helpful in putting the worst of the Consignia trauma behind me. I often think back to it.' Justin is not quite sure why he admits to this, though it is undoubtedly true. 'I have flashbacks, at odd moments, to that table at the back of the pub. I was going through a lot – and it was amazing to have you there for me.'

Joanna smile broadens, imagining that Justin can see her beaming.

'Good to hear that I have been on your mind. You on mine too.'

'Really?'

'Yes, really! And the memory of our stolen time together was part of the reason I called. Apart from catching up. I hear that you are finally off the firm's premises? That is sad.'

'Hm. Not surprised. I bet the whole of Consignia knows that I was shown off the premises by now.'

'No, they don't, silly. And I won't pry. I realise your situation is delicate. You don't have to say anything about that at all. But just to say I was sorry to hear it. You were a force for the good.'

'Yes thanks. I really appreciate your concern. Best not to excavate my history with Consignia again. But good to know that at least one person at the firm has not completely written me off.'

'Not at all. You helped me a lot. And others too. Maybe you were just helping the wrong people?'

'On the money there, Joanna! I have never been very good at separating the goodies from the baddies.'

'Nor me. Even watching a movie, I can never work it out. Until the end. But you are one of the goodies, Justin Drake. How have you been, anyway, since the last time?'

'Oh, okay. I am doing fine.'

'Doesn't sound that fine?'

'Well not quite that fine,' he admits. 'A few little bumps and bruises along the way, professionally speaking. But generally fine. You know this innocuous world of coaching that I am stuck in, where the plan is to treat people like human beings, does seem to have the capacity to stir up hornet's nests.'

'Oh, yes I do believe it. And hornet's stings hurt. I am disappointed for you. And what you say worries me a little too, on the same account.'

'Why you too?

'Well, I was thinking that I might go into this coaching business myself?'

'Oh, Joanna. Sorry. I did not mean to put you off.'

'No, I want your advice about this career move. Your unvarnished advice.'

'I never varnish my advice. Rule 101 of the Justin code of practice.'

'Ha ha. And that is why I am turning to you, because I know you will be honest with me about the upsides and downsides of coaching work, not like the others?'

'You mean the varnishers? The professional bodies, and all of their fellow travellers?'

'Yes, that lot. With all of their shiny surfaces, selling me a dream ticket? And there are so many of that sort queuing up to sell me their version of the dream.'

'Yes, I bet there are. And they all went to the same finishing school, getting the glaze just right on the top surfaces.'

'While ignoring what lies beneath?'

'Quite so. You seem to know this world well already. But don't let me stop you entering the fray, sandpaper at the ready. I am happy to offer any help you might need.'

She interrupts, 'I would love that. I hoped you would…'

'Why me?'

'I think you know why. I trust you to tell it like it is. You were fearless enough in your work with my company – even taking the time to listen to the women's side of things, when you didn't have to.'

'Aw, that is kind of you to say so. And I am more than happy to assist. From the little I have seen and know, I would say that you have all the natural talent in the world for this line of work. Great listening, empathy, strong intuition.'

'Well thanks,' she says, glad that her blushes are unseen. 'And, modesty aside, I feel that my talents are wasted in marketing.'

'Couldn't agree more. Let us take time then to explore your choices further – but not on the phone.'

'Yes, please! It would be great if we could meet. Soon?'

'Yes, soon. But before you go - how is your life anyway. Generally?'

'Good question. It is okay really, beyond the normal frustrations that come with being a woman in a man's world, and having to promote products that may not be exactly what the world really needs right now. Well, I say okay. but some small things are getting to me.'

'Such as....'

'Hmm. Such as? Something really embarrassing and a little shameful actually, but I may as well tell you, though it is nothing you can really fix. But best to get it off my chest. Do you mind?'

'No, of course not. Off-load all you wish, I have the time. And I owe you one,' Justin does his best to keep his tone impassive, while inwardly hoping that her confession will have some juice in it.

'Well, thank you. And really, you owe me nothing.' She sighs, audibly. 'The thing is. I got caught speeding last month. I know. Gulp. And now I have to pay the fine or go to remedial speeding school. Oh, and the other not so minor thing is that my car has broken down. Not speeding related – quite the opposite. No speed at all. Zilch. Neither me not it is going anywhere right now. Grounded.'

'Really? Not nice at the time, but that is not such a big deal. Lots of people are getting done for minor traffic violations nowadays. Dare I say even me?'

'Honestly?' asks Joanna.

'Yes, honestly, and I commiserate with you on getting caught. On both of us getting caught.'

'You too? We should form a speed-trap victim's club on Facebook.'

'Please send me the entry form. I got done last month too – speeding, nothing serious -and face having to attend a similar remedial session, too. What a coincidence. We might even end up at the same class, though I see the bookings are some time off.'

'I like your thinking. You're helping me look on the bright side. You on Facebook too?'

'I am.'

'Good. I am often on there, even at work. And at home my hubbie says I spend far too much time responding to pings from mysterious strangers I have never met. Shall I send you a friend request?'

'Yes, please do.'

'Could be easier to text than use the phone all the time. I promise I won't stalk you. Well, only a little? Nothing too creepy?'

'Ha ha, as they say on Messenger. Nothing much to stalk, I am afraid. Really boring. All you will see is that I am a family man. Kids not kittens.'

'Same me. I save the private stuff for messenger.'

'Look, it has been great to talk but I have to go pick up the children. I am late as usual. And I think Joy said she would be late this evening – as usual – so the wonder of cooking supper falls to me.'

An Inspector Calls

Joy stands in front of Brenda's imposing door, pleased that she has progressed Sharon's dare so far as to be meeting with Brenda face to face. She is glad, also, to have had good reason to leave work earlier than usual, after a particularly testing day. Perhaps this encounter with Brenda might offer some escape from her preoccupation with her woes in Carpet Land. She reminds herself that she does not intend to take this meeting beyond the dreaded chemistry test, which she pretty much plans to fail. Thinking of how often Justin must have stood poised at this self-same threshold, she rings the bell, ready to enter her husband's world.

'Good afternoon, Joy,' says Brenda in a level tone, ushering her through the hallway, past the antique hat stand. 'Do come in. I realise all of this might feel a little strange for you. But I salute your courage in taking this first step. I will do all I can to put you at ease.' Brenda walks her through to her consulting room, where Joy espies the dull brown tapestry once described by Justin. She is beginning to feel at home.

Joy settles in a high-backed chair, facing Brenda, who composes herself in her larger facing chair. 'Thanks for agreeing to see me, Brenda. Tell you the truth, I am a little nervous here. And I have had such a full day, not a moment to myself. Sorry, I did not even have time to brush my hair, never mind refresh my make-up. My mind is all over the place.'

'Worry not, that feeling of not being prepared enough for these sessions is not at all unusual,' soothes Brenda. 'Sometimes clients seem to think that they must arrive here with all their problems sorted, that they need to know the answers before they get started with me. But in fact, the whole purpose of these sessions is to sort the confusions and conflicting pressures, to help you to understand more clearly what to do. And don't worry about the make-up. No need to apologise for anything.'

Thank you, that is a relief,' says Joy, continuing to wear the mask of confusion and puzzlement.

'So, tell me what you are facing, and how you think I may be able to help.'

'I think my coaching is going okay,' reflects Joy. 'Staff tell me that I listen well and help them to clarify their future direction. But I have little real support at work for this coaching I do. HR, where I work, is really transactional. It does not much support me in bringing the human touch to my work.'

'That is a shame. But do you not have corporate core values, a code of ethics that encourages the supporting of staff?' asks Brenda, looking concerned.

'Oh yes, we have those plastered up all over the place! But what did Shakespeare write in Hamlet? These values are "more honoured in the breach than in the observance."'

'I see. Are you a Shakespeare scholar?'

'No, hardly that. But I did my first degree in Literature. First Class Honours actually, though a fat lot of good that has done me in the harsh commercial world I now inhabit. But those learned by rote quotations do tend to stick in my head, though. Not that I use them much at work. Not too many in my line of work would get the references. Simply think I was showing off. It is all Gradgrind in our place. Sorry, Gradgrind is a character from Dickens. There I go again. Doh.'

Brenda bridles, stiffening in her chair. 'I am aware of Dickens. I love the Christmas Carol. I re-read it during Advent every year, without fail.'

'You must love that book! I am more a Hard Times girl myself.'

'Leaving aside the fictional world and returning to your situation. If we may?' suggests Brenda, leaving Joy looking apologetic. 'From what I hear, you feel that in your coaching you are quite often at odds with your organisation? That they do not support – and sometimes oppose – your human, empathic approach?'

'Good summary. I would say that is fair.' Joy says, her gaze drifting towards the tapestry.

'So how do you envisage these sessions going?'

'Oh, what a question,' says Joy, 'Well, I imagine that I sit here and off-load my problems and dilemmas, say where I am getting stuck, and seek you support in educating me, listening and supporting and. and. what was the third thing on your list of what you do?'

'Ensuring that you are maintaining standards. The standards as set by your professional body. And, of course, the standards set by your company.'

'Oh - so you would be acting on behalf of the company? Didn't expect that.'

'Well, not directly, but that is a factor yes that we must keep in the background. Context is all. There would be no feedback to the company of course, that goes without saying. Unless you reveal something criminal, seriously criminal, then I would need to go to the police.'

'Oh, that sounds quite scary,' says Joy, simulating apprehension. 'How would you define seriously?'

'Well, murder in the extreme case. financial malfeasance. That sort of thing, though it very rarely happens.'

'What if I were giving advice to staff that was contrary to company policy or rules? I have to confess that sometimes I do that. It seems the only decent thing to do.'

Brenda considers this carefully. 'That is a tricky one, and would depend on the seriousness of your complicity in rule-breaking. But beyond involving police or lawyers, I would, in my role, be duty-bound to dissuade you from reckless or unethical practice. If you persisted in the face of this advice, then I would have to terminate the contract. And in extremis report back to the Fraternity, as all supervisors are required to do anyway, in such instances. Such a report could put your professional licence in jeopardy.'

'I see. That all sounds really Draconian. So, I would need to be particularly careful as to what I what I say to you in here?'

'No, quite the opposite!' insists Brenda. 'You would need to be completely honest.'

'Okay, so allow me to pose a hypothetical case study,' says Joy, consulting her mental crib notes. 'What if the company were asking me to collude in a barely legal or even illegal summary dismissal? And I acted in the individual's interest, not the company's?'

'That would be a complex one. I must say, this is proving to be quite a challenging chemistry meeting!' says Brenda, picking at a buttonhole of her cardigan.

'Ha! From my experience, chemistry is rarely simple,' replies Joy. 'I was awful at it at school. If it wasn't the formula, it was the uncontrollable Bunsen burners that defeated me.'

'I can imagine,' says Brenda, not sure if she herself had ever studied chemistry at all, while alluding to it often. 'But back to your case. We would need to unpick the situation, view the ethics from all angles, and work out a way forward from there.'

'Well thanks, that is very helpful. So, these sessions would not be all – what do you call it – UPR?' asks Joy, rolling out one of her husband's favourite three-letter acronyms.

'"Unconditional Positive Regard?" No, not entirely, because as I told you there are standards that I must uphold, on behalf of the profession. But I would hope that I come across as empathic. My clients tell me so, at any rate.'

'That is reassuring for you to know. And I feel sure they say the same things about you when you are out of earshot, too.'

'I am sure they do,' says Brenda, primly.

'This is all really helpful, thank you. Let me try another case study?'

'Yes?' says Brenda, looking agitated.

'How might I phrase this? Okay here we go. What if, in the course of a supervision, a supervisee found him or herself in conflict with your direction?'

'Oh yes?'

Joy presses on. 'What if she felt that you were doing little to support her personal values?'

'Well, we would need to work that through. But there has never been a case when.'

Joy interrupts, "What if, hypothetically, you become defensive when the supervisee expressed anger at the whole premise on which the profession was based - and challenged you as part of that?'

'What an improbable case! Let me think.' Her gaze shifts out to Downs where children are playing football. 'Well, I would need to know more of the challenge before I could act. but if it became personalised around me, then I would need to stop the whole session, before it escalated. A strange case, I must say. Do you worry that we might get to that point, in these sessions?'

'I dunno – just speculating. Can I try another chemistry test?'

'Yes, of course, I am intrigued. These meetings are usually quite straightforward, with me outlining the ground rules. But do go on.'

'What if the partner of one of your supervisees become suspicious, or hurt, that confidences shared with you were not being shared with him or her?' asks Joy, treading carefully. 'And that they insisted that their partner reveal all that was discussed during supervision. How would you advise your client, facing this dilemma?'

'That is easy enough. I would say that the client is right to make it clear to their partner that the confidentiality boundary must be respected.'

'I see,' continues Joy, her finger now on the red button. 'So, what if the partner suspected that your client had a crush on you?'

'Well something called transference can happen.' Brenda shifts in her seat. 'We trained supervisors know well how to head that off, without damage being done. I must say these are most unusual questions.'

'I am sure they are. But these are the questions on my mind. For example, do you allow your supervisees to go deeply into personal dilemmas or problems that are not work-related?'

'Sometimes I do, and there can be some really interesting parallels between domestic problems and those issues that hit the same impasse at work.'

'Do you directly advise on personal problems?'

'Rarely do I get directive. Look, can I ask, do you have a pressing domestic problem that you would want to bring to me?'

'I think I might well do, yes,' answers Joy, pulling a troubled face.

'Well in that case, I would need to refer you onto a counsellor who could work with you. This would not be my territory. It would muddy the waters.'

'Thank you. So, what is your main contribution then? Maintaining standards?'

'That is a large part of it yes, as well as support and education.'

'May I ask, have you, Brenda, ever fallen short of the standards set for supervisors?'

Brenda pauses. 'Yes, to my shame I have. We all have off-days. And when that occurs, I take it to my supervisor's supervisor.'

'Always good to have one of those. And have you ever reported a client to the professional body?'

'Yes,' `Brenda admits, 'I have had to resort to that, once or twice, when the situation has not been resolved in here.'

'Last question on my mind, you will be pleased to hear. Have you ever been reported for failing to live up to your standards? Given that you have admitted that sometimes you do?'

'No, never have been. What a question,' says Brenda, crossing her arms over her cardigan in a gesture of self-protection.

'I see. Have you ever considered reporting yourself to the authorities? To your professional body?' Might you ever turn yourself in, if the circumstances demanded it?'

'Yes, I might, but heaven forefend that it might come to that. Look, Joy. Time is marching on here. We have covered some really unusual terrain. Are you satisfied that you now know enough for us to proceed?'

'Oh yes, I am satisfied. It has been most educational. I will need time to think about the chemistry we have created here, and where it might take us. Stick it in the test tube, turn up the Bunsen burner to max. I can see we would have many stimulating ethical and procedural discussions during our time together, should we proceed.'

'Yes, I can well imagine. Would you like to leave me your email, give me some way of getting backing to you? Let me know your company address?'

Joy pauses, surveying the tapestry for the last time. 'You know, this may sound irregular, but I would rather not. I have your number and I will get back to you if I need to. I am the one considering paying for your services after all. And there are other supervisors that I need to meet, do my due diligence, buyer beware, and all that sort of thing.'

Brenda nods uncertainly, saying, 'yes, I fully understand that you have a choice.'

'Yes, there are other providers.'

'But before you go, can I leave with a brochure of my scale of charges and method of engagement?'

Joy reluctantly accepts this offering, then shoves this document into her bag, roughly, saying, 'thank you, I will scrutinise it later. I imagine you have a complaints procedure?'

'Oh, not explicitly. But my brochure and online site do direct you to the Fraternity's code of conduct that covers complaints?'

'And you did say upfront that all of this is entirely confidential? You need to assure me of that,' says Joy, gravely.

'Yes of course it is. Always.'

'And that you will not breathe a word to a soul concerning this conversation?'

'Hmm. I may have to work it through with my supervisor's supervisor – you have given me much pause for thought.'

'I am afraid that I do not give you permission to do that, even anonymised. My company is pretty paranoid. My husband can get very controlling. So not a word to anyone, ever. Do you promise, on your Fraternity's standards bible?'

'This is quite extreme, but yes I do. Promise.'

'I appreciate that reassurance. And now I must go. Thanks for your time.'

'And you for yours.'

Brenda closes the door thoughtfully, a small shudder of fear running through her system. Instead of signing up a lucrative corporate client, she feels exposed, as if she had walked into a viper's nest. Who was this Joy anyway? She could be anyone. A Fraternity mystery shopper? Surely not! They protect their own. A snoop from another professional body? Cunning, if so. An investigative journalist? That would be so upsetting. She reassures herself that even if it were such a reporter, she has revealed nothing untoward, stuck to her guns. Or had she? Then there was her swearing to confidentiality, while she had not asked this Joy to reciprocate. Schoolgirl error, she berates herself.

She questions why she is letting these paranoid fears run so. Perhaps this woman is just who she said she was. A potential customer who had done her homework, and wanted to put her through her paces? But who was she? She picks up her tablet to Google her name: Joy Highbury–Harcross. Nothing comes up at all.

Maybe this woman operates on that dark web thing she hears so much of? Maybe she should have checked her out more thoroughly before letting her through the door. Why had she sworn not to let this go further? Not even to talk to her supervisor, when she really wanted to do. But what if this woman knew whom my supervisor was? She could easily find out, Brenda imagined. She would put nothing beyond this ill-named Joy.

She sighs as her cat mewls for food, food that the cussed creature will probably leave. She noticed this Joy looking at her tapestry a lot. She is tired of clients staring at it, tired of it altogether. In an uncharacteristically violent action, she tears the hanging from the wall, and, following her cat into the kitchen, throws the tapestry onto the cat's bed. 'There, puss. You can have it. Desecrate it all you want. I am having an early night.'

Domestic Bliss

With some reluctance, Justin closes the lid on his laptop, wishing he had had the time to finish off his journal article, but then the chat to Joanna had proved an intriguing distraction. Jumping into his car, he hurries up the Henleaze Road, just in time to pick up his children, whom he finds loitering in the sun inside the school railings, where an anxious and somewhat aggravated teacher hovers nearby. Justin mutters an apology to the teacher then bundles the children into the car before he has to explain himself. Yet again.

'You were late, Daddy. Teacher looks mad at you,' mutters Adam, glancing over his shoulder, furtively.

'No, I was just in time,' protests Justin.

Amelia seizes on this opening. 'Oh yes! We will call you Justin Time all the time. But you were late. But Justin Never-in-time sounds all wrong. '

'Oh well, 'Justin concedes. 'I was late. Again. But better late than never. And did either of you know that "Just-in-time" is one of the principles that drives modern businesses?'

Adam scratches his head. 'Surprised you know about that, Daddy. Were you asleep during that class? Or was it pure theory?'

Despite the teasing, Justin is glad to find the children in fine fettle, even though they are clearly set up for another rally of the dad tormenting that so amused them this morning. He plays along with the ribbing, letting them know that the Ponzi factory is going well for a change – and that in fact, after this morning's work, he may have some new Ponzi people to play with soon.

Amelia grins at this news. 'That is good, Daddy. We like you having new playmate Ponzi's to tell us about. But Daddy, why does your breath smell so funny? You have never ever smelled like this before. Are you dying? Did you catch something horrible at the Ponzi factory?'

'Oh sorry,' Justin says, cupping his hand to his mouth - when one sniff confirms her unwelcome feedback - then reaches for some gum in the car door drawer. 'No, I am definitely not dying, though sometimes I feel like I am dying inside, when my Ponzis don't love me enough. The funny smell must be from the hummus I had for lunch in the Lebanon place.'

Adam, the car fanatic, picks up his ears at this mention. 'Hummers, Daddy? Isn't that one of those humungus American 4x4 trucks with blacked-out windows that bad men drive in the movies? Did you eat one of those? Wow. Respect.'

Adam offers a high five from behind, nearly causing his father to crash. 'No wonder you smell weird. Did you eat the tyres as well? Your lips look a bit rubbery.'

'No, I did not eat a Hummer. Well at least not a whole one. The headlights are really chewy, with all that chrome mashing up your molars.'

This serves to send Amelia on an adjacent track. 'You might need some chrome braces, Daddy, like the coloured braces that lots of our classmates have. Our teeth are all funny dad, it is so embarrassing not to have braces.'

'Yes Daddy, can we have braces Dad – instead of filings?' chirped Adam. 'Please dad. I will never get a girlfriend with gnashers like these. They look like wonky tombstones, Daddy.'

'And I will never get a boyfriend without braces either.' Hardly pausing for breath, Amelia digs out another question. 'Daddy, did you say that you ate your Hummer in Legoland?

'What?' Justin at this point has lost all recall of where this line of questioning began. Searching around, he at last responds, 'No. Not Legoland. I said Lebanon.'

Adam decides that a follow-up question might push their father over the edge of sanity. 'Is Lebanon a branch of Legoland? '

Seeking to change the subject, as they were definitely winning this exchange, Justin says, 'I have just been to see a series of tapestries illustrating the folly of cosmetic consumerism – such as unnecessary dental braces - and the worrying power of celebrity images to persuade children to pester parents to buy things that they don't really want or need. Like more Lego. Or Hummers. Or braces.'

'But Daddy,' protests Amelia, 'it is our job to pester you for things we don't need.' Amelia thinks it might be time to give their father a break. 'You went to see tapestries today? Like in a church? Were they smelly?'

'No, they were modern tapestries. Woven on a big computer-controlled machine. They smelt of nothing.'

'Did you spend all day looking at them?' asked Adam. 'Don't you ever work Daddy?'

Amelia does her best, once more, to rescue her Daddy. 'Or are you training to be a weaver? We like weavers. Thy work on big machines called wombs. And we like beavers too. Eager weaver beavers. Can we have a beaver for a pet dad?'

Adam goes for the killer punch. 'And a Hummer to drive our beaver around in? Your silent Prius is so uncool and embarrassing. We want a Hummer. '

The banter continues in this vein until they pull up at their semi-detached 1930's home, set in its leafy, secluded Westbury Street. Justin enjoys the secure feeling of pulling the front door behind him to sink in, shutting out the world for a while, even if the Better Bank do own more than half of their blessed sanctuary.

His return to the kitchen reminds Adam of the morning's unfinished business. 'Daddy, you still have not shown us photos of your problem Ponzi people. Please show us, Daddy. Are they real at all, or did you weave them?'

To mollify them, Justin opens his laptop to bring up the website of the Whole Health Hub, showing then the mug shots of all of the practitioner's resident therein.

Amelia pours over the evidence base. 'Oh Daddy, you have so many Ponzi Pals that you have been keeping from us. What nice healthy smiling faces. They look like a lot of emojis. Are they real people dad? Are you sure they are not emojis? Gravitars?'

'I think you mean avatars. But then I think I like gravitars better.' Justin is aware that he has never properly scrutinised this rogue's gallery before, looking only for his own picture and brief biography, nesting as it does besides that of the colonic irrigation specialist. 'Some of them are trying to look so serious and wise.'

Adam detects a pattern among the photos, in this game of spot-the-difference. 'Daddy, why are you the only one without a white coat? We need you to get a white Ponzi coat dad. You would look so cool, just like all the others. You look out of place Daddy. You need to fit in, or you will stick out.'

Justin hardly needs this pointing out. He is already painfully aware of his lack of fit in the world of therapy. 'Quite so. Never a truer word said. But now I need to go upstairs to change out of this stuffy suit – and before you say it, not into a white coat - then head on down to feed you and lot and Mummy, if she ever makes it home.'

Feeling more like himself in his favourite pair of worn denims, Justin

struggles to evict some fish finger and oven chips out of their
respective frozen packaging's, a move which results in most of them
ending up on the floor.

'Daddy, where is Mummy? She never drops hot food on the floor,'
says Adam.

'I am sure that is true,' agrees Justin. 'Now make yourself useful and
help me pick these fish fingers off the floor before she gets home and
declares them inedible.'

'Daddy, could we eat them off the floor, like little doggies?' asks
Amelia. 'Woof, woof, woof.'

'Yes, Daddy, we hate knives and forks and plates and stuff. Mummy
will never know,' says Adam, joining his sister on the floor. 'If Mummy
never comes home, then we could live like little animals all of the time,
and never have to wash.'

Joy walks across the Downs towards her car feeling elated after her
show-down with Brenda, her curiosity sated for now as to her modus
operandi. She experiences a buzz of almost sadistic satisfaction at the
impact of her forensic line of questioning on Brenda, feeling glad that
she unsettled her. It proved uplifting indeed to wrest control from this
woman who normally assumes such power over others, most notably
Justin. The tables have been turned, if only for a moment. She is
relieved that she did not reveal her true identity to Brenda – but then
she did not falsify it either. She doubts if she could be traced, but even
if so, she had neither said nor done anything incriminating, beyond
tweaking the witch's tail. She notices that this uncharacteristic act of

infiltration has given her momentary uplift, quite taking her mind off the Carpet cloud that hangs over her every mood.

She is bursting to tell Justin all she has discovered but knows she cannot. She is the one always chastising him for being reckless – and now here she is, taking crazy risks with the woman who may be seeking to get him barred. But she needs to talk to someone about her undercover operation. Oh yes, Sharon, who teed this up in the first place. She needs to report back on her successful accomplishment of Sharon's dare. Then set her a dare all her own. A scary one.

The sight of a group of children playing football on the Downs reminds her that she has her own brood to attend to, left once more to the mercies of her husband, who could be getting up to almost anything in the name of childcare. As she picks up her pace towards her waiting car, her phone rings.

'Joy, hello, this is Angela from HR. I couldn't find you at your desk earlier? Is there a problem?'

'No, not really. I simply left work – on time for once – to deal with a personal matter. How can I help you?' says Joy, not feeling at all helpful.

'Well, that is unfortunate, as we needed you to deal with an aggressive packer who was threatening violence. You are usually at your desk.'

'I know, I just needed some personal time.'

'Okay, but you should have told someone you were clocking off. While you are on, we need to fix a time for your personal disciplinary interview. Some new evidence has come up, which suggests we need to deal with this asap.'

'Okay, so you want to move the date forward. As you know I am in most of the time, so you name the date. But I would like to hear of this new evidence beforehand. This is hardly the way to break bad news, after work.'

'Yes of course, I will email details of that to you tomorrow – so would Friday morning suit? The head of HR from Birmingham is in town then, and she is taking a personal interest in your case.'

'Friday should be okay by me, but I do need time to prepare. Is there anything else? I really do have a home life you know.'

'Yes, we appreciate that. Goodbye for now, but don't forget Friday.'

Joy rings off, any elation that she as feeling from her guerrilla mission into the world of coaching punctured by this exchange. Her mood darkening, she returns home, hoping her family might provide some light relief from the privations of the day. Arriving home, she makes her way into the kitchen, crashing her laptop case onto the faux marble worktop. She sighs heavily at the sight of food smeared all over the floor. 'What is this mess?' she asks of no one in particular.

'Woof, woof,' barks Amelia, rushing from under the table to give her mother a hug. 'It is not a mess at all. Adam and I were little doggies and Daddy spilt our dinner on the floor so that we could get on all fours and munch it all up.'

'Is this true?' Joy asks of Justin.

'Well, not quite darling, though some spillage did occur. Never mind, I have saved some of the rescued fish-fingers for you, after such a long day.'

'Well, thanks for pushing the boat out. Mind you, I need some comfort food after another soul-destroying day at the deeply unfulfilling Fulfilment factory. Why couldn't they just carry on calling it the Distribution Centre? Or the Warehouse? Or the Depot? It is only top-level management that call it Fulfilment Centre, and that is just to copy Amazon.'

Justin feels a need to contextualize. 'We call that phenomenon "competitive convergence" in strategic management circles.'

Joy does not look at all pleased to have her rant interrupted by this attempt to frame what personally assails her as a global trend. 'I am not really interested in how the Harvard Business Review explains all this away. It still leaves us at Magic Carpet having to deal with the fallout. As I was saying, all we ever do is copy Amazon. But then again, the change in name may be because the top managers are the only ones getting fulfilled. And even they seem stressed to hell most of the time. But enough already of my moaning. You can all take off your conversational crash helmets now, Mummy is re-entering the domestic atmosphere from planet work. Give us a hug, kids. That is better. How was your day?'

'It was okay, thanks. Mummy, did you know that Daddy ate a Hummer today. And became a weaver. Then he went to Legoland and he smells funny.' Amelia impresses herself – and Adam - with her summarisation skills.

Joy welcomes this surreal account of her partner's day, glad to find that her children's imaginations remain fertile. 'Really? That all sounds very different. What an exciting life he leads.'

She turns to her husband, the man who inspires such tales in their children.

'But hey Justin, hello. Thanks for your text; it lifted me up during a full-on day. It sounds like the recovery meeting with Richard went well? Back on the coaching pony again, are we?'

Justin is pleased to receive some adult attention, after his children's conversational diversions. 'Oh yes, I do hope so. Good, isn't it? It went really well, and I am back in business again, and cash should be on its way towards us, on at least two fronts. Not just from Consignia, but with that agency, Parallelogram. That is even before I commence my weaving career.'

Joy smiles encouragement. 'Well, thank goodness for that. Though your skills in weaving these fantastical coaching stories has not gone unnoticed, so I am not sure, always, where the truth lies.' Noticing that Justin makes a face at this remark, she says, 'seriously, this is all good news. But wait a minute. Doesn't that mean you will need to find another supervisor to authenticate your heroic endeavours at the listening loom?'

Justin just knew that she would return to her obsession with coaching supervision sooner or later. 'Ha ha. Yes, it does mean I have to source a Mark 2 Brenda, and I am giving that task the highest priority tomorrow.' Not wishing to pour fuel on the supervisory bonfire, he resists telling her that he needs to produce two references before he starts work at Parallelogram, one of who might need to be his next Brenda equivalent. To divert the conversation away from all matters Brenda, he asks instead what the specific cause of her gloom has been this day, beyond the normal excruciation.

In pursuit of this inquiry, he decides to settle into 'Clean Coaching' mode, while rather wishing that he had the clean coaching prompt sheet in front of him, as he was feeling rather rusty on the Clean front. The technique had seemed easy enough during the role-plays he successfully navigated during his coach training workshops, but less seamless when faced with a real-life human being struggling to make sense of things. However, he needs to start somewhere. 'Enough about me. Tell me about your day then, please. I am all ears,' he says, essaying his best attempt at active listening posture.

Joy sits on a stool by the kitchen counter, head in hands, pushing her hair back. 'Oh, it is just going from worse to even worse at Magic

Carpet. Every day we experience more and more pressures from the Stateside HQ to reduce headcount. And for more frenzied implementation of their precious automated solutions that will, in the end, make the few of us who are left in work slaves to the robots we serve, handmaidens of the almighty algorithm.'

'Say more,' he says, interested to see if his Clean Coaching techniques work, as well, of course, as caring for her plight. A voice in his head says that he needs to hear this account, fresh and for the first time, though he knows that he has heard variants on this broken record many times before.

Joy leans forwards, welcoming the opportunity to open up on her woes.

'Well, today I had yet more immediate staffing problems to face. There was a pregnant woman who almost gave birth in the toilets, so afraid was she of not making her hours. It took some fancy footwork to rescue that drama, to confine it to the lady's room. Nice baby though, lustily celebrating her debut, and luckily escaping being packed away in one of our boxes by a high-speed machine. Someone had tipped off the press of this oh so human-interest story, so the cameras were waiting outside the warehouse doors to follow the ambulance down the road.

'Say more' Justin ventures again. Nothing to this clean coaching really. It is all clicking into place.

'Well, on top of the workplace becoming a virtual maternity ward, one of our contracted drivers nearly had a fatal on the motorway junction just before pulling into the depot – what a nightmare.'

'And then?'

'Well he was okay, luckily, but that meant that yet another ambulance was visible from the office windows – and the motorway traffic was building up outside our building, with all of the lollygaggers staring our way. Magic Carpet was beginning to look like a warzone. All of which means that we are bound to be on the local news again, tonight, for all the wrong reasons. We never seem to "get ahead of the narrative," despite being constantly told to do so by our seniors. That is all they really care about, "the narrative," and its equally important sister "the optics," the look of the thing as it is seen by the outside world.'

'And else?' He is not at sure this is a clean prompt, but it is the best he can do, while suppressing an urge to ask more detail of these dramas.

'And then, of course, sure as eggs is eggs, a posse of belligerent drivers rip off their hi-viz jackets and march into the office, up in arms about their working hours and shift patterns, which they claim are making them vulnerable to yet more accidents, such as the one inescapably visible through the office window. They are complaining about the spy-in-the-cab cameras monitoring their every move. And they are threatening collective action, even unionization, which is against all of the free-market beliefs of sacred Magic Carpet doctrine. I was forced to speak to the drivers off the laminated corporate hymn sheet - "we seek to create working conditions where collectivisation is unnecessary. Where every colleague has the freedom to design their own work pattern, to suit their work-life balance." Huh.

'And more?' asks an impassive Justin.

'Yes, there is more. There is always more. Amid all of the pressure to implement new supply-chain processes, I have to spend half my day mopping placenta off the floor and cleaning up the blood off the tarmac as well. No one cares or thanks me for this - they just continue to push me relentlessly through their imposition of their godforsaken

KPIs, forever tightening goals sent down from on high, decided at meetings that local management is never a party to.'

'KPIs?' Justin asks, hoping he has not violated the Clean Coaching orthodoxy entirely.

'Key Performance Indicators. Key Perdition Incarcerators more like.'

'And the feeling is?'

'Vulnerable. Shaky. Angry. Emptied. Yes, deep down I feel as vulnerable, as precarious as those on the floor, as well as those sad individuals stuck in their short-order vans, always behind on their deliveries, never catching up with themselves. Then there is the threat of moving the entire operation to the distribution nirvana of the Golden Triangle, near the Birmingham interchange, to allow our trucks to be within two hours of every major city in the country. Just like Amazon have done. Bristol is seen by our logistics and supply-chain geniuses as being too far-flung for delivery optimisation. So, it is really quite likely that all of us West Country bumpkins could soon be sent back to the cider presses and pasty-plumping sheds from which we were loving plucked, to put us out of our corporatised misery.'

'What does this remind you of?' Oh, no, a misstep from Justin. He realises too late that that was not a Clean Question. Oh well, damage done, he offers her a consoling hug instead, which is accepted, though hugging is strictly not in the Clean Toolkit.

She steps back from his arms to say, 'what does it remind me of? Good question. You know that theory X and theory Y you became so enthusiastic about when you were studying for your coaching qualifications – the theory about how the world has now left autocratic X management style behind? And how we are all now living in a consensual world of Y, where managers can no longer tell people what to do. That instead they need to be coaching their staff all the time through soft power – and that the managers in turn need to be coached by folk like you as well?'

'Yes, I do. And more?' Ah good, impeccable clean mode restored once more. He can stop feeling guilty and give her unconditional positive regard once more.

'Well, that theory came into mind today when I was sat in a disciplinary of a "colleague,"' Joy waves sarcastic finger commas in the air, 'who had exceeded the "three-strikes" rule on the number of breaks taken in a shift. It was a gruesome meeting. He was near tears, just kept on saying "I just need this job, I have a young family, please give me one more chance."'

'And you felt?'

'A bit hopeless, useless, sad, a bit frightened too. It is so hard to listen when our workers' stories restimulate my own fears of destitution. I guess the two of us, as secure products of middle-class upbringing have more internal resources, more economic security to fall back on than many of the folk on the shop floor. But it is still hard for me to put on the management white-face when their stories, their worst fears, and mine, collide.'

'And what would you like to see happen?' Justin asks, knowing that his Clean Coaching mask of expressionless support has slipped alarmingly.

'I hate to see us do that to people. You know, the longer I slave away at Magic Carpet, the more it seems to shift, probably permanently, towards the X factor way of doing things. And I would like to stop.'

'To stop?'

'Sure. We say all the right things, call our staff "colleagues," (more finger commas), saying "going forward" all the time. And we have the laminated corporate values framed on the wall to ventriloquize our responses when we run out of real things to say to our employees that would make any sense at all. Yet the staff are not stupid and are growing increasingly fearful, while all they get in return for expressing their fears is to be scolded like errant children. Magic Carpet may look like a new style, all-singing, all-dancing, zeitgeisty global company. But the grim truth is that underneath all of that pizzazz lurks pure Victoriana, pure Gradgrind, the shadow of the dark satanic mills.' She pauses for breath, taking time to think.

Justin allows the silence to run for a while, then, a little lost as to how to proceed, interjects with a minimalist, 'and?'

'And… and our staff may as well be cleaning chimneys as delivering parcels on a just-in-time basis to customers who want everything now - even though they certainly do not need half of these products at all, never mind now. In fact, chimney cleaning old school style might be more ethical than this. Can we get off this now, please? I am tired and hungry.'

Justin takes a pause, glad for the break from searching for simple questions when a complicated, clever question would do. But then the simple questions do seem to be doing the job of eliciting strong, articulate expression. Not for the first time, Justin muses on the power of Joy's points of reference, many of them drawn from her English degree, but it is not only the cleverness that impresses him. It is more her sheer lucidity, even when emotional.

Or maybe especially when she is emotional. It reminds him of why he fell in love with her in the first place, in those bygone days. He thinks that in another life she would have shone in a serious educational role – not trapped like this, in the maws of capital at its naked worst. But the coaching rules bar expression of such sentiments. Instead he searches around for another form of question, given that his Clean repertoire, and his patience, is now exhausted. 'Look, I may be wrong, but it feels like there is something more you are not saying?'

'Justin, are you going to carry on playing coach with me all evening?'

Justin realises that the game is up. Time to pack away the Clean toolkit. 'Sorry. Really sorry. But I do care, and I think there is something else out there that you are not saying, beyond stating the wrongness of the Magic Carpet business model. No more coaching techniques, promise.'

'No, it is okay,' she admits. 'In fact, you are doing really well. And yes, there is something more, probably much more that I have not said, and should have said, a while ago. But I need you to respond as husband not coach, as this news will potentially affect us as a family quite badly.'

'Okay, my inner coach is back on the naughty step. Husband all present and correct. Do tell me please. In your own time,' he asks, though he is not at all sure anymore what husband mode might entail. No one had slipped him a manual for husbanding before he approached the altar rails. He was too worried at that point in his life as to whether his cummerbund would slip, to listen to the full import of the vows that he was mechanically repeating.

Confident that Justin had stopped coming over all coach on her, Joy takes her time to say, slowly, 'Well the thing is …I don't quite know how to say this. Okay, I will just come right out with it. Do you remember about a month ago there was a shop-floor worker came to me desperately pleading not to be sacked – yes, another one - and she asked me to provide some kind of cover while she dealt with a family crisis.'

'Yes, I do remember that case – you were a hero,' says Justin, trusting that this response was husband congruent.

'Maybe so – but a reckless hero I am afraid, because management spotted the cover-up.' She winced at this confession, feeling a rush of shame passing through her gut.

'Whoops … and?' asks Justin, still finding it hard to kick the Clean habit, after being in the monosyllabic groove for such a while.

'I was formally interviewed and given a verbal warning. Dragged over the coals. Management confected disappointment that someone from HR should be the one flouting the rules when I should be the exemplar, the role model, blah sanctimonious blah. I can't tell you how galling it was, to allow those ethical pygmies the opportunity to sermonise at me.'

Justin searched around for a response. 'Hmm, not so good. But not the worst. You just need to be a bit more careful, take care of your own job security some more, not everyone else's all the time.'

'Well, that is just it. You know we have that system on the floor where ''colleagues'' peer assess each other, and can pass performance issues up the line? The "snitches charter"?'

'Yes, I well remember hearing from you with some disbelief of that disgusting Kafkaesque practice. How dare they!' He retorts, allowing full husbandly indignation the vehemence it demanded.

'Exactly. Foucault's panopticon in perfidious action. Well, last week, one supervisor came to me to dob in another supervisor whom he felt was not pulling his weight, and making it harder for the others, especially him. He claims that the suspect was falsifying some of the rota registers.'

'I see. Ratting his mates in. I do hope the wheel of karma spins in his direction really soon. And?'

'The "and,"' continues Joy, 'is that I went through the motions of filing the complaint, let the dobber-inner see the report, but in fact I smuggled out the whole file, and never entered the complaint in the electronic system. I thought it would go undetected, but not a chance. The annoyingly persistent rat in the camp mentioned the incident to the Ops Head, who said he had heard nothing of this from me. My cover-up was revealed. Yet again. But this time more seriously so.'

'I am so sorry honey. And?' he asks, feeling genuinely protective.

'I do wish you would stop that reflexive questioning thing! Please. But yes, the "and" this time was another really uncomfortable interview with corporate HR, this time resulting in management issuing me with a final written warning. That was yesterday. Then today, on top of that, so much has come my way, from babies being delivered in sordid toilets, road collisions, and yet more needless inhuman disciplinaries.'

'That is so bad. It does not help to say this, I know, but you should have told me about the final warning. I would have understood,' he says, at last understanding what has been preoccupying her for the past few weeks.

'I know. I know you would have understood … but I felt so ashamed and did not want to put more pressure on you to provide when you are struggling. So, this is where we are. "It is what it is," as they say. I could be out on the streets unless I choke back on my instinctive sense of justice; give up on the idea of HR being the conscience of the organisation. Simply adjust instead to the idea that HR is the Stasi, running surveillance on our employees, and doing the dirty work that management want to keep distance from, turning employees one on another, dividing and ruling, while management keep their hands free of the blood.'

'Honey, this cannot carry on.' Justin is emphatic, sensing the fact that she is near breaking point. 'We need to find a way to get you out of there. Somewhere under that magic carpet there must be a magic trapdoor.'

'That is sweet… but where to from here? …HR jobs the world over now are variants of the same psychological medieval rack. Well, they are if you want to earn decent money – and I need to earn decent money. Anyway, thanks for listening – that is a weight off. I will see if I can organise some chimney sweeping after all.' She leaves her stool, to give Justin a kiss on the cheek.

The kids wandering downstairs at the tail end of this conversation, no longer able to contain their curiosity as to what it all might mean.

'Mummy, we heard some of that,' says Amelia. 'We weren't listening, honestly, but there was this echo coming up the stairs. We could go to work, to help out. Please Mummy, can we sweep chimneys? And then we could get dirty all day, and no one would mind.'

Adam adds his employment ideas. 'Or pick-pockets in the Mall just like Oliver Twist did.'

Joy is touched by these suggestions. 'Aww, best that you do not give up on your education at this stage, but thanks for the offer. There again it might have to come to farming you out to work, if Daddy and I don't find a way to earn better money soon.'

Amelia is not finished yet with her helpful suggestions. 'Mummy, we could become child actors. They earn loads of money and get to wear make-up and stuff and pretend to cry.'

'They do, but it is not that easy to get in on that. Best you concentrate on your schoolwork and stop dreaming of shortcuts to fame.'

Adam feels his mother might be underestimating their children's potential. 'But Mummy, I am really good at football. You could send me to soccer school permanently and I will be a star and all your worries would be over.'

'That is very sweet but very, very few boys make it through. Do they

Daddy?'

Justin does not want to kill all the raw ambition freighted in his children's plea – knowing also that the media feeds the idea that the "journey" to fame is attainable to all youngsters. 'No, I am afraid your mother is right, sadly. I used to dream of being a soccer star too, though they were not paid so much in those days. I had real potential. But then all of us lads showed promise, it would seem. Not one of my soccer-loving friends ever made it through, even the ones who signed for schoolboy trials with local clubs.'

Adam scowls at the injustice of this. 'So instead of becoming a soccer star, you had to work in the Ponzi Problem factory. A Justin-time factory. Waiting for your white coat. That is just not fair.'

'My white coat? Straitjacket more like,' Justin mutters.

Joy feels a need to break away from the topic of parental impecunity. 'Now come on you two, stop dreaming and get stuck into your homework or your careers will be going nowhere.' Turning to Justin, she says, 'and as for you, super coach, ace listener, and not to mention gourmand extraordinaire. You had best get off to your "peer network meeting". You said it was at that fancy Clifton Club, hosted by that posh bloke with the cravat? What was his name again?'

'Tarquin Crouch. It may even be Sir Tarquin Crouch.'

She relishes being offered yet another reminder of the idiocy of the coaching world, and its attempts to seek respectability through reference to the old orthodoxies. 'Oh yes. The one who coaches Prince Andrew, or says he does? Or was it Prince Charles? Do tell me if you meet any real Peers of the Realm at the Peer Group meeting. Or is it the "Road to Wigan Pier "meeting? I think Wigan Pier would be better, given that most organisations nowadays seem to be taking an Orwellian turn. Or even the 'end of the peer show' for theory Y based soft power schemes such as coaching? You don't need to answer that. So, are you are going or are you not? The bus awaits. And I need to eat what remains of dinner, preferably on a plate though at this stage, off the floor would be fine, then I could curl up and die afterwards.'

Justin takes this ribbing in good spirit. 'Yes darling, I am, but I don't want to leave you with the washing up and everything, after the horror of a day you have had, and these threats hanging over you.'

'No, on you go,' says Joy, with a sigh of resignation. 'Though I must say it is all right for some, swanning off to carouse with the knobs while I have to slave over an unfinished spreadsheet. There you will be, at that swanky club, up to your cosseted armpits in all that old money that hides itself away so secretly, so discreetly. Make sure you do not mention Bristol's legacy of slavery. Those Mercantilists get quite twitchy about that subject. And bring me back a canapé, please. Oh, and a bottle of milk - we need milk.'

'And a hummer burger please, Daddy,' came Amelia's voice from under the table. 'And a woven Ponzi pizza for me,' re-joined Adam. 'And don't forget to wear your white coat.'

Collision of Worlds at the Gentleman's Club

Boarding the #1 bus as it lurches to a stop just around the corner from the house, Justin finds himself shoulder to shoulder with all sorts of shapes and sizes of Bristolians. The sheer diversity of this motley crew prompts him to speculate about how the "vanity of small differences" plays out along this bus route, as it processes from the furthest north to the darkest south of Bristol, touching upon most social class and socio-economic groups along the way. Some passengers are clutching fancy bags scored from megastores at Cribbs Causeway, the out-of-town shopping Mall not far down the motorway from Magic Carpet.

Other passengers hail from the depths of the downbeat Southmead estate, heading for a night out in the emporium pubs around Corn Street, later to process to the all-night bars on the Waterfront. He suspects that for this group, some pre-loading of cheap vodka has been indulged in at home, to give the night a kick-start, and the wallet some relief.

Justin notices a well-heeled, elderly couple from Henbury, sitting in front of this group, and trying to distance themselves from it. They are clutching their theatre tickets for the Old Vic, and probably wishing they had booked an Uber instead of rubbing shoulders with the hoi poloi. But there again they do have their free bus passes, and it could well be that their lives are those of the shabby chic, their fortunes in decline, just like Tom Rakewell of tapestry fame, despite keeping up appearances to the contrary.

It occurs to him that no one on the bus talks across these class divides; the expression of any sense of excitement at the prospect at the evening in store is repressed until they are safe amid their own tribes. Justin is reminded that everyone is accepted in Britain until they open their mouths, at which point they are betrayed by their accent, when their class is revealed, and the judgment of others not of their class invited.

After a valedictory 'Cheers Droive' – the mandatory parting phrase to all Bristol bus drivers - he strides up Queens Road for the second time that day towards the Clifton club, snuggled inconspicuously in the Mall, within the heart of Clifton Village. It looks undistinguished from the front, but it extends a long way back, deep into the Village, without attracting attention towards its true size. He had walked past it innumerable times without giving it a thought. Yet now he is poised at the point of entry to this cloaked world.

He is greeted at the polished door by an extremely polite young man, who apologetically beseeches him to 'bear with' and wait in the lobby, while he runs an errand for an elderly guest, who needs help to climb into his waiting limousine. Justin is more than happy to be left alone to browse the information board and assorted brochures scattered across the entrance hall. He learns that the Club is "not a place to network... rather one comes to be connected by your club." Justin enjoys this dig at the modernisers who reduce all human conversation to a networking opportunity.

But he is not so sure about the notion that human bonding is dependent on elite tribal affiliation. Not when one man's bonding is dependent on another man's bondage. He holds back on that thought, remembering that he promised Joy not to bring up the topic of slavery too early on his first visit. He reads the next notice:

'190 years old, the club bears a strong mercantilist tradition with links to the Merchant Venturers. Historically, the club's membership has included the heads of major Bristol businesses, local landed gentry and the "higher echelons of the professions."' Justin guesses that by this they mean lawyers, doctors, judges, the odd professor. And probably estate agents. It could even include old-school bank managers, but he doubted it. Reading on, he learns that. 'Exclusively men only for most of those years, the club did not permit women members until 2006. Membership must be gained on the invitation and recommendation of at least two members of good standing who have each known the candidate for at least three years.' Before he is able to learn more of this fascinating den of protected entitlement and white privilege, the well-scrubbed young man returns to escort him along the panelled corridor – passing venerable paintings of endlessly unsmiling men - to a chandeliered room, where he is warmly greeted by the supposedly royally-endorsed host for the evening, Tarquin Crouch, who asks, 'have you come far?' And then, determining from Justin's response that Westbury was not a suburb he wishes to spend any conversational time on, Tarquin encourages Justin to 'grab a glass of bubbles' and go mingle with the others. Bubbles duly in hand, Justin circles the throng, pausing to listen for a while to the distinctive susurrus of coaches sniffing each other out, while ostensibly talking shop. One clustered conversation concerns the impossibility of parking in Clifton, a conversation Justin avoids lest he reveals that he came by bus. Another cluster is subtly, but nevertheless competitively, comparing coaching courses and conferences they have attended at various venues throughout the world. It would seem that the further-flung the event, the better the quality of learning.

Much of this chatter relates to celebrity coaches they may know, or claim to know, or are close to: which leads in turn to discussing which of these celebrities is trending and which is not; and whom among the fashionable gurus has introduced the latest ground-breaking idea. All of this bragging is interspersed with sad tales of erstwhile coaching luminaries whose ideas have been thoroughly debunked; those whose flame is now dimmed; those who have been recently disgraced; and those who are ill or have recently died. Justin detects a barely contained schadenfreude underlying these tales of fallings from grace of the once great ones, even a grim satisfaction in knowing that in the end, celebrity does not protect their mortality.

Another rather more plebeian group seem transfixed by the grandeur of the club itself, unable to talk of anything else, all eyes fixed on the cherubs around the dado rail, while the cluster in the centre of the room are loudly selling their latest coaching products and toolkits to each other, or at least practising their elevator sales pitches. One of this merry group is waving a copy of her latest publication, 'Making your Client's Parachute Fly', which she thrusts high in the air, for all to see and acclaim. Justin is well aware that such publications are as much elaborate visiting cards, as they are evidence of freighting ideas of intrinsic worth. He has seen these books used a vehicle to capture prospective clients' attention; an attention gained through the suggestive power that a publisher somewhere deemed their ideas worthy of print, without anyone bothering to delve deep enough to discern whether in fact, between these bright covers, there were was any wisdom that has not been released on the world before.

Justin floats among these threads of conversation, clutching his now flat Prosecco as some sort of amulet, as he has not yet landed on conversational gossamer that he would wish to weave into something more substantial. On the other hand, he is bursting to share his good news regarding his newly acquired client work, with someone, anyone, but holds back on this impulse, in part through not wishing to brag, but also through fearing that pride may come before the fall.

Not before time, the flamboyant host, somewhat ruddier cheeked than before, puts an end to this frippery and calls the congregation to order. He welcomes all participants to the first meeting of the "Coaching Chrysalis network," trusting that all will feel renewed and enlightened by the end of the session, enlightened if not 'exactly bursting from their pupa.' Clearly, the idea of naming the group 'Chrysalis' was not a title that Tarquin enthusiastically embraced, but one that he would sardonically indulge, in a nod to modernism. He thanks all those who had paid their subscriptions online, while glaring meaningfully around the room to scout out those who might be freeloading. He warns them all that embossed CPD certificates will be issued only to those who have paid up.

He then invites the group, in 'time-honoured fashion,' to go around the room, one by one, and introduce themselves. Some look more awkward and less confident than others at this prospect. A newcomer mutters something about suffering from 'impostor syndrome', while others take centre stage with aplomb, elaborating their well-garnished histories. Justin feels some discomfort that while everyone seems to have dressed up specially to match these auspicious surroundings, he sports oven-chip grease and traces of dried baked bean on his jeans. He is consoled, though, by the fact that the man sitting to his right did not seem to have received the email regarding dress code either. In fact, he seems even scruffier than Justin, with his jean's legs fraying where they met his scuffed and worn trainers. While scanning the group, Justin half listens to the various declarations of coaching identity that echo around the room.

'I am freelance, have been for many years'

'I am an executive coach who specialises in strategic reframing.'

'I work in the educational sector'

'I have just completed my basic training and am so excited to be in such awesome company'

'I am university based, both researching and teaching coaching'

'I was an in-company coach, but am now I am branching out on my own, and need to build my support networks.'

'I am a retired HR director, who has moved into pro-bono coaching, to give something back from all my rich experience.'

'I am a recovering management consultant.'

'I am a full-time coaching supervisor, and trainer of other supervisors.'

'I am a qualified master coach, and also for my sins I am Chair of the national committee of the Coaching Fraternity, UK division.'

This ritual survived, Justin gazes at the twinkling chandelier that has surely illuminated more august gatherings, when the cravatted host announces that,

'Thank you for those pen pictures. Now for the main event. We are graced with two speakers to enlighten us tonight, one to speak on "Neuro-catastrophic approaches to systemic breakdowns" – Tarquin sniggers somewhat as he stutters over these words on his prompt card – 'while the other speaker will cover "coaching credentials and how to choose among them"; a topic that I feel sure close to all our hearts, in this increasingly regulated world.'

The enthusiastic Neuro-catastrophic speaker delivers a Ted Talk light, dazzling all before him with colourful videos of brain synapses 'firing and wiring.' The talk is polished but the content somewhat thin, unless one is easily convinced by a blizzard of quasi-scientific terminology. Furthermore, in the light of recent personal events, Justin did not need more reminders of the imminent demise of his own at-risk family. Despite the chairperson Tarquin seeming to fall asleep at the side of the podium, the speaker ploughs on deeper and deeper into the world of quantum physics, elucidating the power of strange attractors, before grinding to a synaptic halt with his grand finale – a waving of his 'Neuro-catastrophic Toolkit for Coaches', now available online and in hardback.

The question and answer time is mercifully short and sweet, partly because most of the questions relating to practical applications of these concepts were diverted by the speaker towards the need for his questioners to read the toolkit -or even better, to come along to his next weekend workshop and become licensed in the technique.

'Discounts will apply to all Chrysalis members. And save even more if you take up my early bird offers, or indeed my bring two friends, come free yourself offer, which is on special this week.'

Of more common interest was the second topic addressing "Choosing Coaching Credentials." After a preliminary sharing of statistics revealing historic coaching credential choices and their apparent efficacy, the speaker invites each in turn to reveal their orientation towards credentials, whether at a personal level, or in general way. He explains that his interest in these responses is far from casual. In fact, he would like, with permission, to audiotape responses, then add them to his growing research database. No one demurs from this request. Justin feels flattered that his half-baked opinions might be research worthy at all, while remaining sceptical that this vox pop of the converted might be construed as critical research. Tarquin loudly declares that his own paper on credentials, written ten years ago, was probably the last word on this matter, though he was prepared to be open-minded, as always. Justin allowed that this non-sequitur was an attempt at irony; though he was swiftly coming to realise that one can never be sure what might pass for irony at this club.

As participants declare their interests and credentialing biases around the room, they hear at first from the Pollyanna-ish newbie, who believes that coaching will save the world, and who wants to never stop learning and collecting credentials, even up to doctoral level. She is countered by the far more sceptical and fidgety newbie sat alongside of her, who wonders even now if his investment in basic training will ever pay off. Next up is the retired grandee who would like nothing better than to mentor them both, though he himself has no appetite for more honorifics after his name, as he has, 'been there and got the waistcoat'.

They hear from a coach who has newly graduated at master's level from the University of Bristol, whose main concern is that credential awards must in future must be evidence-based, with particular attention being paid to measuring outcomes. The Fraternity of Coaching grandee, who is clearly our self-appointed guardian of professional ethics, supports her view. He reminds us of the need for professional bodies to protect us from the predations of bogus licensees. Somewhat oblivious to this, the woman with the parachute book (said publication now lowered somewhat discreetly from above her head to rest, outward facing, in her lap,) says her approach is entirely validated and proven through a peer-review process conducted in California. Neuro-catastrophic man is quick to add that his toolkit licences are kosher too. Justin's ragged-trousered neighbour - who reveals that his background is in grief counselling and conflict resolution - says that he feels there is little need for any credentials at all, just as long as unconditional attention and deep empathy are present at any coaching session, to cause 'the shift in the room.'

The wellness expert has some sympathy with this sentiment, while the ex-sports coach says that, 'It all comes down to winning and losing at the end of the day. It is all about seeking marginal gains, however microscopic. Coaching is fine and dandy, but you have to ask: does it make the boat go any faster?' The meditation guru simply smiles at all of this, indulgently suggesting that, 'were the Buddha present, he would keep pouring tea into each of the cups of we apprentices until the tea spills over.' Justin feels sure the guru was pleased that his esoteric wisdom was captured on tape, to be added to the research database.

The credentials speaker who has unleashed all of this does his best to somehow pull this conversation into some sort of synthesis. 'What I hear from around the room – and I do thank you all for contributing to this seminal research - confirms my preliminary findings that the field of coaching credentials is highly fragmented; and that, putting modesty aside, that my ten-point template for credential integration – you will find the flyers at the table on the way out - is one of the few hopes we have of ever unifying the field. My intention of course is to anonymise all of your responses and to fit them within my proven frame. But if any of you wish for your quote to be specifically attributed then do please let me know. Equally if you want to engage with this inquiry further, then I would be delighted to include you. Please come speak to me afterwards and register your interest. And do take a sneak-peek at the toolkit too.'

The chairman Tarquin – perhaps the most commercially successful and acclaimed of all there present – smiles benignly, saying how fascinating it is to hear all of these contrasting views being expressed within the same room, from people supposedly pursuing the same line of work. He says he is particularly intrigued to hear of the need for supervisors to have supervisors of their own, to keep them out of trouble. He muses that it all rather reminds him of the time when the denizens of this club had a 'gentleman's gentleman', though he felt sure it was not quite the same thing. Pausing for the laughter that does not come, he concludes that the whole conversation reinforces his personal position that he will not commit to gaining any coaching credential whatsoever until he is convinced that this qualification will cause his clients to think even more highly of him than they already do. Which he so far, he thinks is highly unlikely. Again, Justin's virtual irony detector wobbles all over the place, the needle never settling. On that modest parting note, Tarquin thanks the speakers for taking the time to lead the group out of their pupa towards enlightenment, then invites them all, 'to relax within the confines of this room over coffee, but please not to go AWOL anywhere else within the rest of the club, where members' privacy is sacrosanct.' In the silence they hear from the next room the sound of snooker balls rattling one into another, following a set of rules laid down centuries ago, rules that will never be subverted. Justin's dishevelled neighbour turns to whisper, 'how reassuring it must be to live in a world where everyone knows exactly what they are doing, and how far they are allowed to go.' Rather than linger in the confines of this cloistered holding pen, where Justin knows he might be under pressure to buy a toolkit or even a parachute book, he makes his way towards the door, clutching his embossed CPD certificate. Casting his eyes back for one last lingering glance at the portraits in the hallway, he catches the eye of his neighbour who is making in the same direction. 'Fancy a pint?' his grief counselling neighbour asks.

'Yes, I do, I really think I do. How about Somerset House on Princess Victoria Street, do?' Justin is not at all sure this is the right venue, but it is one he favours from his student days.

'Yes – anywhere but this suffocating place. I know the pub. My name is Tony by the way.'

'Hi. I am Justin.'

Huddled over pints of Guinness, they find a quiet corner to share impressions of their time at the Club, by way of getting to know each other better. In their shared dissection of the evening's proceedings, it would seem that in many ways they are kindred spirits. Both have moved towards coaching out of a belief that they each can make a solid contribution through the intensive development of others, and - without getting too much up themselves - to uplift society through emancipatory action. Given the slide towards professionalization, they agree that, for the sake of business survival, they need to keep onside of the need to credible and qualified, and to keep learning. Reflecting on the conversation on credentials this evening, they conclude that the field of coaching is mired, and is likely to be taken over by the rules and regulations fanatics, who Tony says, 'are stinking up the joint.' He goes on to voice his fear that coaching professionalisation must somehow match the corporate shift towards surveillance and intrusive regulation of every employee move, while undermining the old verities of trade union protection and the power of the collective. By way of example of this, Justin decides to share with Tony Joy's current agonies at Magic Carpet, and the threats to her livelihood posed by her resistance to becoming a handmaiden of managerial oversight. Tony is concerned to hear of this, and wants to know more. He is a good listener and Justin feels relieved to offload this personal predicament. In talking it over, he discovers just how vulnerable and guilty he feels about Joy's plight, while also kind of helpless to do anything material to help. Tony reassures him that he is already doing more than he knew, just by being there for her and listening. 'She is at some level grieving, and you are holding that boundary for her.'

Tony reveals that much of the coaching he does is with those who have been marginalised or hurt by the boot of Big Brother. He also indicates that, should Joy face the sack, then he knows not only of Human Rights lawyers that might be able to help, but that he also knows some journalists who would be more than happy to take her story further. On the other hand, he is happy just to simply be there for Justin, as a sounding board, should he need to discharge his feelings further.

Justin thanks him for these kindnesses, taken aback and a little humbled by these offerings from a stranger. The conversation swings back to sharing impressions of the Chrysalis network and those within it, as well as to ponder as to the ancient power contained so securely, still, within the Clifton Club walls. Their impression is that the network comprises a fractal of the deeply fragmented coaching world. They ask whether it was in fact a profession, distinct in its own right, rather than coaching comprising an activity that people do from a whole variety of positionings, professional and otherwise. They go on to question whether professional coaching was purely in service of further molly-coddling the already entitled professional middle classes, many of them the salarymen occupying bullshit jobs? At which point they ask whether coaching itself has become yet another bullshit job? Then agreed that if coaching were to truly contribute to the emancipation of the workspace, then it would need to take an entirely different direction from the current one.

Tony says that for his part, his practice is now is following a liberational route, though there is little money in it.

He has set up a small office and consulting room in Stokes Croft – 'Yes, the "Peoples' Republic of Stokes Croft," – where he is surrounded by clusters of alternative practitioners of all shades and descriptions. He also works with many Non-Governmental Organisations, or NGOs, as they are known, and charities within the city. He asks if maybe Justin might be interested in joining him in these endeavours at some point, as he feels that Justin's values and time in life might be right for it. Or perhaps Justin was too busy currently seeking to subvert capitalism from the inside, to have time for projects on the margins of respectability?

Justin chuckles at this exaggeration of his current workload, feeling a need to reveal the sorry state of his threadbare order book. He talks of his struggles with Consignia and of the dangers of taking that work underground with Richard; and of his recent hook-up with Parallelogram.

Tony's ears prick up at the mention of Parallelogram. 'Oh them,' he says, with a grunt.

'Yes them. What do you know of them then? Pray tell. Do not spare my feelings.' Justin fears he is about to learn something that he would really rather not know.

'Well, I have heard of them, but have never been approached. Have they asked you for a finder's fee up front?'

'No, but they will take a significant chunk of fee for sourcing work, which might be an okay trade-off, as I hate all that selling stuff,' says Justin, while worrying that he might have been sold a pup. Another pup to add to the over-stuffed kennel.

Tony realises that Justin, like so many before him, has been seduced by the prospect of an easy ride. 'Well, yes, don't we all hate the grubby work of selling? But do beware of selling your soul into the bargain, which can be the price of not selling for yourself. I would be most interested to hear how you get on with Parallelogram. All I hear is that they are highly ambitious, and are aiming for domination of the corporate coaching scene, swallowing up smaller companies and independent players such as you and me along the way.'

Justin looks chastened. 'Oh, they had not made the swallowing up bit clear to me. But their naked ambition is right up-front. At some point no doubt I will run into a values crunch with them.'

Tony nods, meaningfully. 'Well, I would think that is highly likely. So far you are passing through their corporate culture screening process. But their antennae are acute, and it will not take long for them to suss out your true egalitarian leanings, the moment you drop your professional guard. Which you probably will. We all leak our true values at some point, despite our best attempts to don the conformist mask. Sorry, I should not be so discouraging. But once you do reveal your true self then I would say they will cut you out like a virus, eliminate all traces of you from the system.'

'How dramatic. But I get it. What you say is fine, advice well taken. Right now, I am torn between not compromising my values, and putting food on the table, especially with my wife's work under threat. Do you have kids, Tony?'

'No, I do not, not yet leastways. And I openly admit that that freedom allows me to take economic risks that might prove really different than if I had dependents. But we all compromise at some level. While training as a coach I did sacrifice my white-man's dreads. And I am careful to cover up my tattoos when coaching. It is strange how we move to camouflage who were really are. Have you seen Grayson Perry's show at the museum?'

Justin is delighted to hear of this cultural common ground. 'The Vanity of Small Differences? Oh yes, I loved it and it has lived with me since. It was top of mind for me when looking around the Clifton Club, and the people in it, tonight, through the prism of the Vanities. I was alive to the social gradations on the bus coming into the city, with all of Grayson's tribes present and correct. But oh - talking of buses – I must be off before the last one

disappears back to the great depot in the sky. So great to meet you, Tony, and I feel sure we will meet soon. Here is my card.'

'Yes, same here, and here is mine too. The quality of this chat was way in advance of what I expected to get out of tonight. And it has given me hope of what like-minded coaches might achieve together. See you soon.'

Justin makes the last bus by the skin of his teeth, self-consciously clutching his ridiculously embossed CPD certificate.

Sat in the middle of the bus, he is openly ridiculed, in a good-natured way, by a group of drunken nightriders, returning to Southmead, who taunt him as the 'poster boy.' He finds this mockery of his certificate amusing, and laughs along with them, which serves to diffuse any tension. At home, he finds that everyone one has gone to bed. There is a note from Joy, saying that she fell asleep during Newsnight, and that he was not to wake her, as she has an early start and needed a lift as her car has broken down. She also predicts that he will have forgotten the milk. Which he had. Not ready yet for sleep, he lies on the sofa, his brain spinning with all he has heard and learned today, and all that he must attend to tomorrow. He scribbles a to-do list on the nearest thing to hand, his CPD certificate, then promptly falls asleep, sliding off the sofa towards the floor.

The Path of Least Resistance

As Justin awakens, he rubs his eyes and staggers downstairs, bemused to see his smudged and crushed Chrysalis certificate languishing at the spot where he had tumbled off the sofa. He turns it over, to see that at some point before sleep he had scribbled upon it a 'to do' list designed to direct this brand-new day. Despite the grogginess attendant on spending most of the evening on the floor, he feels a sense of awakening, an urgency and that were absent several days ago. There is also the added imperative to get some cash rolling in to take the pressure off Joy.

Tomorrow's to do list

- Draw up and land new contract with Parallelogram – push for earliest start time
- Brush up CV for Richard
- Find a new supervisor
- Find references – for Parallelogram - ask Richard and? New supervisor (some guided materialisation needed here Justin!)
- Fix Joys car
- Get kids to school and back

As if to get the list accomplishment rolling, Brian, the peripatetic mechanic – "I pick up from your home!" boasts his flyer - is knocking at the door, early as requested. After a quick chat about Joy's car's ignition problem, Brian drives the stuttering Astra down the road, followed by his shadowy mate in the support car. Justin is glad to see it go, while hoping the car returns fresh and renewed, never to need treatment again.

Showered and suited, Justin wastes no time in rustling up breakfast, then decants his wife and children into their remaining car. Dropping the children off at school – mercifully without too much banter on the way – he has a conversation with Joy about the Clifton Club, which confirms all of her worst suspicions of the place. In fact, the reality was worse than even she imagined. She describes it as a mercantilist Masonic Lodge. She is amused by tales of Tarquin the Mighty, and is not surprised that Chrysalis is a mixed and confused bag; but she is really curious to know more of Tony, saying that he sounds like a really promising connection to make.

'He sounds like our sort of person,' she declares, prompting her to think that they had never really sat down to define what 'their sort of person' might constitute. Instead, they had simply allowed people to drift in and out of their lives, especially people from the work context. Near Almondsbury intersection wherein sits her workplace, their conversation turns to Magic Carpet. They think through survival strategies that could leave her in place, without destroying her soul. Joy finds it releasing – despite how hard it was to tell him - that Justin now knows of the degree of threat she is under, and of the need for her to pull the rug on Magic Carpet sooner rather than later. As she steps out of the car, he sees her greets a few colleagues in a perfunctory way before this group click into robotic, automatic pilot mode, leaving their home selves behind for the day.

Justin drops the car off at home then takes the bus into town, stopping off at an independent café at the top of Black Boy Hill, where he takes out his laptop to update his CV for Richard. This does not take too long, as there is little to add to his last update, beyond his crumpled certificate. Pressing send, he eases back in his chair to gaze out at the traffic crawling down towards Whiteladies Road. Whiteladies, eh? Black Boy Hill? Some would say that these street names were slavery related, some say of much older provenance. He is tempted to research this on Google, but resists, instead disciplining himself to go supervisor hunting instead. His morning list must be obeyed; there must be no backsliding. He reminds himself that goals must be pursued without distraction, never forgetting the need to make marginal gains along the way.

Ping! An email arrives from the Parallelogram agency, saying they need to see him urgently – the power of materialising the list is working strongly. After several short email exchanges, he agrees to meet Parallelogram early that afternoon at the Marriott Grand Hotel on College Green. They remind him of the need to forward his most recent CV, and to bring details of two professional references along with him. No problem, he replies, while knowing it may be a problem unless the gods of supervisory materialisation get to work pronto.

Ping! A return email from Richard saying that he has received the CV, and, having seen his draft contract, that he is broadly agreeable to the terms, saying the pricing looks right for this stage. He asks would it be possible for Justin to meet him tomorrow to sign up, then to be ready to get started before the end of the week?

Justin replies in the affirmative: then decides to push his luck by asking if Richard would be prepared to provide a reference for him – at short notice. Surprisingly, he receives an immediate reply from Richard, confirming the reference request, and suggesting that they meet to ties things up at the Marriott tomorrow, 12.30, in the coffee lounge. The Marriott again. Justin thinks that he may need to enrol for a Marriott reward card at this rate.

Taking breath to count his blessings, Justin delights at his hit-rate of list manifestation so far. The next vital item on his critical path is the immediate sourcing of a supervisor who is prepared to start pretty much immediately. He is not sure of his selection criteria but ABB – Anyone but Brenda – features highly.

Which in this instance means someone who is flexible, and can start pretty damn quickly, as there is the highest urgency to get a supervisor back on board, now that the other pieces are falling into place. If the criterion of immediacy is met, he speculates that major chemistry tests are surely optional, but he does need to find someone credible enough to put in front of his professional body, to meet their minimum requirements.

 His search begins by scrutinising the professional bodies websites for their respective listings of recommended, qualified supervisors. Most of these look much of a muchness. Justin is dismayed to find that most of these candidate profiles read much like Brenda's, which means - if their sign-up process is as demanding as hers - more time dedicated to matching and assessing fit than he could possibly afford. Moving away from the coaching specific websites, he decides to take a punt on Google, to see if there is anyone local who could be fast-tracked into position. His search reads 'coaching supervisors in the Bristol area.' This search yields many more Brenda lookalikes, including Brenda herself. He is just about to give up when he comes across something quite different.

'Coaching Supervision but Mainly for Men. Male coaches are different! And I
understand where men in the helping professions are coming from. For a full and frank discussion, ring Bert Thompson now on 0117 4556841.'

Bert's website pitch is unusual, to say the least, but it sounds promising. Justin is not sure if he cares so much about the 'men only' tag, which sounds a bit grubby. But on the other hand, Bert is well qualified, experienced, and lives just around the corner in Redland. Ringing the number, Bert picks up immediately, sounding affable. In fact, he emanates a 'hail fellow well met' sort of vibe.

Bert is quick to talk about himself. An ex-Marine, he has done active service in several theatres of war, and was a great sportsman in his day – he played rugby for the Army and is now a grandee of the Rugby Football Union, the highest sporting power in the land. After military discharge he went into sports coaching, which was something that he really enjoyed. But when his knees began to give up, he diversified into more general coaching, while doing all the necessary coaching training and credentialing along the way.

'And more?' asks Justin, back in the clean groove.

Bert confesses that while he chimes with much of what was preached during coach training, he did feel that much of the tone was quite parental and rule-bound, as if written by an HR person with time on their hands. He declared that he preferred to work instinctively, by the seat of his pants stuff, which works well for him and his clients – an approach that he is now encouraged to stick with.

The success of this manly approach suggested to him that much of classical coach training and support is quite feminised. He surmised that there might well be a niche in the market for a more masculine approach, more yang, less yin. The demand that he has attracted since testing this market is proving his gut feel right.

Justin wondered if Bert might take pause, but he does not. Clearly, he has much to say. He has learned more personal back-story from ten minutes of Bert than he had from two years of the inscrutable Brenda.

153

'Tell me more,' says Justin, disingenuously, his phone now hot in his ear. But then he does not want to discourage Bert's flow, thinking that a supervisee in need will listen endlessly to engage – well almost anyone, really, who is readily available.

Bert continues with his well-grooved monologue, to say that - once he had established this male-centric niche - he decided to point his approach towards the trend for regular supervision becoming a necessary requirement of a coach's licence to operate. He notes that most conventional supervisory practice tends to follow clinical, psychotherapeutic and counselling models.

'I notice that too,' says Justin, thinking back to Brenda and all her parallel process Jungian shtick.

'Glad to hear that,' puffs Bert. So, seeing a market opportunity, he explains that he decided to get in early, at the top of the supervisory pyramid. He gained a quick basic credential in supervision, but then saw no need for additional credentials, as no one in the profession could decide or agree what these should be. All they were agreed upon was that everyone needs a supervisor. So, he 'set up his shingle' as a full-blown supervisor, in particular supporting men, feeling that as of now no authority in the world could challenge his right to work in the supervision space.

Eventually Bert needs to pause for breath. 'Gosh, that was a lot, thanks for listening to all of that. But I feel sure you get the drift. You sound like a smart chap. Does this sound like the sort of thing you might be looking for?'

Justin ramps up his enthusiasm to maximum, despite the hot phone burning in his ears. 'Yes! It sounds most promising - and refreshingly lacking all the fuss and pomposity generally surrounding supervision – to the point where folk start to make a religion of it.'

'Totally agree. So, tell me a bit about you. You have heard quite enough about me, but I felt it important to give you the full background.' Justin welcomes the invitation, though he rather thinks that Bert may have put the phone to one side. And he knows for sure that his fragmented story will never match the completeness of Bert's soliloquy. Instead of answering the request, he says,

'Sure. I will tell you all about me - but first of all – how soon could we get started? Cheeky I know but I live just around the corner and I need to switch supervisors really quite quickly. With regard to the demise of my last supervisor – well just to say that she and I fell afoul of – ahem – artistic differences, and now I am in supervisory transition.'

'Say no more, old chap, say no more. I get your drift completely. In fact, I have heard a similar story many times before from other shipwrecked coaches. The answer to your question is that we can pretty much start as soon as you like, as long as you pass muster, which I feel sure you will. And as long as you like the cut of my jib. Look, I am not too much of a one for all this remote video nonsense or booking teleconferences – for goodness sake, what a waste of time all of that is. Why not just pick up the phone, like you just did just now? So, are you free to meet up today? I am free as it happens. Free as a bird.'

'Yes, me too. I am free this morning though I am busy after lunch.'

'Okay, so no time like the present – what is your poison?' asks Bert. 'A coffee or a pint or a glass of wine – I find social settings conducive to contracting meetings, though it does not have to involve alcohol. I am not totally blokish.'

Justin grabs this opportunity to meet soonest with alacrity. 'All of those options sound good – which do you prefer?'

'Well, I am a member of the Clifton Club. I do a lot of my stuff there..'

'Oh, yes I was there last night 'Justin says casually, wanting to sound as if he were a familiar in that exclusively masculine world.

'Well we could meet there, seeing as you know it. Mind you, it is a bit stuffy this time of day. But how about we meet at the Clifton Wine Bar, just along the Mall, right next to the club? Been going there years – in fact I met my third wife there.'

'Yes, I know it. Sounds great to me,' says Justin, relieved that he will not be returning to the club so soon. Shall we make our way down shortly? I am only up the road, on Black Boy Hill.'

'Sure, half an hour or so is fine. You will find me at the back of the room. And look, I sense the urgency of your situation. No need to dress things up for me, for the sake of respectability. I have seen most things in this business so no need to sugar-coat for me – the best thing is for you to be totally honest.'

'I will be honest, don't worry. See you there.'

Debrief Behind the Bike Sheds

After a meeting of eyes across the dividers in the open-plan office, Sharon signals via a series of elaborate mimes that is time for a break outside. And a conversation.

'How are you, Sharon?'

'Oh, living the ideal life of the single woman. Loving my choir, the Wildfire Chorus that I told you about, and my yoga classes of course. Not to mention collapsing on the sofa after those excursions, to enjoy a boxset and guzzle a tub of ice-cream, undisturbed by manly blandishments.'

'Sounds blissful. Yet I accept my married lot. Such a complicated business, bringing two lives together. In fact, make that four lives, two of them as yet unformed.'

'Joy, that is a lot, and quite a complicated jigsaw to manage. But thinking about Justin - I just remembered. My dare! Did you ever enact my plan to ensnare that supervisor woman? I bet you didn't!'

'Oh, ye of little faith. I did, I did – and thanks for the nudge!'

'I am impressed. How did it go? Tell me all,' Sharon asks, as she lights a cigarette.

'It was outrageous. I was outrageous. It was not what she was expecting at all. It seems that she is most always in charge of the conversation, but not that time. I made the running all the way through. So pleased with myself.'

'How did you do that?'

'How? It was genius.' Joy smiles at the memory. I did it by asking a whole series of hypothetical questions, setting up case studies that were anything but fictional.'

'Sounds amazing. So you stitched her up?'

'Not yet, but I could do. I certainly left her much to worry about.'

'Good for you girl. Did she suspect the Justin connection?'

'No, not at all I don't think,' says Joy, betraying some doubt in her voice as she replies.

'Do you think Justin might have had a thing with her? Had a "thing" thing?'

'No, I do not. Not at all. In fact, I can now quite see how in the end she drove mild-mannered Justin Drake to near violence.'

'Could you imagine him coming onto her?'

'Oh no! The woman seemed completely sexless. Sorry to speak ill of a sister, but she did. It would be hard to have a crush on her, unless you were a man seeking a dominatrix.'

'Hmm. Well many men do seek precisely that - and pay handsomely for it. Especially public schoolboys. And politicians, so I am told.'

'That is true enough,' agrees Joy. 'Dastardly Dominic who crucified us at the bank during the dying banker tableau probably needs a dominatrix. It is all in the name.'

'Nominative determinism?' offers Sharon. 'I heard about that on the radio this morning, driving in. How some people's names reflect what they do. Like Sue Yoo, the American lawyer.'

Joy is impressed. 'Nice term. Must use it. Though with a name like Joy, I challenge the theory.'

'So, is this banker Dom needing dominating?'

'Probably. I, for one would love to be given permission to whip him.'

'Oh, like you do with Justin, all clad in black vinyl?'

'Of course!' says Joy, 'though I mainly torture him with sarcasm. Nominative Determinism, eh? And then there is my dying banker Mr Fear, he was fulfilling his given name. Anyway, I do not think domination was Brenda's attraction. Justin gets enough submission practice at home as it is.'

'I am sure he does, from what you say!' grins Sharon. 'So, was doing the dare worthwhile, Joy?'

'Oh yes – extremely so. Most satisfying to be the one asking the questions, challenging, without overstepping the mark. I felt very much in control, knowing far more of her world than she ever suspected a naïve supplicant to know.'

'That must have been such a rush. What a sleuth!' Sharon claps her hands. 'You should become an investigative reporter.'

'Thanks. And yes, it felt quite forensic. Posing questions such people are rarely asked. Infrequently asked questions. IAQ? Like it?'

'IAQ? You must pitch this acronym to the call centre. Never asked questions. Taboo questions.'

'Ha Ha.' Agrees Joy. 'More questions than answers. I guess I was meant to seek her approval, but I never even tried any of that. She was off-balance most of the time, way outside of her normal control stuff.'

'So, what did you learn about her? And more generally this world of coaching that Justin has fallen into, perhaps never to get out in one piece?'

'Well, what I learned about her confirmed my gut instinct. She is highly rule-bound, nice on the surface but officious underneath, was probably a grammar-school head-girl of the worst possible sort. She is a cog in a bigger surveillance operation. It is one-way cameras, mind. Can't imagine they are ever turned on her. One day, one day, maybe. I dream.'

'And about the coaching world?'

'Oh, a place designed to tie ingénues up in knots. She is up there atop the pyramid, and such folk have so much power.'

'Maybe it all gets down to power in the end.'

'You are probably right' Joy concedes. 'But this time around I felt empowered. It was exhilarating!'

'I am sure,' encourages Sharon. 'Even better than having a submissive hubbie under your control. But talking of which, what if Justin finds out about your surveillance trip?'

'Not sure how he would unless I tell him. He would be upset of course, and fearful that I had taken an unnecessary risk, exposed him when he least needed it.' Joy shrugs. 'But hey, if he has meetings where he keeps the conversation secret, then so can I!'

'If he found out, might he think you were seeking vengeance?'

'Hmm- he might. Why, do you think that?'

'Yeh, I do a little. You seemed to enjoy it a lot. So how did you leave it?'

'Don't call me, I will call you. Made her swear on her coaching bible that she would not chase me down.'

'And how did it leave her?'

'Puzzled and chastened, I think! Non-plussed, having been put through something quite out of her experience. She was clinging to maintain control – and failing.'

'Oh well glad you did it. I am proud of you,' says Sharon, giving her a small pat on the back.

'Good. At some level so am I. And now I am wracking my brains to think up a high-stakes dare for you!'

'On no, don't think too hard. I am such a coward really. And – skilfully changing the subject - well not entirely changing it, because it is about surveillance. Have you heard the rumours about a massive Magic Carpet data breach, a huge leak in the firewall?'

'Oh, yes I have. And I am being co-opted into sniffing out what it might be, and who might responsible.'

'I thought they might push that towards you,' says Sharon, finger pointing at her friend. 'Getting anywhere with it?'

'No, not really. But then I am not exactly putting my back into it – too much else to do. I am just saying I am finding nothing so far.'

'Me too. And I really do know nothing. Come on, lunch break nearly over. Back to the hamster wheel. Under his eye.'

'Yes indeed, back to that. What are these jobs turning us into?'

Sympathy For the Devil.

Justin steps out of the café and onto the # 1 bus, harbouring a really good feeling about this coming encounter. Stepping off the bus, he sees sunlight sparkling among the trees on Queens Road, now his habitual passageway to good things. On arrival, the wine bar seems a bit gloomy. Two older gentlemen in tweed jackets, shiny brogues and matching red trousers occupy the seats outside, looking as if they are engaged in a conversation that has gone on forever. Towards the back of the room he glimpses a chap sporting a sleek mane of glossy salt-and-pepper hair, wearing a seasonably de rigour linen suit. He beckons Justin forward, rising to shake hands then inviting him to be seated.

Bert says he has already started on the wine, indicating his glass. 'Well, the sun is over the yardarm somewhere in the world. The sun never sets on the Empire, and all that.' Justin begins to wonder if Bert's whole discourse consists of blokish clichés, but holds his tongue, while courteously accepting a glass of Sauvignon.

'Okay' Bert says ' Chin, chin. Let's cut to the chase, shall we? We are all men together here. Tell me all about this supervision transition business. I liked the euphemism about "artistic differences" by the way.'

Justin takes his time to run through the whole saga, including the Brenda bust-up, and his impetuous part in that. Bert oozes reassurance. 'No need to feel bad about that, old chap. These things happen in the heat of the moment. And frankly, at some level it sounds as though she may have had it coming. Whoops – should not have said that. But I do know how we men can be provoked beyond reason.'

'Thanks for listening and understanding. Here, take a look at my CV, maybe give you some idea of my background.'

'Ah, your CV thank you, let me have a scan through this.' Bert flicks through the document at speed. 'So, let me see – you are well credentialed – tick. Evidence of good private work. Tick. You seem to have one or two prestigious clients. Been in continuous previous supervision. You have client references. You are a member of a professional body and of the prestigious Chrysalis group, plenty of CPD. Tick, tick, tick. All looks legit and above board to me. For my part I am more than happy to take you on. In fact, you are just the sort of chap that is ready to be taken to the next level – I feel I know what you are facing. So how am I doing on the biology test, in your eyes?'

'Don't you mean the chemistry test?'

'I do,' Bert attempts a twinkle, 'but I do like to be playful with words, mix it up a bit, undermine the jargon. Make people think, disrupt their mental models, get them out of auto-pilot, that kind of thing.'

'Well, that is refreshing to hear.' Justin says politely, while hoping further disruptions to his life are kept to a minimum. 'So, what is your fee rate, if I can raise the sordid question of money?'

'Oh, I never do hourly rates or any of that stuff, far too limiting. How about £1000 for the year – pay when you can afford to? If you feel I am adding value, then pay more. If you feel I am wasting your time, then pay less. We can meet as often as you feel the need, within reason. If it feels too much, then squeal.'

This payment regime was more than Justin could ever have hoped for. So different from Brenda's insistence on perpetual direct debits draining his bank account. 'Perfect. Thank you. A bit impertinent as this stage, I know. But would you be prepared to write endorsements or give references for me – I would pay you to do so, obviously.'

'Of course, of course, old chap, I do that all the time! And I have a swanky letterhead, using the club address, or my private one, whichever floats your boat. '

'That is so good to know,' says Justin, feeling emboldened. 'Just to push things a little further along. Would it be at all possible for me to cite your name right now, as my supervisor? I have a couple of pesky forms I need to submit to endorse new work that really have significant urgency behind it. Sorry to put that on you, to impose, you may need time to think about it.'

Bert does not need to dwell on this request. 'Yes, of course old chap, go ahead and cite away; I sense a lot is pressing on you. Would be a pleasure.' With that, he passes Justin his impressive business card, while Justin reciprocates with his far less impressive KwikPrint cardboard effort.

'Good!' Bert declares, rubbing his meaty hands together. 'All that is left then is for you to sign up an ethics form.' Bert retrieves the document from the depths of a shiny executive briefcase, the likes of which has not been seen since the height of the 'loads-of-money' eighties. With a flourish of Bert's gold-plated Parker pen they complete the deal. Signed sealed and delivered.

Bert smiles, while draining his glass. 'Just let me know when you want to meet next and we can fix a time.'

'Yes, of course I will. And thank you for being so clear and speedy.'

'It has not been difficult with you at all, Justin. You are my sort of chap.' Allowing a silence, to indicate a change of subject, Bert continues, 'By the way, you need to know that with my lifestyle – and my train of ex-wives and errant children - I cannot live on my coaching earnings alone. In fact, coaching is as much a hobby as anything. On the back of the life planning coaching that I do, I also offer investment planning for clients. I am not a licenced Independent Financial Advisor, but I do know chaps who are. And through my connections with high net worth individuals, I hear of many excellent investment tips that are well worth a punt. So, if you want me to have a look over your portfolio at any time – or if you have friends that might benefit from the same, then do let me know. Even as we speak there are some excellent investment opportunities opening up in West Africa.'

Justin is not surprised to hear of this rider, on the back of the sweetheart supervisory deal. 'Well, thanks for that. I will be sure to let you know, but right now can we get the supervision going first and see how we get on? Oh, and just by the by – do you keep records of our supervision meetings?'

Bert shakes his head. 'Oh, not really – I just make a few notes. Fortunately, I am blessed with a great memory. Few have as good a memory as mine. If someone or some professional body needs detailed notes - which in my experience they rarely do - then I am quite able to produce a nifty and convincing summary of our meetings. Look, this supervision business is not to my mind a surveillance operation – I had enough of that in the Marines. I am here to support you, to be a critical friend, not to be someone that spies on you, or dobs you in.'

'Thanks for that,' says Justin, pleased to know that these meetings would not leave a long, written evidence trail.

Bert makes to move from the table. 'Oh well, I sense we are done for now. That's it. I think I will pop along to the club for a game of snooker. And so good to do business with you. I have a good feeling about this one.'

Out in the sun again, Justin is so happy to have this potential obstacle of on-going supervision ticked off his ever-diminishing to-do list. But he has little time to linger and bask in today's successes though, as the time has come for him to head down Park Street for the contracting meeting with Parallelogram.

The meeting with Parallelogram takes place in the coffee bar of the Marriott Grand Hotel on Cathedral Green. The Parallelogram Client Relationship Manager Doris Pinkington, and the New Business Development Manager Graham Smart, sit at the back of the room, in a private setting replete with rococo chairs. Dim lighting lends an air of seriousness, almost solemnity to the proceedings. Both Graham and Doris bristle with urgency, getting through the perfunctory pleasantries at speed, while alternately sipping from tiny espressos and elegant glasses of water. Justin accepts a glass of fizzy water, as they get straight down to business.

The Parallelogram agents take it in turn to deliver their spiel, saying that they know this assignment is happening all of a rush, but they need someone local, fully qualified and available now to fill an opening that has just recently come up. Doris briskly thumbs through the documents she asked Justin to bring along, declaring them all in order, with the exception of references. Justin shows her both Richard and Bert's cards, indicating that she can approach either of them at any time; and that written references from both would follow shortly. Taking a photo of each of the cards on her phone, she seems happy enough with this evidence, indicating that they are now ready to proceed.

'Okay' says Graham, 'so here is the deal. We have a client in the global distribution business. They are facing some exciting challenges in their call-centre out at Aztec West. Coaching is needed for a significant number or their first-line team leaders, and perhaps some team coaching too. We see you are credentialed for that … '

Justin jumps at this opening, 'Oh yes, fully. And I currently have a team coaching assignment on the go.'

'Good – sounds like you are just the man for the job.'

Pressing his advantage, Justin says, 'I am pleased to hear it. So, when would this assignment start?'

'Next week – the need is pressing,' says Doris. 'We estimate it will be 100 coach hours for the first phase, spread over three or four weeks.'

'And thereafter?' says Justin, not forgetting his lessons on on-selling.

'We visualise intensive follow up subject to satisfactory performance,' assures Graham.

Justin is impressed by this seamless handing of the baton between the two. He feels he is picking up on the quick tempo exchange really well. 'May I ask, how do the financials work out between us?'

Doris's turn to speak, this time around. 'Well, we will work in accordance with our usual associate arrangement. We will waive the finder's fee in this instance, given the imminence of the deal. The rate we have agreed with the client is £95 per hour – we like to keep the hourly rate under three figures, for the optics. From that gross fee we take 50% per hour. So, you take about £45 an hour gross, for at least 100 hours. The good news is that the client has already signed up for this, as long as you pass the chemistry test with her. We feel that you will be great with her – she has already seen your profile and she likes it.'

167

Justin tries his best to hide his excitement on hearing all of this. At some level this news and the timing of it all is like manna from heaven. All the dirty bits, the selling, the contracting, all done for him, all laid out on a plate, with even a second phase in the offing, and all the downside risk carried by Parallelogram. Sure, the fee rate is not that great, but then it is volume work. Despite his rising anticipation, he does his best to maintain his poker face, saying 'Sounds great – so tell me more about the challenge, and about the company.'

'Well, the company is the US-owned Magic Carpet, Amazon's biggest rival, and most feared competitor.' Justin recoils from the table at the mention of this company name, despite himself.

Doris is quick to pick up on Justin's alarm. 'Oh, what has elicited this reaction? What have we said? Have you had a bad customer experience with Magic Carpet? Been fired by them in the past? It is best that we know now, at this stage. We do not want to run into any hands from the grave.'

'No nothing like that.' Justin gives himself time to breathe. 'It is just that you took me by surprise when you mentioned that company name. By coincidence my wife works on the distribution side, in the warehouse - sorry, the Fulfilment Centre, for Magic Carpet. And no, I have not been fired, nor have I had any bad experiences with them, quite the opposite. They quite often leave parcels at our door, and always deliver on time.'

Doris's eyebrows noticeably lower. 'Oh, is that all? Your wife works there.' She considers this a while, looking over to Graham for a cue. 'Well, that should be no problem. The Fulfilment and call-centre operations are quite separate entities – the bosses like to keep them behind Chinese walls for management purposes, different KPIs etc. In fact, it could be a real benefit, your wife working there. You might know something of the culture already - such a go-ahead firm, disrupting the business model all over the place, no doubt she has told you. We think they will park their tanks on Amazon's lawns soon enough. And we at Parallelogram are proud to partner them on their journey. But just out of interest, what does she do there?'

Justin replies, 'She is on the HR and performance management side, been there a few years now.'

Graham nods at this. 'Perfect – she must know the place inside out. No doubt your TV dinner chats may take on a different note once you are on board. But be aware, nothing you pick up or learn while on the premises on our watch goes beyond the office door. You will be required to sign up to the strictest confidentially agreement, with no exceptions. It will only take one small piece of leakage that can be attributed to you, and you will out the door at fastest speed imaginable; and you will be gone not only from Magic Carpet but from Parallelogram also. This might sound heavy, I know, but this must be understood. In fact, thinking about it, it is probably best that you do not mention your wife's job in Fulfilment at all at your chemistry meeting. It could muddy the waters. And we know the Chinese walls will take care of data exchange risks anyway, don't we Doris? Understood?'

Justin hears the warning loud and clear. 'Yes, I quite understand all of that. And as a coach and former HR person, I am well used to observing confidentiality. I will not say a word about my wife's role to the client. And I see no reason why they might ask what she does anyway.'

Doris placates him. 'That is good to know. And yes, there is no reason why they might pry. Look, time is pressing, so please look over the associate agreement for this assignment right now.' Doris places the document on the table in front of Justin, in a vanilla folder. 'I know it looks a lot, but we must be thorough, for all our sakes.'

Justin hurriedly wades through the documents, then indicates that he is agreeable to signing off to this.

Graham starts to shuffle his papers, clearly impatient with this associate dance, now that he knows that they have Justin in the palm of their corporate hands. 'Great!' he says, emphatically. 'So just to put some added pace on this, some grease on the wheels, given we are motoring along so well so far. Are you free right now to go meet the client onsite? That is a lot to ask, I know, but we can whizz you off straightaway, if you are ready. The client is keen to get this signed off as soon as possible. We could swing by her offices to make this happen right now. Which would mean that we can both get back down the motorway to our Swindon HQ, to report back on a deal well sealed, and with a new associate to boast about, too. If this goes well, then you could be an integral part of the growing success of Parallelogram.'

Justin, admiring Graham's close technique, makes a brief pretence of checking his diary, then agrees, 'Yes, there is no time like the present, my diary is free.'

With that they descend into the bowels of the Marriott, to pick up their shiny Parallelogram leased Audi, to head up Whiteladies Road towards the motorway. Justin sinks into the black leather seat, brushing some lint off his posh suit, feeling quite grown up, quite executive for once – so different from being the 'bones or groans' coach of yesterday. Doris phones ahead to the client to say that they are on the way. Leaning over towards the rear seat, she says to Justin,

'You will be meeting Dolores Wilson, the Operations Head. Be aware that she is all business. Do not expect or offer any social pleasantries. She will need to get down to business at speed; and you need to make sure that you pick up on every cue and impress the living hell out of her. I think you will get on though. Just don't fuck up, as they say. Any questions? '

Of course, Justin has a million questions. What is Dolores really like as a person? Why has she chosen Parallelogram? Any hidden agendas he needs to know about? How secure is Dolores within the hierarchy? Is she an agent for the theory X culture that Joy laments so much? But he asks none of these, instead stays quiet, while muttering under his breath, 'Justin, please, please don't fuck up. Just don't fuck up.'

Beyond the Almondsbury interchange, the Audi arrives at the offices of the call centre, located in an unprepossessing business park. Parking up in the sole visitor's space, they pass through elaborate security, picking up the requisite badges and lanyards as they pass through. So bedecked, they are then escorted by security through the noise and flashing lights of the call-centre operation desks, to be led upstairs to an office located high on a gantry, with windows overlooking the whole shop floor.

Dolores welcomes them brusquely, saying she is glad they were able to come at such short notice. She says that the purpose of the meeting is for her to run a slide rule over Justin, to check him out for fit, before they roll up their sleeves and get down to work. She stands behind a set of screens, her short, bleached hair scraped back rather savagely off her face, her blue trouser suit and white shirt looking like a uniform, while an identical outfit hangs behind the door.

Justin listens closely as she puts him through his paces, short question after short question demanding concise answers, which he duly provides. He does not mention his wife's role, as advised, but picks up vibes enough to suggest that the call centre might be operating on a similar command and control basis to Fulfilment, underneath it all. Though Dolores is clearly listening, and continuing to offer a logical line of questioning, her eyes are frequently diverted towards the many flashing screens in front of her.

Near the end of the interrogation, a rising of voices outside the window jerks her attention towards the shop floor. Her visitors lean over also, to witness an animated argument breaking out. They witness a call centre operative tearing off his headset, throwing it to the floor in a temper, then stomping towards the door, closely followed by someone whom Justin conjectures must be a supervisor.

Dolores turns to them hurriedly, saying, 'Look guys, this may be turning into something I need to deal with quite quickly, nip it in the bud. We have had some troubles with that guy's melodramas before. He terminates far too many calls for my liking. He even suggested to one customer that they might not need what they were ordering, and to think twice about it.' She looks out the window once more, satisfied that the commotion has subsided somewhat. 'Ah well. It seems the floor is calm again. Shows over folks, back behind your partitions.' Returning her attention turning towards her visitors, she says, 'Look, Justin fits the spec well enough, and he is local, so no hotels bills or travel hassles to deal with. You said you can you start Monday?'

Justin is quick to affirm this. 'Yes, I can, and appreciate the trust you are vesting in me. I am sure you will not be disappointed. It would be great to know more about the set up here, now that we are going ahead. '

Waving her hand towards the window and the view below, she says, 'what you see out there are our front line call operative teams – and in the office behind those large plastic sheets is the internet order-processing team. You can see we are doing some structural work behind there. We have twenty front-line supervisors in all, and in my view all of them are adjusting well to the new performance strategy crafted by our US HQ. What we need you to do is to work with each of them on their personal transitions, to gain alignment around these radically changing strategic priorities.'

Seems clear enough to Justin. 'Yes, I get that.'

Dolores continues, 'Over the next two weeks you will have two one-hour sessions with each of them. If they like the support they are getting from you, then they may ask for support through phase two of our 'Going Forward' initiative, which we are rolling out globally. I expect you to take some headline notes from these sessions and then report back a summary big picture of how we are doing at the end of each week.'

'Sounds good,' Justin responds, 'but please be aware that I need to operate within my professional body's ethics code, which requires that we do not report back on individual coaching clients, unless specifically contracted so to do with the clients concerned.' He swallows quite hard as he says this, expecting a kick-back. Which duly arrives.

Dolores makes no attempt to disguise her impatience. 'Oh, sure I know all of that – please don't patronise me. I too have an MBA, perhaps from as good, if not a better, school than yours. I consider myself a consummate management professional. And all my performance reviews confirm that. All I am asking is for you to collect your general impressions of the current climate and readiness for change. And anyway, all of the ethical safeguards you are looking for are written into your contract.'

She looks at all three of them meaningfully, defying challenge. 'Just know that I am happy to have you in here doing this vital transition work. It is best that we have someone from the outside to do this, to ensure objectivity, impartiality. But please do not be coming all Mother Teresa on me if you sniff that some snowflake is feeling victimised. I have enough of that sort of low-grade moaning from our HR and Wellness staff, defending our so-called victimised workers. We have a business to run and I want you to be a team player in pursuit of our overarching goal – which is to become the best online retail provider in the world.'

Before Justin can respond to this, the sound of a further commotion breaks out from the floor below, only this time even louder even than before.

Dolores says, 'Look, it is great to have you onboard, but I need to deal with this. Please drop by security, Justin, on your way out, and fill out all the documents relating to maintaining our integrity and competitive advantage. I will sign them off later, then you can pick up your pass and lanyard on Monday, when I can give you your interview schedule and brief you in more detail. 07.45 sharp on Monday, thanks for coming and see yourselves out.'

With that, she follows the obedient triumvirate down the stairs, before engaging in deep conversation with a brisk man in a suit, who seemed to be at the centre of the melee.

Justin duly signs off all the relevant paperwork at the security desk, and then goes in search of the waiting Audi in the car park. Further back in the parking lot, towards the exit, he witnesses the two escapees from the shop floor breakout standing behind a scruffy car, both of them in an intense conversation with a man holding a notebook. In conversation, that is, until security marches determinedly towards them. As the security man steps up the pace, the two mutineers head back inside, while the stranger hotfoots it out the gate. Finding the Audi, his Parallelogram minders declare themselves well pleased with his performance. They say they feel sure they can leave him to get on with it from here on out. They ask him if he wants dropping off nearby, explaining that they cannot take him into town, as they need to get down the motorway, to report back to Swindon before the close of play. But they can take him some of the way. Justin nearly says, 'Drop me by bus stop,' but that does not feel quite the right look. Instead, he says, 'Oh, no need, just let me just call Uber and they will get me home.'

'You sure?' ask Doris, sounding relieved all the same to be dispatching her recruit without too much personal inconvenience, or even worse opportunity to reopen the contracting conversation.

Justin seems quite happy to leave the conversation at this point too. 'Quite sure. I like Uber. We fellow players in the gig economy need to support each other.'

They look at him somewhat strangely at this non-sequitur, but smile weakly and drive off, deep in conversation with each other. As they leave, Justin harbours a distinct feeling that he will not be hearing much from those two again, unless something goes seriously wrong. As he waits, Dave, his Uber driver rings ahead to apologise, saying that his satnav has taken him to the Magic Carpet Fulfilment Centre rather than the call centre. He asks Justin to bear with, saying that he will be along in a jiffy.

175

Waiting outside the call-centre gates, Justin notices the mystery man with the notebook quietly sidling up to him.

This stranger asks, 'Hope you don't mind, but can I ask, do you work for Magic Carpet?'

No, I don't. Do you?' Justin asks, sensing that this is a conversation he doesn't want to be having.

`No, I don't either. But are you a contractor or such?'

His interrogator is clearly not a person to be easily deflected. 'Well actually, yes, or I soon will be, but before we go further, could you say who you are?'

'Yes, for sure, no secret here. I am Dick Bellows, a journalist covering economic and business affairs. Freelance.' He moves closer to Justin, offering his hand, which Justin obligingly squeezes in half-heartedly. Searching for a question, he finds himself asking, 'You work for Bristol Evening Post?'

'Sometimes,' Dick says, disdainfully, plunging his hands deep into his parka jacket, 'But mainly for The Guardian and The New Statesman, sometimes for the Financial Times.'

Justin picks up on Dick's arrogance. 'So, I take it you are writing a piece about Magic Carpet?'

'Well, at this point researching rather than writing. Can you say what role you will be playing in there?'

Justin feels the hackles rising on his neck. 'No, I really cannot. And you must not ask me.'

Dick is clearly not one to take no for an answer. 'Look, I do not want to seem paranoid, but could we step away from the gates some?' He leads Justin by the arm. 'That is great, now we are safely away from the cameras. So, may I ask, have you met those two men I was chatting to in the car park? I saw you clocking us in conversation as security marched in.'

'No, I have not met them,' replies Justin, honestly puzzled as to where this unwanted conversation might be heading.

'Were you witness to the kafuffle that occurred inside?'

Justin will not be drawn further. 'Look, you cannot push this line of inquiry, I am unable to comment.'

'Fair enough,' concedes Dick, scratching his two-day growth, 'but perhaps you can listen. So, you are new to this place?'

Justin says nothing, choosing silence as the best way through this conversation, while Dick continues with his one-way information exchange.

'Well, perhaps you need to know that Magic Carpet is systematically trying to drive staff out, but without incurring high redundancy costs, or attracting employment law action, or tarnishing their own reputation. Ambitious trifecta, eh? There is no need for you to comment but you are clearly an intelligent and retentive person, and this information might be of interest to you at a later date.'

Not sure how to respond, Justin is relieved when his phone rings. 'Hi, Dave here' his driver drawls, in heavy estuary English, 'sorry Justin old son, but I am still at the other Magic Carpet, driving all around the houses, then satnav bleeding brings me all back here again to Fulfilment. But I will be with you in a jiff. So sorry, mate.'

'That is quite okay Dave, see you soon.'

'Your driver eh?' asks the journalist.

'No nothing so fancy. Simply my Uber ride, lost in the M4 / M5 jungle.'

Dick looks sympathetic. 'Yes, that happens a lot. But then we all get lost around Magic Carpet land. I think that distraction is designed in, to stop unwelcome intrusions. Thanks for listening to me before, by the way.'

'I wasn't.'

Dick grins a complicit grin. 'I know you weren't. Those two at the gate, the ones that you did not witness disrupting the smooth surface of call centre life, have been talking to me for a while. At risk of their jobs, but I guess their days are numbered anyway. And there are others too in there that want to talk, need to talk. Even including some of the supervisors.'

Justin decides surrender is the only option in the face of this. And he is curious to know more, despite his every self-protective instinct saying move away from this seductive but dangerous man. 'Go on, I am still not listening, just playing with my phone.'

Dick senses he now has Justin's attention, despite his surface resistance.

'So, if you meet some of the supervisors, you might notice they are under pressure too. And thank you again for not listening. My Magic Carpet brief is not just the call centre. And not just Bristol either. But here is where the action is for now. No doubt you have not seen anything on the local news about the Fulfilment Centre down the road? Things are kicking off there too. And we are getting info off both Magic Carpet sites out into the public domain, don't worry, soft and hard data, and management are getting lairy. But we do not have enough evidence as yet to build a firm case against them for employment malpractice and so much more.'

Justin simply scans the horizon, on the pretext of looking for Dave. It is clear that eye contact is unimportant to Dick. 'More important still. and this is on the hush-hush. we know of a major data breach of all Magic Carpet customers' data worldwide. It is believed the breach first occurred from within this building. And that the Magic Carpet IT firewalls continues to be breached, despite desperate attempts to patch and to shut the leak down. We understand that, even now, someone is blackmailing Magic Carpet for huge amounts, on grounds that the hacker holds back data. We also believe that all recent management emails and employee records have been hacked.'

As Dick's monologue continues, Justin remains curious, yet uneasier than ever to be listening at all. Relief comes by way of a silver Prius hoving into view towards the gates, scanning for a passenger. As the car pulls up, Dick says

'Don't forget, you have my number; there may be a conversation we need to have some time. Thanks for not listening to anything I said.'

He winks, then moves noiselessly away.

'My pleasure,' Justin says, not meaning it. He pokes his head through the window of the approaching Prius, asking 'Excuse me, are you Dave?'

His surprised tone gives away his assumption that, given the London accent on the phone, he had been expecting a gammon-faced cockney driver; whereas Dave turns out to be a large, black, shaven-headed middle-aged guy who amply fills the front seat of his car. And more besides.

Dave laughs loudly as Justin climbs in beside him. 'Oh, don't worry! No need to look embarrassed. You were not expecting me to be black, right? Thought I was some sort of pale cockney type, some kind of Pearly King?'

Justin unsuccessfully attempts to shield his embarrassment, something that is never easy to do when jammed into a seat right beside the person one may have offended. 'To my shame, yes, I did think you were white.'

'Well, you are not the first to make that mistake. And I do not take offence. In fact, that mistake can open up a good conversation about assumptions we all make about each other beyond the class and accent divide, know what I mean?'

'Yes, I do know what you mean,' Justin stutters, still squirming on the inside. But having broken the ice in this unexpected manner, he declares that he, too, is a Prius owner. This disclosure opens up a chat about Prius's, and their suitability for Uber work.

'Prius are perfect for this job,' Dave says, 'Just perfect."

'So how are you finding Uber?' asks Justin, genuinely interested to know more of this world.

Dave is more than happy to feed his curiosity. 'Well, only three weeks in so far, but going well. I am working on a number of outside projects that need funding, and Uber is doing the job nicely, know what I mean? '

Yet more curious, Justin asks what these projects are. Dave says, 'no problem to talk about them. In fact, I am happy and proud to talk. The main project is my writing a history of black British stand-up comedians.'

While wishing this conversation to flow, Justin chokes on his ignorance of this topic. He fears that he will demonstrate the sin of 'unconscious bias,' an obvious give-away of his bourgeois conditioning that practitioners in the helping professions are so cautioned about revealing. However, hesitantly, he says, 'I confess that, beyond Lenny Henry, I cannot think of too many others – unless Asians count. I know I am sure they don't. That was a crazy thing to say, sorry,'

Dave frowns a little. 'No, Asians don't count. I know how that sounds. I mean Asians can be really humorous, but they do not come within my frame of reference. Afro-Caribbean for me only, get what I am saying? And don't worry. Most white folk do not get far beyond name-checking dear old Lenny Henry, unless they are into the scene. That is a big reason why I am writing the book. Get the other names out there.'

Justin is relieved to hear that his blunder is shared. 'Glad to hear I am not alone, And I really would like to redress my ignorance. I love live performance – and that I am not a little ashamed that so much of my cultural content is now received through internet or telly.'

Dave chuckles, 'no worries, no need for middle-class guilt on that score. Come along to my next gig in Stokes Croft. Here is my card. It would be great to see you anytime. I mean it. We need to spread the word. Dave is the name. Dave Allenday. All in a day's work. Get it? Great stage name, don't ya think? And thanks for taking an interest, and for being so okay about me being late.'

'Worry not. I will give you star rating and a good tip. And thanks too for the racial awareness training.'

Dave laughs loudly. 'You are a gentleman, a real gentleman, Justin. Always a pleasure, see you at my club.'

Home at last, Justin sees Brian the mechanic pulls up, his shadowy mate still tailing him. Brian greets him with, 'hi there Justin. Just a small misfiring problem on the Astra, all done now, should not give you any more problems for a while.' Justin pays him what little he charges, admiring Brian's new portable credit card machine, while commenting on how unusual Brian's level of customer service is. Brian is delighted to hear this, shaking Justin's hand as he leaps into his backup vehicle.

Once again back home and settled at the kitchen table, Justin reviews his morning's "to do" list, satisfied that so much has been achieved in so short a time.

- Draw up and land new contract – tick
- Brush up CV – tick
- Find a new supervisor – tick
- Find references – change references – tick
- Fix Joys car - tick

He is pleased that this emphasis on personal productivity idea, this goal-setting business, learned during his coach training, is at last paying off. He congratulates himself that his efforts at creative visualisation, of inducing the placebo effect, are working at full tilt - or perhaps he has just had a good day, gotten lucky. He feels exhalant – so much achieved, and so much momentum gained. The coaching gurus – especially the sports coaches - talk of the vital importance of momentum, and he is living evidence of it.

He is bursting to tell Joy of all is breakthroughs. He wants to let her hear her husband saying something concrete that will palpably relieve her of some of the burdens she carries, alone, on their family's behalf. But he cannot call her, not just yet. Magic Carpet forbids it, forbids all spontaneous contact with the world outside the fence. Instead he needs to work within those rules that boundary their lives, and patiently await her arrival. Meanwhile, he needs to pick up the kids, once they are free from their scholarly shackles, as he is nearly late for them again. Just in time then, and with them both safely installed in the car, he is happy to surrender to their good-humoured jibes. Eventually - an hour or so late –she makes her way through the door.

Justin greets Joy with a big hug, far more than she was expecting. She allows it all the same, though pulls back to park her bag on the table. Sitting down, Justin asks, 'How was your trip home, without your car. I was wondering how you got back.'

Joy replies, 'I got a lift from a colleague to Cribbs Causeway, and from there the #1 bus home. The journey was not bad, actually. But good to see the Astra outside the door once more. Is it all working?'

Justin replies, 'Yes, it is, thanks to Brian. Did you remember to say 'cheers Droive' before you alighted the bus?'

'Course I did – my baba.' Joy is rather enjoying their inept collapse into cod Bristolian.

Justin decides it best to sit on his good news for a while, preferring instead to let Joy talk her day out of her system. While a selfish part of him would prefer her to deliver her account of her day in executive summary form – with bullet points – he knows that the story of her day will be prolonged, to the point where she has exhausted the awfulness of it.

'So how were things at Magic Carpet, after all of yesterday's melodramas? Was there any aftermath, any backlash from all of that?'

Joy takes the space to ventilate. 'Oh no, it was okay really. I kept my head down, no ambulance emergencies, and no maternity action, no one jumping off the top of the building. In fact, I felt much relieved to have confessed all to you last night. Somehow I am no longer feeling that I am shouldering all of this burden alone.'

Justin looks chastened. 'Give me a moment while I adjust my guilt level upwards.'

Joy waves a dismissive hand at this riposte. 'Look, don't be like that. I know that I never was carrying the whole family support thing alone, but it has felt that way at times. It is certainly true that at Magic Carpet

I have few colleagues I could easily turn to, to trust enough to talk to about what that place does to you, or to your sense of self- worth, probably only Sharon.'

'I am aware of that,' says Justin, recovered from the implied slight.

 Joy continues, 'which is not my colleagues' failure of course, not at a human level. But that is how Magic Carpet is designed, to separate so-called colleagues from each other, to make everyone a snitch. We all know that everyone is being watched, measured, being monitored, every second of the day. And to double down on that, we are each required to be self-monitoring, and to be monitoring each other – no social loafing allowed - no collusion to ease off the endless pressures.'

Justin seizes on this textbook reference. 'Yes, I remember social loafing from Business School. Always sounded quite attractive to me.'

'Yes, but it is designed out of the equation at Magic Carpet. The good news from today is that no one died, and the other good news is that I am no longer feeling alone, given the threat I am under. Anyway, how was your day, dare I ask? I know there were a lot of things hanging in the balance.'

Justin readies himself for the delivery of his news. 'Oh yes, I very much dare you to ask.'

'Well then, tell all. Spill the beans.'

'Well first off, let me remind you of my list for the day. The impossible list? Well …' He brandishes the crumpled list in front of her, taking her through all of his successes, tick by tick. 'On a spin of the wheel of fortune, five cherries have come up, not least in finding a Brenda replacement.'

Joy listens eagerly to the recitation of all of the successes on Justin's tick list, pleased in particular to know that Brenda is finally gone. 'Well, that is great to hear. Well done you. So, the storm clouds are blowing away?'

Justin braces himself for the revelation that he knows will bring a frown to her face. 'Well, not quite all of them. The only cloud in an otherwise clear blue sky is that the Parallelogram contract is with – drum roll – Magic Carpet.'

She looks shocked and surprised, saying, 'I had thought we were planning to rid this house of that Magic Carpet toxicity, not inviting the fog further in over the doorstep again.' She sighs a resigned sigh. 'But maybe we just need to take that hit as part of getting you back on your feet again. And I like the sound of the workflow, the cash flow and the swift entry to the agency, the opening up of doors to other companies – I mean there are other companies in the world are there not, beyond Magic Carpet? Please tell me there are? Or do we have to create our own?'

Justin is glad that she has taken the Magic Carpet news with such relative equanimity, at least for the time being, while knowing that before long she will delve, with forensic precision, into the downsides of him working for the Carpet. 'I wish, too, that the first engagement with the agency was anywhere but Magic Carpet. Maybe a terrible karmic cloud is following us both around. But there we are – caught in destinies maw. On the bright side, Brenda is gone – or at least she is gone unless she files a complaint. That could well be a hand from the grave that we could do without.'

'It sure could. But you have done so well to find a replacement so quickly. Those coaching chemistry matching and contracting rituals, these beauty contests, do seem to take an age, in the normal course of events. And all for something so.' Joy catches herself in mid-sentence, 'no, I should not say irrelevant, that is not fair. But for something so straightforward, you do all seem to make it very complicated. You know what I mean. No offence intended.'

Justin does not rise to yet another invitation to dissect the byzantine rules that govern the relatively simple matter of two people talking over a problem face to face, saying instead, 'Yes, I do know, and I agree with you, Joy. But the new supervisor is quite the opposite of Brenda. He is quite unreconstructed, and probably downright misogynistic – well, not exactly anti- women, but certainly pro-bloke. You would like that he is keen to cut through all that self-referential malarkey that coaching indulges itself in, taking itself so seriously. He is on a mission to cut through all of that, to prise coaching away from its HR and counselling roots, with a crowbar of necessary. And I am all for that.'

Joy wonders if this is too good to be true but wishes to keep the conversation upbeat. 'Good to hear. And I dare I say that I am also happy that you have a man as Brenda replacement. Sounds like he might be less prissy about things then she was.'

Justin grins. 'Don't worry. He is many things but not prissy. And amid all of this whirlwind, your car is fixed – saving you from perpetually tooing and froing on the bus.'

'Yes, that is great. Sorry if I seem to be brooding amid this abundance of good news. But I am thinking about you being involved with Magic Carpet, what that might all mean.'

Justin knew that this would come around again, once Joy had time to process it. 'No, I understand. What exactly is preying on your mind?'

Joy lines up her questions in her head. 'Well, first of all, tell me - Magic Carpet does not know you are married to me, do they? That could be awkward, given I am on notice, and lined up to collect the world's worst employee award for the second year running.'

'No, they know nothing at all about us. Parallelogram does know, but they suggest I keep stum about it. They did not see a problem, but said it would be best if we do not mention our relationship to the company. And no, they do not know you are due to collect the world's worst employee ever award, with stars.'

Joy shows relief at this, but her concerns still remain. 'I am pleased to hear it. But when you do get started, then it is probably best that we travel out there separately too. On the hush-hush. Under cover of darkness.'

'Yes, I agree. We could tail each other – I would feel like Brian the mechanic, who always has his unmarked support car in tow.'

Joy still needs to know more of what Justin is getting into, as she knows that when he has good news, all downsides tend to get pushed away in his eagerness to get started. 'Quite so. Just out of interest, what did you pick up on the management culture at the call-centre? Different from Fulfilment, from all you hear from me? Different from how they were portraying it?'

'Well, of course I did not trust their bullshit one bit. I would say it is identical to Fulfilment, though the workers scurry around less. Just trapped behind headphones and flashing screens, but otherwise the same. '

'Oh dear. Not able to move around. Sitting ducks. At least my lot are moving targets as they skate between the stacks of parcels. Moving at great speed, actually, especially when there is a supervisor in view.'

'Ha ha – there is that freedom in your place, though limited.' Justin feels the moment is right to air his biggest concern. 'What worries me most of all is that I am not fully trusting the coaching client confidentiality deal I have struck with them. In fact, I have got a funny feeling that they are going to want me to spill all I discover from the interviews I do. Sing like a canary. I have learned from you how crazy they are on flipping, wanting to make everyone a snitch. I have a feeling they want me to act as super-snitch, external spy, under the cloak of trusted independent advisor.'

A steely tone in Joy's voice forbids Justin from any slackening of ethical standards. 'Well, if they do pressure you to squeal and reveal all, then just walk away – your integrity is worth more than a short-term contract with them. And there could be real world consequences for one of the shop-floor supervisors' livelihood, should a fateful confession fall into the wrong hands.'

Justin picks up on the gravity of this. 'Yep, I totally get that. And you ask about the culture – well I am not generalising from a study of corporate artefacts, though there are those aplenty. But there were a couple of real-life dramas that occurred on the floor, right before our very eyes, during our visit. And I have a sense that the place is on a knife-edge, all the time. Such a strained environment. This will not be a cosy data collecting exercise, that is for sure.'

'Tell me about it!' says Joy, rolling her eyes. 'And why does that not surprise me! Magic Carpet lives and thrives on dramas, despite it having such tight processes.'

'I think this drama is escalating beyond the office gates. In fact, I know it is. The eruption that occurred while I was there – in fact there were two related eruptions. One of them spilled over into the car park, and then into the arms of a waiting investigative journalist. '

'Really? That is bad. Or good, depending on whose side you are on,' muses Joy, aware that for much of the time she is caught in the tension between management dictat and shop-floor sympathy.

'Quite so. And the journalist is really well informed – and tenacious'. As he says this, Justin sees the can of worms spilling all over the kitchen floor.

'How would you know that?'

Justin knows he is now inviting censure, but then he cannot avoid telling the truth. 'Well, he talked to me afterwards.'

'Where? In the car park? Please say no, not on the premises?' quizzes Joy, clearly exasperated.

'No, it was outside the car park, beyond the gates. And he and I moved away from the cameras at the gate.'

Joy cannot quite believe what she is hearing. But then knowing Justin as she does, and his inability to see the hole he is digging, this progression makes perfect sense. 'This is all quite inadvisable as I am sure you know. You are scaring me.'

'Yes, I do know,' mutters a penitent Justin, 'and sorry to be putting the frighteners on you. But on the other hand, much of what he had to say was really interesting, and will help my study.'

'For goodness sake! I thought you were simply going there to do some listening practice, not conducting a major judicial inquiry. I do hope you said nothing attributable to you?'

Justin somehow knew, even at the time, that this entirely innocent, accidental encounter would result in a relentless grilling from Joy. 'No of course not.' He protests, weakly, wishing now that he had never mentioned this meeting. 'Not that I would have had anything to say for at that moment anyway, as I have not even started yet. I know nothing. I have not talked to anyone so what do I know, beyond the corporate bullshit?'

'Well that is something,' concedes Joy, while feeling that saga is not yet fully out in the open, with all of its attendant jeopardy exposed to the light of day.

Blind to Joy's growing apprehension, Justin ploughs further in. 'But I did listen to what he had to say about the company, and what was behind all the drama. I also learned that his Magic Carpet investigations cover your patch at Fulfilment also.'

'Uh oh. And the journalist was?'

As he passes over Dick's card, he sees alarm in her eyes. Detecting a tremor of fear in her voice, he asks. 'what is it, Joy?'

'Oh no.' Joy's eyes widen. 'Anyone but Dick Bellows. You do pick em. Or maybe they seek you out. He has been after us for months!!! And you talked to him before the ink was even dry on your contract? What were you thinking? For God's sake, stay away from him. We in HR are told to "bellow" at the first signs of Bellow. Start waving red flags and get everyone off the beach pronto. Yet now I learn that my husband is happily making best friends with him.'

Justin looks bemused. 'Oh, I see. He really is that deep into you lot then?'

'He is. Up to his elbows. And he is not going away, despite all Magic Carpet can do to shake him off. Please say you did not make any plan to take things further with him?'

Justin feels a need to defend himself, in the face of this onslaught. 'No, I did nothing of the kind, simply listened to him. He was most insistent.'

Joy is scornful. 'I bet he was. Do you know nothing of journalists, how they operate? He is intimately connected with all of the forces of resistance around the town, with those factions that threaten Magic Carpet's best interests. He is in with the unions, with Human Rights groups, with the Momentum wing of the Labour Party. And with the whole radical subculture based out at Stokes Croft, probably including your new best friend Tony.'

'He did seem slyly tenacious. And I sensed that he is really good at this infiltration stuff too. Felt like he was getting things from me, even when I was saying nothing.'

'Yes, he is really good at what he does. And dangerous. And at some level I admire him. If Magic Carpet had their way, they would hire a hit man, put a contract out on him. In fact, maybe they have already done so. He is kryptonite to us both, you do realise that, don't you? I would say it is best we never mention his name again. Not even here, in the sanctuary of our home. Listening devices are really tiny these days. If you think I am paranoid, then Magic Carpet makes me so. Walls have ears. If we are acting out the Scottish play, then for Macbeth read Bellows. The mention of his name will bring a curse upon us all.'

'Then I will never ever mention him again.' Justin does his best to ham up a dodgy police witness voice. 'Dick who, officer? No idea. I never heard the name, never met him in my life. Rum old name that, Bellows? Not one you would forget. Shake of head.'

Joy allows herself a smile, resigned that the damage has already been done anyway. 'That is the spirit. Now help my anxiety levels by telling me of something that happened today that doesn't immediately threaten our family.'

Justin scratches his head. 'Well, I met a man today – whom you will meet – he is another or my new best friends, as you call them. He is called Dave Allenday and he is larger than life, in every sense. A black guy who is writing a history of British black stand-up comedy. And we are going to his next show in Stokes Croft!'

Joy is not at all sure that this falls into the category of good news, especially when her social life is being decided for her. 'Are we indeed? I did not even know that British stand-up was a niche interest of yours, never mind black stand-up. First, you say you are taking me to a song and dance show about slavery at the posh St Georges Chapel; and now we are heading down among the homies in the People's Republic. I am finding it quite hard to keep up with your list of latest newest best friends and their alternative interests. Did the Bellows tip you off about him? Set up the meet?'

Justin laughs at this. 'No. In fact quite prosaically, he was my Uber driver.'

'I should use Uber more often. You do meet some very different folk while you pay them to drive you around and listen to whatever story pops into their heads. Seems like Uber is as much life story sharing as ride sharing. Hang on - are you sure he was not a journalist?'

Justin realises that no sooner has he shaken off the endless Brenda interrogations that she is to be replaced by Bellows on Joy's radar. 'Quite sure. Look, here is his card. With photograph. He looks authentic enough to me. And not at all the type to go sleuthing.'

'Ah. Dave Allenday. Strange name. Great picture of him too. Quite a hunk. And yes, I would be really happy to go see him, if we can find a babysitter. Talking of the children, what have you promised them to eat tonight? It is all worryingly quiet up there.'

'They have had some crisps to get them on – I know I know, so bad of me – and I have further bought their silence with the promise of a Pronto Pizza.'

'Good idea – get one for me too – a woven Ponzi one please.' Asks Joy. 'Oh, and away from the Magic Carpet hotbed, when do you reconnect with that other psychodrama you are running? Your train carriage chum, the clandestine Richard from Consignia that you might have a Brief Encounter mancrush on?'

'Oh yes, that piece of the action all kicks off again tomorrow. And hopefully he will have a contract ready for signing off. I need to ensure that that schedule doesn't collide with my Magic Carpet work.'

'What a busy boy you have become. Now pour me a drink before I break open a pack of cigarettes.'

'Oh, I know you are under stress but please don't do that. Anything but cigarettes. Apart from anything else, I could not stand any more nagging from the children.'

Joy is not going to let him off the hook. 'A joint then? A line of coke? I feel sure that your new pals Dick, Dave, Bert - and probably Tom and Harry that I am yet to hear of - could readily source both. Why not ring them? You seem to have all of their visiting cards.'

'Not in front of the kids, dear. And, before you ask, I am not planning to get our innocent children involved in 'County Lines' drug running. Let me fix that drink for you now.'

Freemason's Hall.

Justin awakens feeling fresh, having slept better than for quite a while. With renewed gusto he attacks the routine family chores, then sorts out a fresh to-do list, before heading down the road on the bus for his meeting with Richard. They meet in the Marriott, in the self-same spot where he met Parallelogram just the day before. Richard is courteous, saying how good it is to see him again. He says that things at Consignia continue to be tense, and that the CEO, Philip Junior, seems more erratic, more impulsive than ever, his moods swinging the whole company's future in wildly unpredictable ways. Richard concludes, 'they say that in the end all leaders go mad, and I think that Philip is in the latter stages of that cycle, without realising it to be so. Something must be done.'

Justin needs to ask, 'was he always this way? Or is it a more recent turn of his?'

'Good question,' responds Richard, 'and nice of you to give him the benefit of the doubt. I would say he was really good for us when he first joined, two years back. He was a welcome breath of fresh air, and we rallied around him. But the signs that he could turn were always there, now I look back. We were being charmed into doing his bidding. And when we did not acquiesce, then he started to put the thumbscrews on.'

Thanks, that clarifies things some.' Justin gears up to ask his next question, worried that it might be too early. 'Look, Richard, not wanting to interrupt the flow, but before we get too deep in, could I ask how my new contract is coming along?'

'On no, you are quite entitled to ask,' says Richard, 'I can assure you that the contract is in progress, but you need to understand that for contract completion I needs to involve Legal, and that it is best not to frighten those horses at this stage. It is on the way through, do not worry.'

Justin tries to conceal his inner alarm. 'Oh, but I thought. and the initial payment for the first stage of the work?'

Richard is all reassurance, quick to move the conversation on. 'Oh yes, do not worry. That is all authorised and the monies will be with you soon. In fact, I can call up the invoice paid authorisation chit on my laptop right now, if that would help?'

'Yes, please do,' asks Justin.

He watches as Richard fiddles with his phone. "Okay, all done. The payment should be with you really soon. In full. Look, you can see the transaction on my screen. And I have just emailed Legal, too, to let them know that a contract will be on its way too.'

'Thank you for that,' says a relieved Justin. 'So, let us press on. How are your plans to confront Philip going?'

'They are moving along at quite a pace. In service of which I would like you to stay over at lunchtime today to help progress matters further.'

'Well, yes I can, but why?' Justin worries that this may involve a mantrap that he will never extricate himself from.

Richard reveals that some of his colleagues from the executive team will be joining them for lunch to plan next steps, making sure that everyone is on the same page. 'I have booked a private room upstairs at the Freemason's Hall, just up Park Street? Nothing sinister in this, but we need to meet face to face as a group, away from the office. Need to be eyeball to eyeball, make sure everyone is in for the bumpy ride to come.'

'But what about Philip? Won't he notice you all gone?'

'Don't worry; the CEO is away on a sales trip to Dubai. We are not under his eye. This is just an informal thing, some sandwiches and coffee – no wine this time. And for safety's sake we will make our way to the room separately, one at time. I think it best we are not seen as a group.'

Justin is still doubtful whether he should be at the meeting at all. 'Well, I hope I can add value to this.'

'Oh, you will, I feel sure. The team trusts you, and you will be there to represent the survey findings you collated.'

'In that case, that sounds like I will be of some practical use. You seem to have this process mapped out on a timeline?'

'Hmm, yes I do, notionally, but we need to take it one step at a time, as I can never be sure what will emerge.'

Justin moves to secure his involvement, amid these provisos. 'Given that, then could we talk about your requirement for me, time-wise, over the next couple of weeks? You seem to have a plan for me. And I do have other commitments.'

'Not to worry about diary clashes,' says Richard, 'we can do this Consignia work with you in the late afternoon, or evenings. I anticipate that the main work we need you for will come in a couple of weeks' time, dependent on how today's meeting goes.'

Justin is glad he asked the question, sighing with relief to know that both of his current jobs will dovetail together, along his suddenly busy timeline. He has a timeline. Who would have thought it? 'Thanks for clearing that up. It all sounds quite do-able. So, what do you have in store for me, then?'

'Well, right this minute, I want you to make your way up the road to the Freemason's Hall, to the Brunel room on the second floor, to await the others. Just tell the greeter on the door that I sent you, it is all booked.'

The welcome from the Freemason's Hall receptionist is courteous, and Justin is relieved to discover that secret handshakes are not a condition of entry. In contrast to the grandeur of the entrance hall, the Brunel Room is small and stuffy, kept at a temperature too warm for this time of year. Casting his eyes around the room, it is clear that this meeting is not only secretive, but also a low budget operation. On a linen-covered table at the back of the room, sandwiches curl under some plastic covers. A coffee urn has, by the sound of it, been bubbling for quite some time. The door creaks, as the team hesitantly trickle in, one by one, checking out who is in the room, while nervously bidding each other a tentative hello, unsure as to how to behave outside of the cocoon of the C suite. Justin observes that subterfuge is clearly new territory for them.

With the gathering all assembled, Richard moves to open the meeting. 'Welcome, colleagues all. I do not need to remind you of the need for complete secrecy in all that we discuss. Justin is here by way of representing the report that he has sedulously assembled, and also to provide some external facilitation in what might become a sensitive meeting.'

With that, Richard distributes a copy of Justin's report, then asks him to run through the findings once more. Caught wrong-footed by this, Justin nevertheless does what he can to pull the threads of the report together, reading the executive summary along with the team. They nod solemnly as they are reminded of the gravitas of what is freighted therein.

After a silence, the conversation proceeds in fits and starts, mainly revolving around the awfulness of the CEO, and of his palpable unfitness to govern this important company, which is undoubtedly veering, in their collective view, towards the rocks. Allowing this conversation to run for a while, Richard then pulls it back to say, 'All of these concerns are known, and well stated in the report. There is little doubt that our leader is our major stumbling block. We do not need to keep reminding ourselves of that. What we need to do is to figure what to do about it. We must also not forget that our esteemed leader is not the only problem. Some of the content of the report reflects badly on the rest of us as well, and we need to be alive to that fact. We are not invulnerable, not ironclad in this matter.'

As Justin surveys the room, he notices that jackets are now off among this highly masculine assemblage. Armpits are looking damp, while the equally sweating sandwiches lie hardly eaten in the middle of the table, the ageing coffee turning cold in the barely touched cups. He senses from their uncomfortable shuffling a collective denial of the suggestion that each of them might be implicated in landing the company in its current dire straits.

Richard continues, 'the good news – and mainly why I have called you here - is that I have alerted the chairman and a sympathetic non-executive director to our concerns. This was not difficult to arrange, as the chairman had asked for an informal meeting with me at his club, to air his concerns regarding declining sales figures, and also to talk of his alarm regarding the new strategy. He feels that the timing of the launching of this new strategy, among other things, is quite wrong. The chairman strongly feels that this is a time for market consolidation, a time to keep the shareholders happy: not a time to be sacrificing dividends on an unproven market hunch.'

A sigh of relief circulates around the stuffy room. The Services Director asked if the chair knew of the report, and of this meeting. Richard responds, 'Well he does, but he has no wish to see the report at this stage, for probity's sake, though he was pleased to know that the executive were alert to the same concerns as he, and were planning on contingencies should CEO performance be called into question. He did make it clear, however, that he must not be seen to be in the loop at this stage, as he is not completely sure that the executive team - or even God forbid the Board - are blameless in all of this.'

As alarm spreads around the room at this further implication of complicity, matters of personal survival push to the surface. Some of the executives clearly begin to backtrack – while others voice various versions of the sentiment, 'Having come this far, then we must press on.'

With each pronouncement, each protest, Justin detects that they are sussing each other's stomach for a fight. It does not take long, amid all this conversational tension, for a blame-storm to break out. Justin finds it by no means easy to facilitate across these divides, but with some deft work at the flip chart - as the only disinterested person in the room - a review of alternative plans of action begin to settle.

It is eventually decided that the first step should be that a triumvirate of Richard, the Operations Director and the HR Director should take their collective concerns to the CEO on his return, making it clear that they represent the entire executive. Not only will they take our concerns to the CEO, but also convey concrete ideas as to how recover market position. With this, consternation breaks out once more.

'That is all very well, but don't we need a fall back for when Philip pushes back strongly on this? Which he undoubtedly will. What will you say to him at that point of breakdown, when this rebellion needs to be elevated to the Board? Will you say to Philip that we have the ear of the chairman? He will go ballistic.'

Richard nods that this scenario is quite possible. 'Perhaps he will. But if push comes to shove, then we will reveal that the chairman is behind us.'

'And will you be completely candid with him with regards to the impact of his behaviour on the company?' asks the quizzical IT director.

'Yes, of course we will. We need to take our courage in both hands.' Another voice chimes in with, 'and will you bring up the fact that not only senior managers, but also junior staff have been complaining about him? About how some of our female staff have been deeply offended by his lurid remarks and wandering hands?'

Richard vacillates some. 'Well, we could mention that, though I suggest we keep that information in our back pockets, should the conversation break apart completely. But please don't forget that we, too, have been somewhat culpable in suppressing these accusations of harassment.'

'Well, speak for yourself,' protests the HR director. 'I have pressured all of you to elevate these harassment complaints, but you have pushed me not to take them further. And, even in some cases, you have asked me to pay off the women in question. And you know full well that women talk to each other of such things.' This reminder causes an outbreak of coughing among the downturned heads in the room.

Richard says, 'Yes, that would be a tricky path to follow, best kept back at this stage, though the CEO of course knows of these accusations. Let us get back to our proposals, one of which is to ensure that decision-making is shared by the executive, rather than unilaterally handed down by dictat, as written in our governance charter. Are we all agreed on that? And prepared to act on that basis?' He scans the room, noticing reluctant consent to this principle. 'Then, with that agreed, gentlemen, it is time to return to our offices one by one, before our staff notice we are gone. And I must ask you to leave any notes you might have taken of this meeting on the table before you leave.'

With that, the executive leave in a furtive stream, with the occasional clandestine glance over the shoulder. In a short while, Richard and Justin are left alone in the stuffy room to debrief. Richard reflects, 'Well Justin, I am glad to have called this meeting, but honestly I feel nervous as to the level of true commitment around the table. But Justin, well done. You facilitated the storms really well, and that having you there was really helpful in ensuring some degree of objectivity, amidst all the emotion that was in play. You certainly earned your keep today, and great work at the flip chart.'

Justin is not sure this praise is earned, but then again, he was so unused to praise that it was new ground for him, 'Thanks, but all I did was write down the ideas that were flying around.'

'I think you did far more than that, though the flip chart work was, in itself, really helpful. And at least we had something else to look at, apart from each other. Did you notice how hard they found it to meet each other's eyes?'

'Yes, that was really observable, and probably a symptom of their anxieties.'

Richard fixes Justin with a steady eye. 'Now, no one must ever know of this meeting. I paid for the room myself, and that should be undetectable. Now kindly collect up the various notes on the table and pass them over to me, there's a good man. What I would like from you next is for you to be available for telephone or one-on-one support. You and I need to have another meeting prior to the "gang of three" – as I now call us – show-down with Philip. And the gang of three will probably need some facilitation after that the show down, depending on how things go.'

Happily assenting to this, Justin makes his way down the grand Victorian staircase, feeling to some extent complicit and vulnerable, and anxious regarding the possible consequences of his involvement, despite being reassured that he had done a good job.

Finally, at home alone in his office, Justin tries to put aside the Freemason's experience for a while, to spend his afternoon instead reworking his upcoming presentation for the Chrysalis group entitled, "The State of Coach Education Today," the deadline for which is looming. He reads through his draft, and declares it worthy but boring. Really boring. It needs buzz, it needs zing, it needs to cut and bite. His fingers wander freely across the keyboard.

One way to see the purpose of coach education is to conceive it as a process designed to turn us all into virtual varnishers. We learn only how to shine the top surfaces, while concealing the mess that resides beneath. But, try as we may, we know that we never achieve the mirror-like shine that our educators' model for us. When we add a new layer of concealment, then they overlay it with a more sophisticated gloss. We applaud their sophistry, but collapse a little inside, knowing that the current credential that we are striving so hard to attain - one on top of so many others - is in fact just another false summit."

Pleased with this departure from the dull, he spends the next hour warming to this analogy. He feels sure it will ring bells, if only of alarm, among his elders and betters. Amid a spell of mixed metaphor disentanglement, his phone pings with a friend's request. Joanna. *Wave to your new friend Joanna* demands the phone, telling him to click on a large yellow clown's glove. Clicking on the invite as directed, he then adds a personal message,

Hello there, Joanna. Nice to have you as a friend.
She replies immediately.
Oh good, you are online. How is your afternoon going?
Doing just fine. Been working on a conference paper.
Sounds posh?
No not really, but our chat earlier has been an inspiration
How so?
I have been working on the riff of varnishing that we were playing around with earlier
Oh, so you are polishing the varnishing paper?
Ha Ha. Yes, I am. How is your afternoon?
Not bad. But wasting too much time on the phone with the garage about fixing my car. I swear they have dismantled the whole thing and left it in a corner to rust away.
That might be truer than you think. Happens to the best of us when we trust ourselves to the hands of professionals.
That is true.

You know, it is so different, chatting to you in here. Different to when I
can see your face, or even just hear your voice on the phone. No
clues really, what is going on, on the other side.
I know what you mean. I feel the same. it is nice though.
Oh, yes it really is.
Look sorry Justin, but I am right in the middle of sorting out this car
lark right now. The garage is on the phone. Would it be okay for me to
go offline?
No that is fine. Catch you again soon. x

Justin reads through the texts again, thinking this was not something
that you could do with a phone call. He feels he is getting to know
more about Joanna, as a friend. Seeing her name at the top of the
message trail, he clicks on this to reveal her full profile. Nothing much
in there that he did not already know, though the profile picture is of
the face of a woman younger than he remembers in real life. But that
mild deceit is forgivable. Everyone does that on social media, posting
their best selves. Neither is he surprised to see her children and her
family life perfectly curated for the entire world to see, in the same
fashion as presents his own home life on social media.
He returns to his varnishing paperwork, but the messaging has broken
the flow. He pulls up the profile of Joanna on the screen once more
but gains no fresh insight. He researches further, but her work profile
on LinkedIn tells him little more, except about her education –
commendable – and her declared passion for marketing, which he
knows to be false. He would like to hear more of this husband, Alan,
who appears but little in her curated accounts of life. Ping. As if he
had demanded her for more information on her homelife, here she
was once more.

204

Hi Justin, me again. I was getting bored with this spreadsheet that will not reconcile. You are my chosen distraction.

Oh, hi Joanna, nice to hear from you – again. Got the car sorted?

Well yes, I have for now. They are keeping it in for more tests.

Sounds serious.

Yep. And having to run to back-to-back meetings, to relay and unsuccessfully explain dismal sales news, then returning to stare at these endless spreadsheets that refuse to improve, no matter how much you will them to

Sounds rough. Glad you are breaking off from that for a while.

And you?

Oh, just doodling around with the varnishing thing, but got stuck.

You could stick your varnishing brush in some literary turpentine?

Well I could. But it is a distraction from the sales I am not even beginning to land. Just more bullshit to plough through really

Sorry for the pause. Boss just called me in. '" Joanna, can I borrow you a minute?"

I hate that phrase. As if the loanee has any choice in the matter

Well, he only borrowed me for a bit. I am back to you now. What else you been up to?

Well for one thing – creepy confession time – I did take the time to look at your profile

Oh yes. and?

Lovely pics, and your kids are adorable too.

Happy families eh? That is how it is, and – fess up time here too - I have had a sneak peek at yours. God what am I saying? I hate that expression. But yes, I looked at yours too.

What did you see?

Somewhat the same as mine, but with a different cast of characters.
And your two are adorable. And you wife so pretty too. Lucky you
Quite so .... not always sure she likes me posting pics of her though –
she discourages that.
Hmm – my hubbie too. But changing the subject from the perfection of
our family lives. Thanks for you offer of help on the coaching career
front by the way. I am more than curious to know how you got into
that. how did you get into coaching?
Oh, it is a long story. In fact, as part of my coach training I had to write
up an account where my original impulse to coach came from.
Oh, I bet that is fascinating reading.
I am not sure about that.
Why not let me be the judge. Why not ping it over, if it is not too long. I
will I be gentle with it. With you. Anything other than marketing
brochures.
Well okay but it is strictly private
I know that.
Great! Before I lose courage, I will email it to you. What is your email?
it is jojogo123@gmail.com
Hm, nifty email handle. You will get my email address to save when I
send my writing through.
That would be useful.
Great, I will ping it over now.
Let me see it and I look forward to reading. I might even comment if I
find the time or the words to say. Would that be okay?
Yes, it would – don't be too hard on me though – and please don't
mind the grammar and spelling – not my strong suit.

In a quiet moment, once her work for the day is done - and before she faces the bus ride home - Joanna decides to take before the time to read through Justin's account before hurrying home to her family as normal. It is a source of grief for her that her workday is barely out of her system before she has to face Alan and his tales of his day among the motor parts, the details of which she neither knows nor cares about. Yawl rate sensors, for god sakes. They sound so dull that it is little wonder no one stocks them. She is astonished that anyone in their right mind would want one. Live with the warning lights is her motto. And now her car is broken down, which Alan blames on her negligence, on her failure to heed warnings.

The story of her life, as far as he is concerned. She sighs, then steels herself to text her husband, saying that she in delayed at the office – which is true – and that he will need to take care of the kids. She resists adding, "for once." She then settles to read Justin's musings, quite captivated by his account. It captures her imagination, making her want to respond in freestyle mode to what his writing has provoked inside of her. As she reads through for a second time, she pastes in her own comments, while resisting the wish to match his fluency. She just wants to get it out before she gets in her own way. Once again.

Justin: *Did I harbour any notions back in my youth of how I would wish my life to unfold? As much as I search my memory, no picture emerges of my envisioned destiny. Back then I had no job to go to after university. I was turned down by all of the mainstream graduate recruiters, one by dismal one. The last straw I had to cling to was an offer of postgraduate studies in business at a university down the road, which seemed a defensible way of postponing the inevitable.*

Whatever that might be. I knew for sure that I would not follow in my father's footsteps. He was an accomplished session saxophonist who would play in any idiom that paid, but preferred rock and blues, always infused with jazz influences. He was of little help in directly shaping my destiny, except to say 'Follow your muse, your passion. Do what makes you happy. We all die, not all of us live.'

Joanna writes: Your father sounds like a great man. Maybe it was a good thing that you did not go straight into a standard graduate type job. I know I did, and I am not at all sure it was a good thing. I got into the corporate track early on and have never really left it. It has been comfortable and a good living, but I do sometimes wonder.

Justin: *Looking further back, I think I know why idealistic teenage me had elected to study a joint honours undergraduate in Sociology and Psychology. I was, for reasons I cannot now quite remember, captivated by both subjects, an appetite that was earnestly encouraged by both my left- leaning parents. They were stoutly of the belief that it was up to my generation to carry on the work that they, the baby boomers, had begun: to understand then subvert the underlying structures that keep ownership and control in the hands of the few. What they might not have reckoned with was that while there were job opportunities for sociologists in their day – in academia, in politics, in trade union careers, in alternative journalism. But by the dawn of the Nineties, the time that I began to job search such jobs were long gone, unless you were really prepared to fight for them, and to be prepared to exist on a pittance.*

Joanna: Sounds as though you stumbled on a sense of life purpose quite early on. And that it has never stopped nagging away at you, probably reinforced by what your parents wished for you. That might have felt a burden as much as an inspiring model to follow. My parents – well they were not the opposite of yours, but not far off. Their expectations of me were pretty standard. Good degree, good job, stay on the rails, marry a reliable husband, have children, all of that.

Justin: *When I think of the time when I was leaving university, I wince in embarrassment at the naivety of my youthful, idealistic self. Life was so carefree back then, and though some of my student tribe still keep in touch, the pressures of the passage into adulthood, the endless merry-go-round of getting and spending, then the coming of children, has made it hard for us to maintain enduring friendship. Many of my cohort have followed their Daddy's footsteps into financial careers in the City, while others - including me - remained in Bristol in a variety of incarnations, mainly working in teaching or local government. When this generational detritus do get together, we ruefully describe Bristol as the 'graveyard of ambition'. We gently mock exiled friends now caught up in the melee of a highly competitive commuting life of working in London, living in the depth of Surrey, with extravagant lifestyles to maintain and neighbours to impress.*

Joanna: Hmmm – I sound more like your friends than you – unthinkingly following a conventional path, though I must admit that I did harbour doubts about getting into all of that tram-lined life that I could hardly admit to, even to myself. I did the London thing though, for five years, before the wish to settle, stop partying and have a family drew me to Bristol, when Consignia called.

Justin: *However, when I think of my salary-men friends' smug reflections on their own life choices, in their secure jobs, then their current experience seems far away from the hand to mouth struggle for survival I now feel caught up in as an independent player. They acclaim how 'brave' I have been to have stepped away from the stultification of institutional life, in order to follow my own path. I grind my teeth on hearing this, saying we all create our own hamster wheel, regardless of our occupational positioning, whether it is wage-slave or freelance. They pay this pleading scant regard, perhaps because I am vicariously living for them an alternative breath of freedom on the other side of life's sliding doors. They collectively sigh 'It is all right for Justin.' I never really summons the energy to protest that is not in fact 'all right' for me.*

Joanna: I can just imagine – but I would be saying the same if I were one of them. I do feel the oppression of the hamster wheel and do have an urge to step off. But that step is a hard one to take, with all the fears of losing all you have worked so hard to achieve. Coaching could be a good way to go, though the idea of self-employment terrifies me a bit. My husband is an entrepreneur and some part of me says I need to have a proper job to provide some kind of anchor for the family, while he wheeler deals. Though maybe that is just an excuse for staying where I am.

Justin: Many of my old college friends are now entombed in what some of them term 'bullshit jobs,' jobs that they show little intention of letting go of, despite their persistent complaining at the awfulness of it all. Earlier on, their jobs seemed to offer a degree of freedom and choice, but now they are becoming increasingly involved in roles where they are not only the surveyed, but also the surveyors, if that is a word. They inhabit a world of measurements, of targets, of KPIs, of bogus strategies, of spreadsheets run by algorithms, of hollowed out leaders calling town-hall meetings for all employees; but then go on to do exactly what they had always planned to do in the first place, regardless of their cosmetic shows of engagement and inclusion.

Joanna: Ouch. And again ouch. I know I am in a bullshit job, and it gets worse by the minute. I spend so much time monitoring my staff, and being monitored by others. It is such a squeeze. In fact, it squeezes my soul. And I so hate all those false corporate shindigs. We all cringe at them, inside. Or those with any human feelings do. We know we are being manipulated, coerced.

Justin: *Perhaps my left-leaning idealism rendered me unfit for mainstream work, and it was certainly a factor. But I think this lack of fit was as much to do with my own instinctive recoil from working within structures that demand control and surveillance, allied with rampant reductionism in the design of job roles and work processes. After several years working in Human Resources – the dreaded HR - in a chocolate factory, of all places, I then drifted into another HR role in local government. In both environments my listening skills proved comfortably above my rudimentary attempts at bureaucratic control over staff members: while my empathic tendencies eclipsed my forlorn attempts to treat employees as human capital. When the local authority offered me redundancy terms sufficient to fund my launching a career in coaching, then it felt like a merciful release, a release that Joy was highly supportive of.*

Joanna: You describe it well. And you are inspiring me to do the same. HR at Consignia has relinquished all pretence at working the human side. We are resources, pegs in holes that are forced to fit. So a redundancy pay-out was the thing that propelled you to go out on your own? I think that happens to a lot of people. Maybe I should be looking for a package too, at some point. Sorry, this is about me and it is meant to be my comments on you. But yes, I can see now how your step out happened. Which answers the question I asked in the first place!

You know you sound quite a romantic soul, if I may say, unable right now to find the right channel for that romantic expression. Are you saddened at the loss, perhaps forever, of an early state of being in love that has not been replaced by something else, full of buoyancy and optimism – or might you be seeking to rekindle that giddy sense of falling in love? Not necessarily in love with another person – though goodness knows so many of our contemporaries are going through divorces at this stage in life, seeking to break free – but wanting to fall in love with a project, a sense of purpose that was there before, but is now somehow soiled, damaged? Sounds from what you say that your early socialist ideals, while still dormant, have been – what is the word? – maybe brutalised by harsh reality? And that you had high ideals for this coaching work, which you seem increasingly disillusioned with, from all I hear. And then I hear you beating yourself up for being so naive. And yet, and yet the romantic in you is still seeking, searching, needing an outlet. Would that be correct? I am really aware that I am sticking my neck out here.

This is all pure speculation of course and pardon my intrusion. Which begs the question, where am I in all of this? Writing on at speed before I lose my nerve, I have to ask where do I identify with what you write? Well, yes, I am disillusioned with my work, and with my workplace, and with the whole corporate set-up in financial services. I know full well that if I were to jump ship to another corporate, it would be a temporary relief, only to find myself mired in another version of the same old shit, pardon my French.

Am I locked in a pattern with my husband Alan where neither of us can really express what is in our hearts, in our minds? Do we instead play out the same old conversations that block us even further from opening up? Yes, I worry that we are locked in such a pattern, and I am fearful that we might never find a place through it. We both just end up withdrawing, him seething in his man hut, full of unnamed and unwanted parts, me feeling frustrated, and often just sad. But we have a family, all of the things we need, so why?

And do I feel as if I want to break out? A lot of the time yes. Do I feel some yearning? Do I want to fall in love, fully, overwhelmingly, one more time? Probably, but I also deeply fear and pray that that doesn't happen. Not sure I could stand the pain of the nuclear fall-out. I have quite a number of really unhappy divorced friends who have not found the Holy Grail on a long-term basis. So, the fear of destabilising all that we have worked for is just about greater than the pull of taking a different direction towards something that from a distance looks highly attractive, and that my heart moves towards. God what am I writing here, please keep it utterly private.

I don't know, I just don't know. And I do count my blessings. And what is this thing called happiness we are chasing anyway? Beats me. Maybe the truth is that we need to keep going along our allotted – or chosen – path. I am not always this gloomy you know! I am most of the time quite a cheery, upbeat woman. I love flower shows and proverbial maypole dancing. A high-spirited woman who also feels she could be vulnerable to seeking out new paths that I might later deeply regret.

Look, I need to stop. But I am going to send this back to you immediately before I chicken out. Thanks for sharing – and I know I do not have to say to you that this must never – I was going to say fall into enemy hands – go beyond the two of us. Read, eat, and destroy. In fact, I am not at all sure I want to talk about what I have written just yet. Happy to talk about your amazing piece, but I will let you know if ever want to talk about my responses that seem to have come from nowhere Send Jo, send.

Still lost in reverie, she emails off the document before she deletes the whole confessional thing. Sat in the now empty office, she hopes she done the right thing. Panicking a little, she absently checks her phone. Seeing that Justin is online, she messages to let him know the deed is done.

Hi Justin. It is read. And appreciated. Thanks so much for sharing this it was most stimulating.

Thanks Joanna – I needed a reader anyway, and you were a good spontaneous choice. I don't have much time right now, with the kids, but can chat for a minute, before I feed the flock.

That is okay. I need to go find the bus now the traffic has died down. But it was a great read. And guess what?

What?

After reading, I felt moved to paste in some of my thoughts and reactions to your journal. Hope you don't mind

No not at all. How did your writing come out?

Oh, I dunno. Thoughts about you, thoughts about me, all jumbled up. I have emailed them over. Some of the thoughts scared me a bit, never put them in cold print before. Do keep them completely to yourself. And don't titter!!

Oh yeh, I see the email now. Can't wait to read it. But not straight away. And of course I will share with no one.

Good to know that. No rush. In fact, we don't even have to talk about what is in there, just good background on each other, I guess. And you have prompted me to write freely too. Good practice, this type of writing, if I need to be doing it in my coach training.

Yes, there will be a requirement for reflective practice, as we call it. So glad you got started on this. And glad my sharing prompted it.

Me too. Look you need to get back.

Yes, I do. Turkey Twisters are calling.

Ha Ha. Thanks again, your secrets are safe with me

As are yours with me. Even before I have read them. Unless you are confessing to a murder?

Aww, you are a spoilsport.

Yes indeed. Got to go. The kid's twisters won't fry themselves. And these texting fingers need a rest too, before they land me in hot water, alongside the spuds. x

'Mind out,' says Joy, coming through the door, 'those potatoes are boiling over. I give up. Take your head out of that phone, Justin, and pay attention to feeding our kids!'

'Yes' feed us, feed us!' agrees Adam, 'we are not far from starvation. Look how skinny Amelia looks.'

'I have told you a thousand times not to exaggerate,' ripostes Justin, making use of this diversion to put his phone to silent.

'Who were you chatting to anyway?' inquires Joy, not yet ready for a full-on riff with the children.

'Oh, no one much in particular. Just a coaching colleague. We have been critiquing our written work, prior to submission.'

'Well now,' says Joy, hands on hips, 'let me critique your unwritten parental obligations. I have no idea where you find the time for all this. for all this self-indulgence. Get that food on the table. I have their homework to.... to critique, if not redo altogether.'

215

'Daddy, could you make us critique croquettes? Instead of chatting to your Ponzis?' chirped Amelia. 'I am looking forward to having my own phone and chatting to my friends all day long. Between meals. And during them. Like you do, Daddy.'

'Anyway, Joy,' he says, pecking her on the cheek, 'nice to see you home early.'

'Thanks. It is good to be home. And I have done quite enough hours in that place already this week.' Joy sighs, 'and anyway it is Friday, though that means nothing to most of our shop-floor staff. But I don't even have to think of them for a while. I have whole week's holiday to look forward to. Hallelujah.'

'I am glad to hear that you are taking a break. What a week we have both had,' muses Justin.

'Yes, that is true. Quite dramatic. So, tell me about your most recent confab at that posh hotel?'

She was interested but concerned to hear of the latest developments at Consignia, glad to hear that an invoice would at last be met, but cautionary with regard to him being complicit in all of this plotting, should the coup backfire. Agreeing that they should put aside work concerns until next week, they resolve to have a good time with the children, who seem happy that the conversation between their parents is more amicable than earlier in the week

Together with the children, they plan a trip to Bristol Zoo together, and to enjoy the Harbourside Festival. Inspired by the prospect of these outings, the kids continue to imagine the alternative employment for Justin that these trips might open up, including keeper of the penguin house, or lead singer of a traditional jazz band. The here-and-nowness of all of this playful repartee proves a wonderful antidote to all of the corporate shenanigans that their parents have recently endured.

Joy announces to her family in general that, 'this weekend plan is a timely reminder that we live in a wonderful city, with so much on offer. Let us congratulate ourselves that have done well to stay here in Bristol, and to not to have debunked to a dreary Surrey suburb.'

The normalcy of this familial harmony reassures Justin. He settles in the deep knowledge that their family unit is the most important thing in his life, and in Joy's life too. While work and assignments may come and go, he wants to believe that the strength of this family unit will see them through, come what may. The kid's excitement at the prospect of the school holidays helps lighten things up too.

At the Harbourside Festival they unexpectedly bump into Tony Crocker from Stokes Croft. He is helping run an environmental stall, where the kids get to play with models of climate change onscreen. In this, her first conversation with Tony, Joy is able to do some light mocking of the coaching world, which goes down well with Tony, who takes her jibes in good spirit, even to the extent of building on her put downs. While the two of them grow deeper into conversation, and as the children become absorbed in saving the planet online, Justin is not unhappy to be diverted by the ringing of his phone, announcing that Bert is on the line. Justin moves away from the crowd, towards the Harbourside, to take this call.

Bert asks him how things are going, reminding Justin that he is there to listen at any time. Justin lets him know that this is indeed a good time, and starts by recounting the bare bones of the Consignia saga.

Bert says that he is aware of Consignia's problems: and not surprised to hear that there might be trouble in paradise. He says that they must talk this over in more depth soon, but meanwhile he invites Justin and family to a classic car rally Sunday at Ashton Court, where he will be showing off his beloved Austin Healy 2000. Justin thanks him, saying he will check this kind invitation out with the family, whom he must re-join right now, lest he be accused of working on a holiday weekend.

'Who was that on the phone?' asks a sceptical Joy, leaving Tony to attend to his stall. "Your secret girlfriend?'

'Ha ha, no,' says Justin, putting visions of Joanna to the back of his mind. 'Nothing so thrilling. It was only Bert, asking us to a classic car show at Ashton Court tomorrow. Can't imagine you would want to go, though I thought the kids might.'

Joy surprises him with her reply. 'Oh, no, I would like that. It sounds quite different, and the kids would love it. Well, Adam at least. We could go for a morning's walk across the Downs on the way, the forecast is good. And I would like to run a slide rule over yet another of your new best friends, in the flesh, as it were, as Tony was really good company. I never met Brenda – and it would be good to meet your new supervisor Bert, who, after all, holds your professional life in his hands.'

The following day, the trip to Ashton Court Park goes well, not least because Bert is so welcoming, and lets the kids sit inside the car. They take time to admire not just his silver Austin Healy, but those of his mates too. Bert then promises them a ride at some point in the near future, which really pleases them. There is no coaching shoptalk,

218

and Joy judges that he is really old school, but friendly, and probably harmless. Even better, Joy is pleased that Bert has taken a shine to Justin and was interested in his family life, which was no bad thing, as Brenda never engaged in any way with Justin's wider world.

Bert beams in the sun reflected from his shiny bonnet. 'Look, here's a plan. The show will be over in forty minutes. You two go take a look at some of these other classic beauties, while I give the kids a quick spin. Then come back and I will give Joy a ride too. It would be good to get to know her better, give her a break from the family for a while.'

Justin frowns a little at this. 'Well, those are kind offers, but I am not sure if we have the time.'

'Of course, we do!' retorts Joy. 'It sounds like a great plan. And a chance for me to give my inner Isadora Duncan an airing. Shame I didn't bring a scarf!'

The plan duly agreed, and the excitement building, they saunter around the other fine vehicles, feeling that Bert's Healey has the edge. Returning to their kindly benefactor, Bert duly unstraps the whooping children from the passenger seat – delighted to hear them brim-full of tales of the sensation of speed and danger - before decanting them out into the care of their father, while strapping in Joy for her adventure.

'Look, Justin, this is such a great plan,' says a flushed Joy. 'Why don't you amble back home with the children. I feel sure Bert can drop me off later. He is quite right; I do need to experience something completely different. I am sure I will be in safe hands. And I have time with the kids all next week. This afternoon could be your quality time.'

Doubtfully assenting - and anyway given no space to object - Justin gathers up his exhilarated tribe and heads for home.

'Strap yourself in, old girl,' croons Bert, reaching across her to fiddle with the safety harness. 'Sorry for this, but all a bit fiddly, this harness. There we go. Harnessed without harassment. I am not attempting too much invasion of personal space at this stage,' he grins, 'too early.'

'Better not even think of it,' says Joy, adjusting to the cross-belt digging into her shoulders, and noticing that it is sending her dress in all directions.

At the turn of the key, the Healey emits a lusty roar. Grinning at the Healey's familiar growling, Bert pulls on a pair of string driving gloves, then places a tweed flat cap over his luxurious silver-grey mane. 'What a wonderful sound, eh? Makes me feel alive, all the way through. So, I have you all to myself, what a treat! The world is our oyster. Where would you like to adventure, Joy? I am at your command.'

'Well, that is kind of you. Every girl's dream. Let us not venture too far though, please. I do need to get back for tea though.' She shifts in her seat. 'This strap still does not feel right. Can you?' Bert reaches across to pull the harness closer around Joy's waist. 'Do you want to borrow a headscarf? Or just let the wind blow in your hair?'

'Let the follicles flow freely, please,' she says, shaking her hair forward.

Bert pulls towards the Park gates. 'Joy, I just love driving around in this car, gives me such a thrill. Especially with a beautiful young woman in tow. Bliss.'

'Steady on, Bert. I am a married woman.'

Pulling out of the gates, Bert suggests, 'How about we head out into Somerset, go over towards Failand? Get some speed up and some wheel spin action around the tight corners. Put my reactions to the test. And the car's.'

As they race off, Joy at first braces herself against the swirling wind, but after a while relaxes into settles into the rhythm of the open road. Bert chatters away non-stop as his hands cross on the wheel. She nods good-naturedly at his remarks, without hearing even a half of his banter. All that matter for her is the sensation of the wind in her hair, and the sun on her face,

After some hair-raising action through the tree-lined lanes, Bert pulls to a halt in a deserted woodland car park, spitting out gravel as he spins the back wheels. 'What now?' asks Joy, seriously wondering why they might be stopping in the middle of nowhere, just as she was growing to luxuriate in the ride.

'Sorry old girl, nothing sinister. Just had a warning light come on, is all. Best take a look at what is going on under there. Need to pop up the bonnet.'

Joy refrains from telling him that her own internal warning light flickering away too.

'Oh dear,' says Bert, 'the old girl is getting near to over-heating. And I need to let the engine cool down before I top her up with my back-up supply of water. How about a walk in the woods? You are looking a bit cramped there?'

'A walk? Yes, a good idea. Please release me!'

Bert holds open the low-slung door to assist her out, despite her pleas that she can manage the harness quite well herself. 'To the woods!' cries Bert, dramatically. Joy walks alongside him, enjoying the crunch of the fir cones beneath her feet, and the scent of wild garlic. As Bert continues to chatter away about his car, she quietly hums the "Teddy Bears Picnic."

'Do you get much time out in nature, Joy?'

'No, not much unless you call the Downs nature. Nothing like the isolation out here. We are quite alone.'

'I don't do much of this country palaver either. More of a wine bar man. But good to be in among it.'

Joy leans back, gazing up at the sunlight breaking through the canopy, inspiring Bert to say, 'what a lovely sight, the sun dappling across your face. Justin is lucky to have landed you.'

'Ha ha. But yes, you are quite correct. He is indeed a fortunate man.'

'How long have you two been married?'

'Fifteen years.'

'Oh, a long time. Not bored with it yet?'

'Not at all. Things change week by week, especially with the children of course. Nothing stands still.'

'No, it does not. Even at my age, little seems to stay stable. This your first marriage?' asks Bert.

'Yes of course! First and last is what I am planning for.'

'Was Justin your first proper boyfriend?'

'Bert, that is very personal question – but the answer is no. We met when postgraduates here at Bristol – we clicked immediately and have been together ever since. That is much history as you are going to get out of me. How about you? You still in your first marriage?'

'My first? Good god no! I do not even remember much of my first. I am now on my fifth marriage.' He counts on his fingers. 'At least I think it is my fifth, quite hard to keep up.'

She ignores the innuendo. 'I am sure it is. Really? Five? That is quite a thing. Impressive, I imagine, at least in some people's eyes? Like Hollywood actors.'

'Yes, I am quite proud of my record. Sometimes people try to embarrass me about it. But I am not much afflicted by embarrassment. Congrats on the fifteen years by the way. I have never made it past twelve. Maybe less.'

'Really, never? What happens to make you move on?'

'Well, I have analysed this,' muses Bert. 'And the exit pattern would seem to be when the woman in question hits forty? That is the only common denominator I can discern.'

'Oh my god! Wives coming with a best-before date on the bridal gown? Did the wives get forewarning of this end date, or does the auto ejector seat of the Healey just thrown them high in the sky, far away from planet Bert?'

'Joy! Give me some credit, please. I am never that calculating. It has never been a case of me planning to finish a marriage while at the altar. It just seems that the "gone at forty" pattern has been persistent.'

'I see. Maybe I will give you some credit then. Children?

'No, I've managed to dodge the bullet on that one. Kids were never on the radar, at least not until this fifth time around. Being in your sixties is no barrier to parenthood these days. And I am still really quite active. I mean for playing football in the park and all that.'

'Hmmm' I will take your word for it. So how come these women get into marriage, knowing it might be trade-in time for a younger model once they hit forty?'

'Dunno.' Bert scratches his chin. 'Maybe you should ask them. For reasons beyond my instantaneous magnetic attraction? All I know is that they all seemed up for it, at the time. In fact, very much up for it at the very beginning.'

'Fascinating. So, it wasn't a case of serial blackmail or some such thing? Just one date and they were smitten?'

'Ha ha. Funnily enough, I was with some of the boys down the golf club the other day and one of them was asking this question. "Would you marry someone who slept with you on the first date?" Most of the boys thought this a bad idea. I had to confess that it had happened to me five times – every time. They said no wonder then that my marriages never stick.'

'Now that is too much information. But sociologically interesting.'

'So, you are a scientist? Well, at least my confession is evidence that they all got carried away. So did I, by the way. Perhaps I am an incurable romantic. And you need to know that I have been honourable to each of them. Just as well there have been no kids involved. But those ladies still cost me a fortune month after month, year after year, even given all four are now remarried.'

'Did any of this bevy of wives have serious careers while married to you? Just curious.'

'Hmmm. One did – Celia. Think she was number three. The others didn't feel the need to work. And I liked having them around at home to meet my needs and all of that. Lady in the drawing room, chef in the kitchen. etc. I have forgotten how that ditty goes. Something in the boudoir I think…'

'Did any of them work in your businesses?' asks Joy.

'Oh, the second one did, Rachel. She started out as my bookkeeper, then we got into more personal double entry. What a nightmare. She wasn't any good at keeping the books, but thought she was. So I had to be on her back all the time. Then when we broke up, she blackmailed me with all she knew about the company. I was a bad lad back then, business-wise, but all straightened out now. And I had to pay a fortune for her to hand over the files. All very messy. She was a gorgeous looker though. Feisty redhead.'

'So, was it the business thing that caused the split?'

'No, it was simpler than that. I had an affair with a barmaid. Not good I know, but I did own the pub.'

'I see. An impulse thing … that is quite an argument in mitigation, owning the pub. Did they have things in common, as people, these five, or were they very different?'

'Anything in common, beyond being crazy about me? No, they were all quite different to look at, marvellous variety.'

'But were they different inside? Personality wise?'

'Yes, probably. Never really thought about it. Would you ever consider an affair, been tempted?'

'What a question! Never been asked that before. And no, not even tempted.'

'Oh okay. Just that I have had a few affairs with married women. Marriage does not mean.'

'I am sure you have – but not this one, buster.'

'I was not even suggesting that,' says a miffed Bert, releasing the arm that he has latched onto during the latter part of the walk, 'although I can say there is much to be said about affairs with someone who is married, man or woman. It is time-bound. They go home afterwards, and are not into making long term plans. Works even better when both lovers are married, as long as you don't let the guilt and all the secret plotting get to you.'

'I see where you are coming from,' says a doubtful Joy, 'But not sure I could deal with all that clandestine stuff, or the sense of betrayal that would eat at you after a while. And I would imagine endless conversations about whether either party will pluck up the guts to leave their partner. Must be a terrible merry-go-round to be on.'

'And Justin? Affairs?'

225

'Where did that question come from Bert?' asks Joy, pulling further away from him on the narrow path. 'Is there something you know that I don't?'

'No, not at all. Just curious. No evidence of him leaping at the phone every time it rings, or lost in long text exchanges?'

'No Bert, just no. Can we just drop this subject altogether? The car will have cooled by now, and hopefully too the driver. Shouldn't we be getting back?'

'Yes, we have gone far enough already. I feel heady with all this nature. And with this great conversation.'

As they turn back towards the car park, Joy asks, 'can I ask about you supervisors? You all seem quite different? I mean between you and Brenda for example? You seem very different in kind?'

'Well spotted. Do you know Brenda at all?'

'Brenda? No, not at all,' replies Joy, knowing full well that she cannot disclose details of her top-secret investigative foray. 'Only what I hear of her from Justin. He did not seem too enamoured.'

'I have never met her either, but I know her kind. So rule-bound. The coaching police. They love the power. And all that virtue signalling. Gets on my.... nerves. I do it differently.'

'So I hear. He seems happier with your more relaxed style, Bert.'

'Well, that is good to know. We aim to please. And I have a much wider portfolio than the likes of Brenda. Offer all sorts of help. Including investment advice.'

'I hear that. Must be a useful arrow to have in your quiver.'

'It is! Tell me, what do your parents do? I assume they own half of Gloucestershire, friends of Prince Charles? I ask as they might be interested in investment advice?'

She laughs. 'I doubt it. My dad's forlorn hope is to win the lottery. So, no dice there, unless you want them to risk their meagre state pension?'

He chuckles. 'No not all. I will leave then well alone. Hope they have a lucky break. And no harm in asking, I hope?'

'No none at all. They would be amused that you thought them worthy of investment advice. They are most definitely not "high net worth" individuals. Nor are Justin and me. Nor most of the people we know.'

Back at the car Bert prises open the boot to find the water, then tops up the now cool radiator. Returning to the close the boot, he pulls out a silver hip flask. 'A wee snifter old girl, to settle your nerves for the thrilling ride home?'

Joy looks surprised. 'No, I had better not,' she says, recoiling at the smell of whisky. 'Are you sure you should?'

'Oh, yes, I can handle my drink,' he says, confidently. 'Only lost my licence once. Couldn't even get off on a technicality. Bloody useless lawyer. But alcohol and I have a good relationship. Leastways no wife has ever complained of performance impairment. To quote Churchill, "I have taken more from alcohol than it has taken from me".'

With a wink at Joy, he reaches to strap her in again, breathing whisky over her in the process. He brushes his hands down her hip, his head close to hers. 'Apologies for the greasy hands,' he says playing with the harness buckle.

'Yes, they are greasy. Yuk. Just keep them well away from my frock. And I can manage this harness all by myself, thank you.' She plays with the strap, pulling it tight.

Bert protests, 'oh, but I think it chivalrous to help a lady.'

'I bet … but we are well into the twenty-first century, you know.... Did you not get the email?'

'I do like it when you get angry. Your cheeks flush. Pretty thing that you are.'

'Bert, I have to ask. Are you flirting with me?'

'Me?'

'Yes, you! Who else is there out here, in the middle of nowhere?'

'Am I flirting? Well yes, probably a little. I do enjoy the fission of a little flirting. Makes the world a gayer place. All quite harmless. Makes a girl feel wanted too. Especially if there is little excitement in her life. Life would be duller without it. And you have to play the percentages.'

'The percentages? Is this a betting thing?'

'Sort of. Surely you know the old urban myth? Ask ten girls, strangers in the street, to go to bed with you? Nine might slap you, but least one will say yes.'

'Bert, I will not be putting that myth to test. Either in gender reversal, or as a prospective victim. And besides, I could do with less excitement in my life, not more. Shall we head back? It is time for my family. You know, it has been lovely to be out in the fresh air for a while, getting away from it all. And interesting to get to know a lot more about you. You are a one-off.'

'That is right. Threw away the mould and all of that. But you think you have got to know me? Just scratching the surface old girl. You don't know the half of it.'

'Perhaps that is just as well. Let us go home. Now!' says Joy, enjoying a sense of power over this man, and his beloved car.

The Healey roars off away from the countryside, over the Clifton Suspension Bridge and back into town, waving to passers-by as they go. Joy feels they are staging their own mini-festival of the glories of a freedom-loving motoring age, immortalised in Shell adverts, but now long gone. She could get used to this life.

Joy tries her best to navigate Bert through the streets of Westbury, clearly new territory for this Clifton-bound chap. 'Look, we are getting near the house. Off Westbury Hill.' They wind through the streets at high speed. 'Please slow down, Bert. Stop. Yes, right here. Thanks. Do you want to come in, say goodbye to Justin?'

'No thanks, I need to be off. I think I said goodbye to your lovely little family at the car show. Time to see if wife number five and I can get in the family way ourselves.' Joy rolls her eyes. 'But thanks for putting up with me. It has been a lovely chat. Hope you enjoyed it too!' He pulls his cap more tightly over his brow, then roars off, skidding into a three-point turn in a neighbour's driveway, before powering his way onward, waving as if royalty, to all and sundry, as he disappeared out of exhaust filled view.

Joy staggers towards the door, which Justin opens, to greet her with a hug.

'You were a while! I thought he had abducted you. Either that or wrapped you around a tree.'

Joy smiles, glad to be home. 'No, nothing like that. It was all very Bert like!! Everything you would expect from a Bert burlesque.'

'Such as?' he asks, watching tenderly as his wife tugs at her tangled locks.

'Lots of bragging, checking out my parent's credit worthiness. Hearing about his highly chequered marital history. Leavened with a good dose of suggestive remarks, loads of innuendo. And, of course no need to mention some lightweight flirting.'

'My goodness – sounds like a vintage Bert performance. But hey, he is my supervisor for now, so I have to put up with all of that bullshit too. But not the flirting? How serious was that? Sorry to expose you to his predations.'

'It was only half hearted – I managed to wriggle free during the strapping in process. Only just mind. Then there were the oily hands, and the nauseating whiff of whisky. So close I think I could detect its origin as Glennfiddich. Single malt.'

'Yuk. That is too bad. Was it really that bad?'

'No, it was not that bad at all. Don't to worry. In fact, I have arranged to see him next week… see how far we can take the conversation? Probably to the next level, all safety harnesses loosened, open to anything.'

'Seriously?'

'No, not seriously. Just testing your jealousy levels. At some level it was nice to have a man pay me such close attention. But boundaries, you know, boundaries. He is your supervisor. I can't be too careful, strong though my hormones are running for an older man.'

'You wouldn't have an affair would you, Joy?'

'Funny you should say that. Bert was asking me if you had ever had an affair. He was telling me of the warning signs to look out for…'

'I see,' says Justin. "Do let me know if you start to see any of these flashing lights coming on. Anyway, Bert is my supervisor for now, and I am stuck with him. No need for you to be....'

'Don't worry, I will not stick anywhere near him. I think I need a shower. Anti-Bertdruff shampoo. And try to unknot my hair. I might have taken up his offer of a scarf after all. He is so thoughtful. But I did love the wind in my hair and showing off as his part-time Isadora Duncan. It was a gas.'

Your Custom is Important to Us.

After such a freewheeling weekend, Monday morning arrives in the Rake's household all too soon. Joy has taken the week off to be with the kids as they settle into their holiday routine, while Justin heads for his first day at Magic Carpet, making sure that his suit is nicely pressed, and his pencils sharpened. Joy even sends him off with some sandwiches, saying that the food at Magic Carpet is mainly plain fare, delivered by a woman who is clearly bored with outside catering and instead dreams of a better life beyond the confines of her sweaty van. Joy explains that HR has been intending to change the catering contract for some time, but have had other pressing priorities, like laying people off. "Let them eat cake," is Joy's summary of the situation on the catering front.

The traffic is mercifully light due to the school breaking up, delivering him to the door of the call centre in good time, and in a focussed mood. Dolores is briskness itself, stopping only to comment that she is pleased to see that he is fully lanyarded up with all the correct security passes. She ushers him along the gantry to a small, almost windowless room, empty save for a table and four upright plastic bucket chairs. A fan swirls listlessly in the corner.

'This will be your interview room then. Next door is the management canteen where you will find a kettle and some teabags, some instant coffee. Milk is in the fridge, and do put your own food in there too, should you wish to.'

Squatting together in 'his' room, Dolores shows Justin a copy of his interview schedule, which is pretty compressed, with little room between sessions to gather his thoughts.

She barks, 'So, sixty minutes interview time with each supervisor, more than enough to get to the heart of things. They have all seen the schedule and know why you are here. I would say they are curious and looking forward to your support. If you feel you have any questions for me, then you know where I am, but be aware that I am a really busy person. You will see that I have slotted in a time for us to meet and debrief on Friday morning. Thereafter the time is your own, to write up or whatever. Glad to see you have brought your laptop to take notes, though I would ask you not to use your mobile phone for personal calls. You may know that we have strict rules about that which apply to everyone. No exceptions. Not even me.'

Justin emanates ready compliance. 'Yes, fully understood.'

She continues, 'I do not need to remind you of the confidential nature of all of this. Your interviewees are not allowed to bring documents to you, and you may not take anything out of here at all. That needs to be completely understood.'

'That is understood. But I do plan to have a writing pad in front of me, help sketch out personal transition plans for your people, as a memory jogger from our sessions?'

'Yes, you may do that, but I am not expecting my supervisors to be going out with a summary, or even a game plan under their arms. So, if there is nothing else, let us get to it. I see Jim is your first slot – he is waiting at the door.'

Jim sidles in, looking uncomfortable. 'Oh, so I am your first victim then?'

Justin fears that this is not the best of starts. 'Well, I hope you are not a victim. The agreement with Dolores is that your time here with me really is your time, and what happens between us is confidential. I am not here as a representative of management. As I understand it, Magic Carpet is going through significant strategic change, changes that rely on all front-line supervisors being on-board of those changes.' Even as he mouths these words, Justin cannot help but feel that this not the way to invite someone to open up. But they will have to do for now.

Jim replies, non-commitally, 'Well that is fine then. That is what Dolores said to us. I must say it quite unusual for management to be giving us this kind of personal time. So, what is your first question?'

This request takes Justin by surprise. 'Well, I do not really have a set list of questions. I will go with the flow of the conversation as it emerges,' though he already fears this exchange will prove to be more stultified than flowing.

Jim still needs some reassurance. 'And you are not reporting back then?'

'Well not on individuals, of course, but I will talk to Dolores in general terms as to how I think staff are settling with the new direction.'

'But other than that, we can say what we like then?' asks Jim, looking troubled.

Justin feels a need to break away from this circular checking of confidentiality boundaries. 'Sure, I encourage you to speak whatever is on your mind, as far as you feel safe so to do. You asked for my first question. Well. try this for size. How are things going for you, with this new strategic direction?'

'Oh, they are going fine so far. I am happy with things,' Jim mutters, unconvincingly.

'Nothing you think you need to be doing differently, adjusting too?'

Jim ponders this direct question. 'Well I will be managing less staff, what with this automation and all the rest, but the workload will be the same, that never stops. In fact, it never stops ramping up, week by week. And we do need to live with the redundancy programme.'

Justin expresses surprise. 'The redundancy programme?'

Jim looks incredulous, his faith in this interview process diminishing by the second. 'Don't tell me they didn't tell you about the redundancies? Voluntary at this stage, but not many of our staff want to leave, so I expect some will have to be shown the door. Last in, first out, that sort of thing.'

Justin does his best to recover from this unsettling news of redundancies, which Dolores had kept from him. 'I see, so this only applies at operator level?'

'So they say, but the maths say that there is bound to be lay-offs at our level too.'

Justin does his best to fill the gaps in his palpable ignorance. 'Has this been said? In so many words?'

'Well, not in so many words, but it cannot be otherwise.'

'So, your jobs could be under threat?' asks Justin.

'As I say, no one has said such directly but that is the word on the ground. We thought that was why you have brought in, to help select who stays and who goes?'

'That has never been my brief, but thanks for letting me know of that suspicion. So how do you feel about this implicit threat?' Justin immediately regrets asking this question, noticing that it has only incensed Jim further.

'How do you think I feel? But I need to be careful what I say. "I am happy with things" is my report to you, unless you hear otherwise. And you never know, there might be work for me in the new fully automated section they are building behind the green plastic screening at the end of the building. And don't ask me what they are installing back there, cos I don't have a clue.'

'I see,' says Justin, looking puzzled. 'I thought I had heard that there would always be room for tele-operators alongside of online sales. Isn't that something your customers really like, especially your older customers who are not so online savvy? And I heard from Dolores that the Complaints section would always be voice-to-voice.'

'That is as maybe. But I do not work in Complaints. So, to answer your question, I have no problems with this 'transition' thing you are talking about, as long as I have a job here. What else would you like me to talk about?'

'Well, I am not here to force you to talk about anything. This time is your time. And if you choose to remain silent, or just to leave, then that is your right.'

'And you won't report me for doing that?' asks a disbelieving Jim.

'No, not at all.'

'But it would look wrong if I did not stay for the whole time. Dolores would notice.'

The severity of the Magic Carpet surveillance regime is now dawning upon Justin, right before his eyes. 'It is fine for you to stay. I am not going anywhere.'

'Then do you mind if I do some puzzles, the crossword? I have taken the puzzle page out of the Mirror? I normally try to squeeze a few clues in over my lunch break, take my mind off work.'

'Well, that would be unusual.... but go ahead. It is just fine by me,' says Justin, though not sure if any of this is fine at all. His coach training had not included crossword protocols, but perhaps it should have done. What next? Scrabble?

'And you will not tell anyone that I sat here doing my puzzles?'

'No, I will not. Trust me.' Justin has the strongest sense that his probity is being subject to a series of tests that he is probably failing to satisfy.

With that, Jim scrambles in the pocket of his blue overall jacket, producing the 'Lunch Break Fun' pages. He strokes it flat, then finds a stubby betting shop pencil, which he bites the end of, while pondering the clues.

'And you are sure no one will come in?'

Justin is already growing weary with this endless seeking of reassurance. And this is just the first of many such cycles, he bleakly realises. 'Quite sure.'

'Then maybe you can help me? One down, an autocratic leader, six letters, beginning with D?' Jim scratches his head.

'Despot?' Justin offers.

'Could be. Let me go with that.'

Time passes slowly enough, but they settle into a pattern of Jim sucking his pencil, while asking for help with a clue, until he looks at his watch then rises to go.

'That it then?' Jim asks.

'Yes, that's it. Thanks for your help. You may go in peace.'

Jim needs a final reassurance. 'And your report is that I am happy with everything?'

'There is no report directly attributable to you, but, yes, I do note you are happy.' Even if he does not look happy.

During the course of Justin's long day, the candidates roll in, one after another, in sullen procession. As the day unfolds, it is quite apparent that they have talked to each other as a group, and have decided not to give anything away. All Justin can console himself with is that he is getting paid for a not particularly demanding exercise. He eats his sandwiches alone, in his room, blessing Joy for knowing that he would need sustenance of some kind amid this sterile tedium.

With the clock announcing that his seemingly interminable day is now finally over, Justin heads for home, deeply unsettled by this bizarre day. But he is determined not to push the supervisors' collusive silence, this collective omerta, further than it needs to go. On the way down the gantry, he bumps into Dolores.

'Going okay?' she asks.

'Just fine.' he says, flatly, not wishing to give anything away.

'Good,' she says, clearly not that interested. 'So see you tomorrow. And remember not a word to anyone about what you are finding? Not even Parallelogram at this early stage.'

'Yes, you will see me tomorrow, I look forward to it,' Justin lies, not at all sure that anyone would be that interested in the silences he had to report, unless they were into reading ledgers of nothingness.

At home, the kids are wanting to tell him all about the novelty of their first day of freedom from school, while Joy has clearly enjoyed her liberation from Magic Carpet too. 'Dare I ask how it went? You seem really flat,' she inquires of Justin, solicitously. 'Yes, I am feeling really flat, but as you know I cannot tell all of the details of why that might be. Secrecy and all of that.'

She nods in sympathy. 'Yes, I know. But perhaps you could do something non-verbal to give me a clue? A mime? An interpretive dance?'

'Very funny. I can say that nothing much happened worth reporting, even if I were free to say. Now can we all go for a walk in Blaise Castle please, as agreed this morning? I need some fresh air after being stuck in an airless cabin all day, breathing endless supervisor.'
'Sure, we can – and now at least you know how it feels to be under constant surveillance. I have rejoiced in its absence today. Kids, let us take Daddy out to the woods to build us an appetite, and tell him all about your day on the way.'

Returning back to his fetid interview room the following day, Justin finds that the interviews follow that same pattern of self-censured exchange as the first day, to the point where he is dying slowly inside from lack of human congress. He continues to ask the supervisors some general stuff about their time at Magic Carpet, what jobs they did before this one, what skills they had trained for, but none of these lines of inquiry open up much worth listening to.
It becomes increasingly clear that he is just the cosmetic face of this exercise, smoothing the surface of something deeply unhealthy. He sees Dolores a few times but she is always busy, phone in hand, laptop under her arm, rushing from meeting to meeting; or watching stealthily from her eerie all that is occurring in the hive below, hovering over her drones to spy any indications of slacking, or even worse transgressions, such as the abandoning of a difficult call.
With each interview, he is defeated by his respondents' sullen misery and passive silences, interspersed with expressions of fatalistic resignation. He knows he cannot reach into this chasm unless one of them opens a window into his or her soul, which seems most unlikely. The authentic coach inside of him instinctively aches to touch that buried misery, to allow it to be vocalised, to be released through

conversation. But that is not his brief. And even if he were to allow such release, then he could never truly report back on these darker truths.

He also judges that, should he psychologically prise open up one of his subjects, then he doubted that he would be able to return them back to their world of scrutiny and control, without some kind of temporary patch on their exposed vulnerability. Without such a patch, then he fears the cracks would show, and a personal breakdown would be precipitated, for which he would be to blame. But then he doubts that entry to their inner selves would ever be allowed, no matter how skilful his questioning might be.

He conjectures that these supervisors are too well defended after all their time in this regime, too well armoured to expose their turmoil to him. Besides which, they suspect him to be an agent of management. He senses their pain deeply, but feels powerless to do anything about it, given the crooked deal with Dolores that he has bought into. He just wants the whole thing to be over, and to put these poor people out of their misery.

Nor does it help when, on his return to the sanctuary of his home, he is not able to ventilate to Joy his growing sense of suffocating helplessness.

The interviews and the heaviness of time that these conversations freight begins to eat into his soul. He worries that is catching some of the powerlessness his respondents feel, moving into his own version of automatic pilot.

For his own survival, he does whatever he needs to do to get through the hour, the day. The clock on the wall grinds along ever more slowly, the dull featureless walls beginning to close in. He keeps one eye on the door, seeking the hour of my escape, while beginning to dimly understand the wisdom of the coaching gurus who speak of attending to 'parallel process,' the extent to which your own feelings in the moment reflect the field of the client system, but that insight does not really help. Or does it? It could be something that he shares with Dolores, but only at great risk to his own already fragile credibility. Saying to Dolores, 'Here is what my feelings say about the supervisors' feelings,' could be the final nail in the coffin of his already weakened standing with her.

Aware that he is near breaking point, he is quietly relieved, towards the end of his second day when one of his interviewees, post his banal introductory remarks, says she would rather not say much at all. She has heard that is okay for her just to be quiet. With that, she closes her eyes and falls into a light sleep. Jerking awake, she reflexively pulls out her phone, and then thinks the better if it, guiltily shoving it back in her pocket. She chews gum, while making notes on the back of an order sheet that she has snuck in.

Breaking the silence, she sighs, 'I am really tired. Just tired to the bone. But that is not the company's fault, oh no. It is more the new baby and my husband being out of work, all of the pressures of the other stuff going on in my ordinary life.' Justin is happy to allow this expression, without needless commentary or false reassurance from him.

On day three, by way of contrast, his first candidate begins by saying, 'Tell me about yourself, I am interested to know how someone gets a job like yours. What sort of person do you have to be to get this kind of work? You never know, I might fancy it myself.'

Seeing this at first as a diversionary tactic, he then thinks what is the harm? He is meant to be the cypher here, the mirror. But might it not help the candidate to open up if he were to do some disclosure of his own, on the basis of, "I'll show you mine if you show me yours?" At least such sharing would pass the time better, beyond crosswords and mid-afternoon snoozes.

At first, Justin tries to deflect this inquiry into his line of work. 'Look, this is not about me but…'

His respondent counters, 'Yes, I get that, but it would be good to know more about you. I am curious. Please?'

'Okay then, just to move things along, and if it pleases you, I may as well say something about me. But please make this between us, these sessions are not meant to be two-way. This is meant to be about you, not about me.'

Yet it occurs to Justin, in the moment, that nowhere in his brief does it say that the conversation cannot be about him too: and in fact this might be a way in through the impasse that he has hit in all the other conversational cul-de-sacs he has endured during the week.

Challenged thus, he is not sure, in relating an account of himself, where to start, what to include, what to leave out, but he decides to take his courage in both hands, and to let his narrative flow.

He begins his story at an early point in his life, revealing that he was passionate about the study of society and its many injustices at school, an interest that continued into his university studies.

He confesses that he was quite the radical activist in his day, but that there was no money in it, certainly not enough to get by. He speaks of his time working in a crushingly boring job for the council, where he was a white-collar union rep but then went to the dark side, into the management side, to work in HR. Unexpectedly warming to rendering this account of himself, he grows bolder, saying, 'I thought HR might be about showing concern for the people; the word Human was a clue; but I soon discovered it was about Resources instead, fitting pegs to holes, treating people as units of production.'

'Oh, so what did you do then?' asked his subject, clearly full of interest, and delighted that she had asked him to tell her about hid history.

'Mercifully, I was made redundant from the HR job. It didn't feel like a merciful release at the time, but it was. And management could tell that my heart was not really in it, so I left the Council, to retrain as a coach. My first mentor held deeply person-centred values, the training was great, and I was ready, in a different way, to liberate the workers of the world, meaning workers in the broader sense, all those that are waged, including managers. My mission was to make the workplace habitable for humans, not to turn them into robots.'

'Wow – that must have been quite a shift to make in your own head. So how has that worked out?'

Justin, impressed by her intuitive questioning technique, continues, 'It has been okay but not quite as I imagined, to be honest. I have found that to earn a shilling in this coaching business you still have to compromise. Management still holds the purse strings, unless you want to work for a non-profit organisation, where you make little money. And I cannot rely on my wife to do all the earning.'

This window into Justin's personal life opens up a whole fresh seam of inquiry. 'Oh, what does she do?'

'Well she has stayed in an HR role, but she finds more and more that the role is about separating employees from each other rather than getting them to work together, despite all the rhetoric about corporate missions binding us all together. She is not at all sure that we have ever been "in this together," despite politician's blithe assurances.'

'Poor woman.'

'Well in some senses yes. I agree with you. Poor woman. That summarises her plight concisely. But enough about me – that is my story in a nutshell. And here I am, earning a living on zero hours. I am paid by the hour too, you know. Only as good as my last assignment, and all of those clichés. '

She looks on doubtfully at this plea for sympathy. 'Yes, but at least you are doing posh zero hours. You are not driving a forklift. At least you have your freedom, lots of choice and variety. You might in some ways be stuck in a mousetrap just like the rest of us, but it is a far more comfortable mouse trap, with a better quality of cheese.'

Justin concedes her point. 'Well, that is true enough. The cheese is better, and the traps fewer. However, you must still be aware of them, lest they snap you up.'

At this point, Justin is aware that while he is finding this process of open disclosure to a complete stranger cathartic, he panics at the thought that he has let his kimono slip too far, revealed too much. He feels a need to steady the conversational ship before it goes to ground. 'Look, I think I have said too much. You asked me to open up, you listened well, and I have told you far more than I should've done. Please assure me that this will go no further.'

'Oh, would you like me to sign a non-disclosure agreement on your behalf?' she asks, sarcastically. 'An NDA? Magic Carpet is stuffed with staff who have been forced to sign such things, before being bundled out the door.'

Justin groans. 'No, of course I do not want to tie you up in legalities. I just – just want you to be human, to be decent that is all, in your treatment of all that I shared. Sorry, that came out wrong.'

'Don't worry, I was just playing with you. Your secrets are safe with me. And people do say I am a good listener, get to the heart of things. And it has been fascinating to hear your story, thanks for telling me the whole truth.

'That is quite okay. Glad that you took something from it. Was there something else you wished to say?'

'Yes, there is,' she said. 'It is more about you, I am afraid. I get it that you are compromised in your own way – I can hear the frustration in your voice – just as we in this job are compromised by our situation too. Perhaps compromise is part of the price we all have to pay to keep our personal show on the road. Me and me colleagues came into these jobs with our eyes open. The pay is not bad. And I guess my attitude - our attitude - is that at some level we have all agreed to this compromise. And we need the job badly. So, my official report to you, on the record, is that everything is fine here really; nothing untoward to report.'

'Okay, I have got that,' responds Justin. 'Thanks for listening to my story too. It has helped me in a funny way to blurt out all of that to you. Oh, and look at the time. We are done.'

Justin reflects that this impulsive decision to share more of his life feels like a breakthrough, and it could certainly be a move he might make the next time the conversation flags. While aware that personal disclosure breaks all the conventional coaching rules, he realises afresh that it is worth trying something different when all else is failing – and when the client after all is not a volunteer, but a forced subject. If nothing else, personal sharing beats the hell out of hearing that everything on the floor is just hunky dory.

Buoyed by this partial breakthrough, he feels more refreshed, more alive, as his next candidate proceeds through the door. Meeting the usual passive intransigence and lifted by the new energy the last session has imbued, he decides once again to take some more risks, even to the point of dropping his mask once more.

He tries a different opening gambit. 'So how is your day going, anyway? Tell me all about it. We do not have to stay within any conversational rules.'

'Oh, the usual. Quite a few crises to deal with, but all part of the job. I just get on with it. How about yours? You must know all about our work by now. Must be strange, listening to us lot all day. Are you not getting bored?'

Justin is pleased that this opening has short-circuited for now the usual sparring regarding confidentiality. 'Oh, not at all bored, though to be honest it can get tiring. But dealing with 'interview fatigue' is part of what I am trained for.'

'How do you get trained for this job then?' she asks, showing genuine interest.

Taking this question at face value, Justin decides to tell his unfettered story once again. As he concludes once more with his disenchantment with HR practices, his subject responds, 'Well, that is a lot to take in. listening to this story, you sound quite the freedom fighter. And you do not need me to say that you have taken on quite a task, if your wish is to liberate the workers of Magic Carpet. This company is pretty much set on getting the most out of all of us regardless.'

'So, what would need to happen to make it different then? I think we all know what is wrong, where the power is loaded in favour of the company. What needs to change, and how can it be changed?'

After a silence, his respondent thinks aloud about some tentative ideas as to how the shackles might be loosened - but then towards the end of this speculation she makes the same plea as the others for no report back, beyond the official line that they are getting on fine, and that they are adjusting well to the new regime. However, she does say it was good for them each to be open with each other. She had not been expecting that, and that it was a welcome surprise.

Arriving home from this different sort of a day at the interview wheel, Justin feels more in tune with himself, and with those with whom he has shared his room, than he had on the previous days. Joy picks up on this change, reflecting that he seems different this evening, less defeated. She says,

'Hey, good to see you smiling again. Probably the first time this week. Welcome back to the human race. I know you cannot say too much in detail, but what has changed?'

'Yes, something has changed, thanks for noticing, I feel lightened, somehow. I decided to change tack, to mix it up a bit with the candidates, talked more of myself. It seemed to open doors.'

Joy frowns as she listens. 'That sounds like it is breaking every rule in the coaching toolkit.'

'Yes, it does rather, but these clients are conscripts. They are not in the room under their own free will. I can bend the rules if I choose. And there is nothing in my contract to say that I cannot talk about myself.'

She shakes her head slowly, wondering if her husband will ever show a degree of restraint in his professional dealings. 'Justin, have you gone native? This move could be dangerous. '

'I know, I know, but it is yielding results, even if what I am discovering cannot be reported up the line. But my goodness, doesn't it feel satisfying to be touching the truth, at least. My truth and theirs. Surprising how often the two truths actually met, actually. It proved to be a fascinating process, weaving together our respective stories.'

'I am sure it feels cathartic for both parties, even if a high- risk strategy on your part. The truth does not get much of an airing at Magic Carpet.'

'So I am rapidly learning. But enough of Magic Carpet, lest I say too much. Shall we watch the news, catch up on all that is good in the world?'

'Yes, let us do that,' says Joy, 'but do be careful. I know trouble can come your way when you are feeling bored and boxed in.'

Day four of the interview cycle dawns, a Thursday, finding Justin intent on making the day count. He steps up the two-way sharing approach to his interviews, this time around with more confidence, yielding more surprising results each time. His nagging concerns that he might be being consciously manipulative are allayed by the surety that he is connecting at a more human level, which in itself cannot be doing too much harm. And he is pleased to notice that the candidates are leaving the room more refreshed than when they arrived, quite the opposite to first two days of tedium, when his respondents slumped out the door, probably more resigned that ever to their fate.

His final interviewee of the day is with a supervisor named Glynis Davies. While he anticipates the customary early guardedness from her, Glynis immediately presents herself quite differently from her colleagues. She is clearly agitated, looking over her shoulder as she enters. She is impatient of the social preliminaries, saying, 'Yes I get all of that stuff about this going no further. But is this conversation really, really private?'

Justin reassures her, 'Yes, it is. You can count on that. Nothing gets said outside this room unless you agree to that. If I may say so, you seem quite upset…can you say why? It will go no further than these four walls, but can you say what going on for you?'

Glynis looks over her shoulder at the closed door, inspecting each corner of the ceiling – he guesses for cameras – and then, satisfied that she is in no obvious danger, says in a low, urgent voice, 'Look, I have checked you out with my colleagues that you have already spent time with. They say you are a good guy, and have not pushed them at all to say things that might incriminate them. Believe me, we do talk to each other when we are able, mostly after work. But the thing with me is that the case might well be different. I strongly suspect that I am just about to get fired anyway, so maybe you do need to know that. But on no account let that suspicion be known to anyone else.'

This is all new territory for Justin, his curiosity piqued to a heightened level. 'Don't worry, I won't. So why do you suspect that you are going to get fired?'

Glynis continues, 'Well, you must have noticed some of the dramas breaking out around here? And heard some of the raised voices on the floor?'

Yes, I have,' says Justin, unable to pretend that he is unaware of the febrile atmosphere on the floor. 'And I have speculated what might be behind that, but it is not in my brief to take that speculation any further.' Justin ponders on whether such speculation is off limits, as if he were a presiding judge. After some thought, he determines such conjecture can only be allowed if one of his interviewees brings it up.

Which is now happening. He relays this thought to Glynis, asking her if she is sure if she wishes to raise this.

'Well, I want to bring it up,' confirms Glynis. 'And you have deemed it okay to listen in to me. So, we are on safe ground. I have two people working for me, good people, hard workers. They feel that they are being forced out, forced out because they are seen as troublemakers.'

'Forced out? Not being made redundant then?'

'No! That is not Magic Carpet style. They want to spare every penny, and avoid adverse publicity at all costs. There will inevitably be redundancies, the way the new strategy is going, but the company would rather staff just leave. Anyway, I have stuck up for these two. Repeatedly. And management have accused me of taking sides. Say I am not with the project, not a team player, disloyal to the managerial hand that feeds me. And that, if I carry on like this, then they may have to let go. I have a disciplinary tomorrow, my third, and I think that will be the end for me, dismissed on some sort of trumped-up charge, no doubt. '

That must be scary for you,' reflects Justin, slipping into counselling mode. 'How does it feel, to be under that level of threat?'

Glynis's face screws up in pain. 'Awful. And I feel I will not be the last to suffer in this way. We all think that they want to shut down the call centre altogether, apart from Complaints, which is kind of ring-fenced. And even then they are allocating the unfriendliest of staff to Complaints, to ensure they are less than helpful, if not downright obstructive, with complaining customers. Look, I am unhappy talking about this in here. This room may well be bugged. I would not put that past them.'

With that warning, she scribbles a note, which she pushes over to him, with finger to lips indicating silence, writing, 'Could we talk after work?'

He writes back, on the same slip of paper, 'that would be highly risky for us both,' his rational brain working through all the ways in which he could put an end to this idea that they might meet outside. The use of the catchall term 'inappropriate' springs to mind. But his feelings of compassion for her, his own empathic frustrations with Magic Carpet, fuel a genuine curiosity as to where this may be leading. He finds himself hastily scribbling, 'okay, let us do that,' before he loses courage.

She smiles a relieved smile, writing, 'Salutation Inn tonight 5.45 – you know it?'

He writes in turn, "Yes, I do. But we need to be careful.'

'Yes of course,' she writes, then scurries away, well before her allotted time is up.

Nonplussed by this ending to his day – but resolved to make something of his newly-found courage - he packs away his desk for the day, then makes his way to the pub, knowing it is the last thing he should be doing. But there again he is touched by her trust in him, and feels she will not betray him. Furthermore, the curious inquirer in him feels sure that hearing her out will take him nearer to bottoming what is really going on, far more surely than continuing with another week of constipated interviews.

She has chosen the venue well. The pub is a vast, featureless carvery style set up, with very few customers in. Glynis sits in a quiet dark corner, beckoning him over to sit beside her. She whispers, 'Thank you for coming. I think we are safe here. This place lost its reputation quite a while ago, and there are very few staff to bother us. Look, it is vital that you know what is truly going on back at the call-centre. These floor level outbursts are far more than meets the eye. They are just the tip of iceberg of a campaign being waged against all staff.'

'So, there is more?' asks Justin, pleased to know that his wish for the truth to be uncovered is about to bear fruit.

She says, 'Yes there is much more. Do you think that what is going on there is right? Forcing people out? Stopping supervisors from standing up for their people, people who work hard and have done no wrong?'

'Well, from what I hear, it sounds distinctly wrong.'

Glynis leans in. 'So, I can trust you? I have heard from Sue and a couple of others that you have interviewed that you used to be really pro-union, a bit of an agitator in your time? They think you are as much on our side as management's, but that your hands are tied in your role too? That you are a bit trapped like the rest of us?'

Justin blushes a little. 'Oh, I did not think those private disclosures would spread along the grapevine so soon. But I know that people talk, you cannot stop them. And your recounting does sound a bit black and white - but yes, I am really sympathetic to the predicament you all find yourselves in. Stood in your shoes, I would be agitating in some way, if I were you. You are right, I am with you on this one.'

'Good. So, you have gained some of the trust of my friends, as much as any of us are allowed to be friends in here. So, I ask again, can I trust you? Can WE trust you?'

Justin rather tires of this insistence on trust, but fully understands the fear that lies behind it. 'Well, I hope so. But this can go no further, and this offsite meeting never happened.' He looks around nervously, but the place is still fairly empty. 'What about cameras?'

'Don't worry, I have checked, and there are no cameras in this corner.' Glynis takes a deep breath. 'So, have you heard about the data leaks at all, the collecting of compromising data? '

Justin hesitates. 'I have to say I have, but not from management. And I cannot reveal my sources.' The injunction against ever mouthing the name Bellows rings the loudest of alarm bells in his ears.

A complicit smile crosses her face. 'Good that you have at least a whiff of that. We thought you might have been poking around, following your nose. Well, as I said, I am about to be fired tomorrow, and tied in legal knots, bound by an NDA, never allowed to speak, if I am ever work in this town again.'

'That's bad. '

'Yes, and there is more. There is something that needs to get out. I will be searched tomorrow, my desk will be gone through with a fine toothcomb, maybe even my car. So, I need someone who cares, who knows, who can possibly act, to keep this secret safe.'

At that she pushes a USB stick across the table towards him.

Justin is utterly taken aback. 'Look, what is this?'

'Shush! It is a copy of some data that needs to get out there. I want you to have it. I am desperate here.' She pushes the stick further towards him, for emphasis.

'God, I wish you had not told me what this is. As far as anyone knows you never gave it to me.'

'No, I never did,' avers Glynis. 'I have not told you what is on it, you are safe enough on that score. So far. And we need to be getting out of here soon. I am getting nervous, even though I don't see any cameras in this dark corner.' She shuffles out of the booth, pausing to say, 'Oh, and a word to the wise. The management on site have been getting ever more suspicious, even paranoid. Not just of the shop floor and of us front-line supervisors, but of everyone. Including you, I would guess, because you are good at finding out secrets, even if you never share them. So you need to be watching your back too. Just saying. And I hope to God I have not got you wrong – and I pray that you are not a management spy. But I do sense you are one of the good guys, on the side of right.'

His inner knight in shining armour glows at this, his rescuer preening himself over a good deed done. He knows that the coaching manuals say beware the rescuing impulse. But sometimes, just sometimes, some rescuing is needed, even at risk of falling into the 'drama triangle', where the rescuer ultimately becomes the victim.

'No, I am not a management spy,' Justin assures her. 'But nor can I be your champion, explicitly. But there might be something I can do. Especially if I am shown the door, too… though I do not want that to happen. In the best chemistry experiments, the catalyst never gets consumed,' he says, cryptically, though never quite sure what this aphorism might mean, despite his own company bearing the Catalyst name. Another chemistry test failed, he tells himself, losing concentration for a moment.

'Thanks for that,' says a quizzical Glynis, 'though I am not at all sure what you are on about. Now, we need to leave separately, give it five minutes after I am gone. And thanks so much for meeting me. It is a weight off my chest.'

After his prerequisite wait, he drives home anxiously, disquieted, with a headful of questions, accompanied by no small degree of self-flagellation. Why would she take the risk of leaving this with him? Why did he ever accept the USB? Perhaps she trusts him because she knows his contract is crooked? Either way, the USB burns a hole in his pocket. He knows that he cannot mention this to Joy, for - beyond the fact that she would go ballistic - she would be compromised by association too. Arriving home, he furtively buries the USB in the garage, deep in his little-used toolbox, hoping at some level it might just dissolve, forever.

On his arrival home, he puts a brave face on it, summoning a forced jollity in an attempt to conceal his rising anxiety. 'Well, that is my first week under the Carpet almost over then. It has actually been pretty boring, but I have survived to fight another week. Well at least until the review meeting tomorrow with Dolores.'

Joy is pleased to find him upbeat, while not fully trusting the bright and breeziness of it all. 'Well, good luck with that one that. Such reviews are rarely an unalloyed joy.' She occupies herself with preparing the family meal, while he retreats deep into a newspaper, reading the same editorial over and over, with none of it sinking in. His mind can focus on nothing other than the jeopardy lurking in the garage – and a growing fear that during his review meeting, Dolores might somehow have caught wind of his harbouring such incriminating evidence.

Barely able to sleep, with his mind still restless with all that has gone before, Friday morning at the call centre dawns all too soon, to presage Justin's review meeting. Dolores opens proceedings with an unceremonious poke of a finger in this direction, snapping out the question, 'So how is it going then?'

Justin bats this unfriendly opener straight back. 'Just fine thanks, everyone turned up on time. The interviews were productive and …'

He is given no chance to continue, as Dolores interrupts,

'And your conclusions so far?'

'My conclusions, such as they are, is that, as far as I can see, the individual transitions are going fine. It seems like you have it pretty much under control on the shop.' Even as he says this, he knows this tissue-thin truth will not survive for long under her scrutiny.

Dolores ratchets up her scepticism. 'Hmmm. So, they are telling you everything, do you think?'

Justin prepares to offer a defence, in partial mitigation. 'Hmm, it has taken time for me to build the right degree of trust with them. I suspect they might think me an agent of management, and may well be holding back on that account.'

She exhales a raspberry of exasperation. 'For goodness sake! All employees think that of visiting consultants at the outset. It is your job to use your skillset to gain their trust, to get them onside. During my MBA we did countless role plays to do just that, building rapport, putting them at ease, using probing questions. It is consulting 101.'

Justin struggles to maintain his composure. 'Yes, I am well aware of that, and I was indeed deploying those skills. It could well be that is nothing much under the surface to dig up; that they really are okay with the new strategy, with their transitions. You said yourself when you commissioned me that you did not detect any major issues, and that you expected that I would get full cooperation.'

'Yes, I did say that, and it remains broadly true. But we do have a few troublemakers, I have since been learning. And you do not seem to have picked up on that, or the dissent they may have been stirring.'

'I am not sure what you mean,' asserts Justin, knowing precisely what she means. He feels a trap is closing in on him, slowly, inexorably.

'Well, for one thing, I hear that Glynis Davies slipped through the net yesterday, and that you got to talk to her. That should not have happened. We didn't mean you to see her. That was a mistake, an oversight. She should never have been alone with you. We have for this past week or so been assembling a case against her, but we were too busy to remember that she was on your list. But for goodness sake, you should have known.'

Justin feigns innocence. 'How was I to know that she was being investigated? You never gave me an inkling of that. I was simply following your schedule. She was one among a number, and I treated them all the same.'

'Okay, so maybe we should have removed her from your list,' Dolores concedes. 'But things have moved on. We had to fire her this morning for gross misconduct. She had no case to argue back, simply left with her miserable tail between her legs. You sure she did not say anything bad about Magic Carpet? Did she not try to poison your view of us?'

Once more, Justin dissembles. 'No, not really. She seemed agitated, I supposed, seemed like she had other things on her mind. I thought she just wanted to get out of the room, and now I understand she had more pressing things on her mind. Anyway, no harm done to my transition project, given that she is gone.'

Dolores is clearly tiring of this game of cat and coach. 'Okay, so let us set Glynis aside for a moment. So, you have finished week one, one whole long week, and you are telling me that it is all going fine? I mean are you quite sure? We are picking up on signs of covert resistance going on, encouraging working to rule, and probably falsifying worksheets? You are not upwind of any of this?'

Trying to stay calm in the face of this barrage, he reminds her, 'you never mentioned this suspicion of resistance to me before.'

'No, we did not want to contaminate your views. But the supervisors must have been telling you about this?'

'No, they honestly have not,' Justin says, trying his best to put to the back of mind Glynis's revelations.

'Are you sure? Are you not picking up on all of this underground activity? Are you colluding with them, even feeding them ideas?'

'No, how fanciful!' retorts an indignant Justin. 'What sorts of ideas? Where did you get that from?' His deepest fears that she is now onto him are now confirmed.

'Walls have ears. So, you say you are not colluding?' Dolores asks.

'No not at all, I have behaved professionally, ethically.' He swallows as he says this. 'I have shown a degree of empathic listening, which as you say is part of the skill-set. But there is nothing too serious coming out of the woodwork, just the usual grumbles that you might expect about work, nothing more. And it is my job to listen sensitively, to be there for them.'

She runs her summary of his innocuous findings past him once again.

'So, they seem reconciled to the change, by and large?'

'Yes, I would say so. Not all love it of course, but then few people do automatically embrace change.' As he says this, he realises he is getting nowhere.

'And the redundancies? What do they have to say about those?'

'They did mention redundancies yes, in passing. And that was the first I had heard of it. In fact, it would have been helpful to have known about this beforehand. I really wish you had informed me.'

'That information was withheld deliberately,' Dolores reveals. 'I just wanted to see if it came up. And it did. Okay, so who mentioned the redundancies then?'

'You know I cannot say specifically, but a few did mention it. I would have been surprised if they had not. But they seemed reconciled to it – it seemed like something they were anticipating.'

'Hmm. Did you pick any evidence of any kind of a collective conspiracy against management?'

'No, not at all. No inkling of that whatsoever,' replies Justin.

'Are you sure they were fully cooperating with you, telling you everything?

'Yes, as I have said before, I am sure they were cooperative, if not fully disclosing.'

'I see. But you know what? Gloves off here. Much of what you are reporting back feels like a whitewash to me,' says Dolores, fixing him with a stare.

'We are only in week one!'

'Yes, well you have one more week to come up with something more than this blanket, "everything is okay, nothing to see here" assurances. I need you to probe harder, or else I may decide to pull the plug. How can I fully support their transitions if you are giving me nothing to go on to know how best to support them? I care for these people!'

He is dumbfounded by this display of brazen ingenuousness. 'I do feel that I am gaining their trust, and more might come out from the second round of interviews.'

'Oh, so they have they asked for more of you?'

'One or two have, yes.'

'So, you were pushing for more time?'

'Well no - we all knew that a second round of conversations was in the contract …'

Dolores shrugs, dismissively. 'Well, it does not surprise me that they have asked for more time, on my nickel, if only to have an hour off their proper duties. You know, I think I will ask them directly if you are doing any good, before we extend your contract to the second phase.

But at this point in time, I am not happy this is a good investment of my time and money. If what you are saying is true - that they are all happy with the change – then why should I need you? But let that pass. Can confirm that, from the supervisors' perspective, the transition is on track? And that I can pass that message up the line to my executive?'

'I think you can, though at this early stage that might be premature,' says Justin, all caution. 'We did agree to an interim report only after phase one was complete.'

'That is by the by,' scoff Dolores. 'The reason for you being here at all is to show good intent, to demonstrate that we are doing the right thing in supporting our people. I now I wonder if this exercise was a mistake.' She ponders for a moment. 'I was talked into this exercise by HR, then by the hard sell from those charmers at Parallelogram. I need you to find something more; something gritty I can get my teeth into. Let me think this over, and we will see you next week. But be aware that I am not happy with the way it is going. I am now committed to asking some questions myself of the supervisors, to find out what has been gone on in that room, while the long hours have passed by. That is all for now. Have a good weekend.'

Justin's walk across the Magic Carpet car park is a slow thoughtful one, suffuse with the sensation that his time with Magic Carpet is probably up. The feeling is a mixed one. He knows that there is little pleasing Dolores, and he knows he would hate to work for her directly. She is never in the wrong; everything that goes wrong gets turned on the nearest person in her firing line. He is not altogether upset to be threatened with termination, but nevertheless feels somewhat irked to have been manipulated like this. In fact, the experience of the whole week has shaken him.

Knowing what he knows now, he asks himself why he was so keen to get into highly commercial coaching work in the first place, given that he is now realising, painfully, the compromises and tricky traps that are freighted within.

He muses that he could just drive away for Magic Carpet forever, but what of his reputation with Parallelogram being terminally damaged at this early stage? A sense of defeat begins to seep up through the floor well of the Prius. Why did he ever listen to Glynis, never mind meet with her offsite? Banging the steering wheel in a vain attempt to discharge this feeling of having been trapped, his phone, now liberated from Magic Carpet purdah, rings out. He prays that this might be a friendly voice, to vent his frustrations onto.

His screen announces an 'Unknown Number.' What now, ponders Justin? An unwanted sales call? He will give them short shrift, let them be at the receiving end of his ire. He feels sure they are used to copping flak. Let someone else be the 'nearest safe object' for him to dump on, just for a change. But then he knows that his heart is rarely set on wishing to dump on anyone at any time, no matter what the provocation.

'Hello, is that Justin Drake?' asks a level, official-sounding male voice. From the tone, he senses that this may not be the person to offload his frustrations upon.

'Yes, it is. Whom may I ask is speaking please?'

'Yes, of course. This is James Abercrombie speaking, solicitor, acting on behalf of Consignia.' Justin sits bolt upright, putting his Magic Carpet woes to one side for a moment, to listen intently.

'Oh yes, good morning, how may I help you?'

'Well, we are led to believe that you have been acting as a coach and consultant to the Bristol executive team?' the tone of this stranger, measured, clearing following a pre-planned line of questioning.

'Yes, that is correct,' confirms Justin, who holds his breath, knowing that there is no room here for any casual, giveaway remarks.

'Thank you for confirming that fact. We need to talk to you regarding your engagement with our client. It has come to our attention that you may have been involved in some – how shall we say? – irregular activities with some of our executive team members. Activities that are not quite within your contract as we read it?'

'I see,' responds Justin, every part of him tightening. 'And the purpose of this call is?'

'Really, there is nothing to be alarmed about,' says James, his voice smooth as silk. 'Just one or two matters have come to our notice that we would like to resolve informally, rather than getting into any form of litigation at this precise moment. We would like you, if you would so kind, to drop into our offices to talk this over? Nip it in the bud, so to speak.'

'I see, well I have no objection to that,' breathes Justin, trying to match his inquisitor's level tone, while harbouring every visceral, yet unspoken objection in the world. He seeks to establish just how shaky the ground on which is barely standing is. 'Do I need my own lawyer?' He essays, fully aware that he has no such legal representative, but wanting to sound as though this is all quite regular business-as-usual for him. But he does his best to channel his inner Bert. Or Tarquin. Abercrombie oozes surprise at this defensive over-reaction. 'Well no, not at this stage, unless you insist. We just wish to resolve matters as informally and as swiftly as possible. In fact, would you be free this afternoon, rather than have this matter hang over both of us over the weekend? I feel sure it is nothing to worry about, perhaps just a misunderstanding that we can clear up quite quickly.'

'I see no reason why not, I have nothing to hide,' Justin replies, while fully aware that his every recent act of complicity is pressing at the back of his tightening throat. 'I suppose we may as well get this dealt with, whatever it may be, then get on with our lives. Where will I find you?'

'I am glad you can make it this afternoon. That would work perfectly. Rather than come into town, why not come into our Knowle office? It is a more informal setting and beats parking problems. I trust Knowle is not too far out of your way?'

'No, Knowle should be fine,' Justin says, while thinking that it in reality it is a significant diversion. But he surmises that it would be preferable to meeting them in some swanky, intimidating office complex in the city centre.

'Good. We are on the Wells Road, on Knowle Broadway, just above Lloyds Bank. You can park right outside.'

'Oh yes, I know that location. Yes, I think I can make that. What time do you suggest? And do I need to bring anything?' he asks, not sure anyway of what it is that he might bring along, besides a noose.

'Can you make two o'clock? And no need to bring anything along, just yourself.'

'Yes, that would work.'

'Splendid. See you then. Just ring the bell and ask for James Abercrombie, of Abercrombie and Stills. We look forward to a productive conversation.'

Befuddled and bemused at this turn of events – and still struggling to deal with the undertow of Dolores's hostility and implicit accusations -

Justin's first instinct is to ring Joy. But he knows she has taken the children to the movies with some friends, and for a happy meal afterwards out at Cribbs Causeway. Besides which, she has quite enough on her hands, after a week of non-stop excitement with the children and their friends, without her husband bringing her down with yet more work dramas – all of his own making, or so she would believe. After all, she has been counselling caution all along, while he has been reckless, so he knows he has it coming, unless he finds a way to wriggle out of this tight spot.

He takes the Bristol Ring Road towards Keynsham - that place memorable only for the fact that no one can spell it - then winds his way up through Brislington with its interminable traffic jams, towards Knowle. At the bottom of the Bath road, feeling too preoccupied to drive safely - and somewhat early for his meeting with destiny - he pulls into the Arnos Manor Hotel for some lunch, hoping to collect his thoughts, and to deal with the rising panic in his stomach.

The hotel is mercifully empty, even of a staff member to offer him lunch. Eventually someone appears, to say they only have sandwiches and chips. Happy to settle for this, he begins to run a movie as to what Abercrombie might want to talk about. At his last meeting with Richard he remembers mentioning some subterfuge regarding his new contract, and of the need to keep below the radar of Legal. Perhaps Legal had caught up this attempt to sideline them, and wanted to thrash this out in person?

He tries to ring Richard to find out what he might know, but his phone goes immediately to voicemail. He leaves a garbled message, then a following text, asking Richard to contact him asap if there was anything he needs to know, in order to prepare him for this most unwanted of encounters. He realises that he has not heard from

Richard for a week or so. But then the monies owing had been paid into his account, and he was assuming from that that all was in order with the planned executive team putsch.

Still not sure of what this meeting might be about, he submits to a mood of fatalistic resignation.

With the clock ticking by, he pushes the flaccid chips to one side, alongside of the crusts of stale sandwich and the caustic coffee, then makes his way up the hill to Knowle. With his emotions already high from the recent Magic Carpet turn of events, he cannot help but feel that the forthcoming event will spike his remorse levels to an all-time peak.

The Knowle office looks quite unprepossessing, the neglected door seemingly little used. He feels sure that Abercrombie and Still's city centre office are far more prestigious. James himself answers the door, a tall, imperious looking gent in an understated grey suit. He offers his business card, then ushers Justin into a back room, apologising, 'I will be with you shortly, sorry, but I have something urgent to attend to.'

Time passes, but no James. Justin thinks of trying the door but decides that might seem to be a little desperate. Eventually, after a seemingly endless delay, James reappears clutching a large buff file in his hands. Talking a seat across the bare table, he lays down the file, saying, 'Sorry about the delay. Now let us get down to business. You are Justin Talbot? Of Catalyst Coaching? Would that be right?'

'Yes,' Justin replies, drained of emotion.

'Do you have any proof of identification? I do have to ask, for data protection purposes.'

'Yes, I understand,' Justin says, somewhat reluctantly fishing in his wallet, eventually to offer his driving licence.

'Thanks,' James says, 'that looks all in order. If you don't mind, I must take a photocopy of this, won't be a moment.' He exits, leaving Justin alone once more with his thoughts, the room seeming emptier by the minute. He could have sworn that he could hear the door locking as he departed, but he could have mistaken, just a symptom of his growing paranoia. He is more than curious to know what is contained in the buff file, just out of arms reach across the table, but a cautionary voice inside warns him to not even think of peeping at the contents. On return, James apologises once again for the delay – 'Problems with the photocopier,' then brusquely returns the plastic licence across the table, saying, 'so, these formalities over, let us cut to the chase here. I am given to understand that you were asked by the CEO of Consignia to provide consulting services to the CEO and his executive team, would that be correct? And that you have subsequently prepared and presented a report of your summary findings to the CEO and his team?'

'That would be correct,' says Justin, deciding to fall into the lexicon of the many legal dramas he has watched on TV, while never dreaming that he would ever need to recourse to such phrasing.

'I am also given to understand that, post the delivery of your report, you have met on several occasions with the Finance Director Richard Finch and members of the executive team – latterly at the Freemasons Hall?'

'Correct.... but wait, where is this heading?' asks Justin, knowing exactly where this was headed. Into hot, hot water.

'Let me finish. I put it to you that at these meetings you conspired with the executive team not only to undermine the authorised business strategy, but that you also conspired to remove the CEO, based on the evidence contained in your report?'

'No!' Justin protests, 'that is not the case. Absolutely not the case. I was invited by Richard to support him. He had no confidence in the CEO … and the CEO fired me and sent me packing.... believe me, Richard was sympathetic towards the treatment meted to me. And he asked me to help; it was not me pleading with him.'

'We have no evidence of the CEO firing you, as you say. This is pure hearsay, a self-serving confection of yours and yours alone. The CEO was simply waiting for you to come back to him to plan next steps with the team. But he is clear that you left the room before he could finish speaking to you, and that he has never heard from you again. Instead of continuing the dialogue with him, you chose to undermine him: and then you explicitly encouraged a coup on behalf of the team.'

'That is simply not true. He fired me. Summarily. Then Richard hired me separately, to continue my developmental work through him.'

Justin is growing the realisation that his version of events – which he used to know as the truth – will never stand up, in the face of executive denial.

'I am afraid we have no record of any of the events you describe. We are aware that you put an unsigned contract in front of Richard Finch, which he duly, and professionally, ignored, as it was usurping your original gentleman's agreement with the CEO.'

'But the CEO refused to sign off the original contract,' Justin blurted, feeling, for the second time today, trapped in a corner that he has no chance of escaping from.

'The sole reason that the original contract was unsigned was because you walked away, to seek a separate deal with Richard Finch. Furthermore, we are aware that you were paid in full for this original work, as evidenced by this bank statement.' He lays the statement in front of Justin, then continues,

'Your efforts were rewarded in full, without demur. Given that payment, there was no need for the contract to be signed retrospectively. You acknowledge that you were duly paid?'

'Yes, I was paid recently,' Justin sighs, feeling wrapped up in knots.

'But then, even though you were paid, you took it upon yourself to attempt to destabilise the entire enterprise, bringing the company and its chief officer into disrepute. In short, I put it to you that you were singlehandedly attempting to damage the good name of the company and furthermore to urge removal of the CEO by underhand means.'

'But the chairman?' pleads Justin. 'The chairman had full knowledge of my report, of this action by the executive!'

James raises his trimmed eyebrows to the sky. 'The chairman? What about him? I suggest that you are now clutching at straws. Were you seeking to undermine the chairman too?'

'No, of course not. I have never met him,' Justin sighs, realising that at this point that he has nowhere to go.

'Have you any evidence to disprove any of this?'

Justin splutters, 'What about Richard, the meetings I had with him, the contract he was prepared to sign....'

'Yes, we are aware he is not entirely innocent in these matters. But you misguidedly influenced him at that time. His actions are subject to a separate inquiry, and until such time as they are resolved he is suspended on full pay. As far as we are concerned, he remains an employee. Have you made any attempts to contact him of late?'

'No, not for a week. Well, no, hang on. I rang him this morning, after you summoned me. He did not pick up. I only wanted to see if he knew what was going on.' Justin is painfully aware that the corner he is getting backed into grows tighter by the minute.

'May I see your mobile phone please?' asks James. 'It would be in your own best interests to unlock it and let me see the call register. If not now, then we could demand that this action should this go to criminal court, then your phone records would be required to be produced by your provider.'

Reluctantly, Justin hands over his phone, duly unlocked, for James to discover the clear evidence that he had been trying to get in touch with Richard, as recently as today.

'So, yes, I see you called today, though, as you say, he did not pick up. Very wise of him I would say. Were you looking once more to draw him into your web?'

'No, I just wanted to ask what this meeting with you was about.'

'So, you were looking to cover your tracks.'

'Not at all. Simply seeking information. But the new contract?'

'The unsigned contract you were forcing on him?' James clarifies. Justin collapses inside. He is wanting to say, 'fair cop' but instead barely whispers, 'so what now?'

'Well, we are very much afraid that the evidence we have laid in front of you here is extremely damaging, and as far as I can see, totally undefended. The likelihood is that we will be suing you for this despicable attempt to bring this highly respectable company into disrepute. Consequently, we shall be seeking significant damages commensurate with the gravity of your misdemeanours.'

Justin lets this sink in. He cannot face financial damages, not with the state of his finances. The house would have to go, the car, the pension, the children's lunches.

'We also need to know who else was conspiring with you in this endeavour? Consignia's competitors' perhaps? Radical anti-capitalist groups? Never fear. Once we hand this case over to the Criminal

Prosecution Services, they will track down all of your fellow co-conspirators. They will also discover if you were seeking to blackmail us, with the commercially sensitive information you have surreptitiously acquired.'

'Look, these accusations have gone far enough. At this point I need to seek legal representation,' his mind scrambling as to where he might seek such a thing.

'That is your right, of course.'

'And I will report how I was inveigled here under false pretences?' insinuates Justin, seeking any sort of finger-hold that might gain him leverage.

'You may make that claim. But all we know is that you came here voluntarily, of your own free will, in full knowledge of the nature of this conversation. But why not call your lawyer now?'

'I will,' Justin says, with no knowledge of where he might turn to find a lawyer he could trust, to defend the indefensible. But then for all he knew, that was a major part of a lawyer's job.

'Please do that. Meanwhile, if you do not mind, I must step outside for a moment and consult with my client Consignia as to next steps. You are free to go but I strongly advise that you wait to hear the outcome of that conversation.'

With that James disappears, leaving Justin scratching his head as to how to find a lawyer at this notice. Google would not cut it at this stage. A light bulb goes off. Bert! If anyone might know a way out of this circle of hell, then Bert would. Justin rings him, and mercifully Bert picks up.

Bert exudes his customary bluff affability. 'Hello old boy, you were lucky to catch me. I am at the Bristol and Clifton Golf Club, having a quick livener before going out to play in the Rugby Old Boys annual golf competition. Foursomes. How might I be of help?' Realising he has little time, Justin blurts out the bare bones of this sorry incarceration at the solicitor's office.

Bert ruminates, audibly. 'Well old chap, I hate to say, "I told you so", but my gut rumbled the minute you told me about this rum set up with Consignia, the last time we spoke.'

'I know I know. I should have listened to you then. But do you have a lawyer – do I need a lawyer? What should I do?'

Bert needs to know more before they proceed. In Bert's book, lawyers are the last line of defence. 'Do you actually have any co-conspirators; or are they just making that up to frighten you?'

'No, of course I don't have any conspirators!' says an exasperated Justin.

'Good to hear. And now I need to ask, what is your loyalty to this Richard Finch right now?'

'Good Question. None. Absolutely none. I feel totally betrayed by him.'

Bert is satisfied that he knows all he needs to know now to move towards giving advice. 'Well, in that case I suggest you agree to do all they may ask of you – even if that means shopping Richard – then you get out of there pronto. I know Abercrombie's practice, they are tenacious, and Consignia has really deep pockets. Anything else? It is near my tee time. I think that is the best advice I can give you right now, but it gives you something to go on. Just get out of that room alive, and then assess your position. Bye now, and good luck.'

As the call ends, James re-enters the room. 'I have consulted with my client to give an account of our meeting. It is obvious that we could sue you for massive damages – and even have a case for imprisonment. On the other hand, we know you have little money and could never pay.'

'That is true. And I have a wife and family.' A pleading tone breaks through Justin's attempts at neutral delivery.

James ceases to attempt to contain the scorn rising in his throat.

'Well, perhaps you might have thought about that before embarking on this scurrilous action. Here is what a deal might look like. I am acting here on behalf of the Chairman, not the CEO. We are asking that you are prepared to disclose all you know, under oath, regarding the behaviour of the Financial Director Richard and his fellow executive team members? And we require that you are prepared to stand up in court if needs be and defend those statements.'

'I see,' replies Justin, weighing this offer up. 'But you have to understand that those disclosures were made in confidence. I have ethical standards to uphold, professional standards....'

James had anticipated this ethical plea. 'Yes, we have investigated those standards you claim to represent. We understand you are a member of a professional body, the Coaching Fraternity. We have seen and scrutinised their ethical code of conduct. Did you, as you were required by that code, share those standards and associated complaints procedures with your Consignia client prior to starting work?'

'No, well I didn't think it necessary I ... I forgot...' says Justin, weakening still further in the face of this fresh angle of attack.

'So, you have already betrayed those standards, even as you secured this work. Heaven knows what other parts of the code you have violated since. As far as we read the code, I would say you have wilfully contravened most all of the standards conveyed therein. We are confident on this evidence we have gathered that we could report you to the Coaching Fraternity and have you struck off. So now - are you prepared to tell us all you know? The whole truth and nothing but? I will leave you for a minute to consider your decision.'

With that, he leaves Justin to the empty room again, where Justin is sure that he can hear the sound of a key locking the door once more. He knows that he has nowhere to go. He just wants to escape this makeshift cell before it morphs into a more real imprisonment. He has nothing really to think about, no options left. After what feels like another age, James returns, bearing a document. 'So, what is your decision please?'

With a gulp, Justin finds himself saying, 'That, after due consideration, and consultation with my representative, I am prepared to listen to whatever actions it is that you require.'

'Excellent. We would require you now to look over this document I put in front of you. In it we are prepared to hold back on pressing for damages, and refrain from reporting you to your professional body, on the basis that you sign off this full statement regarding your report, and the behaviour of the executive team members. We also require that, if necessary, you agree to appear in court to testify in line with your statement, the facts surrounding this case. To help things along, and on the basis of what you have told us, we attach a summary statement that you may wish to agree or amend.'

Justin reads over what they have prepared. It is pretty damning of the executive, but mercifully paints him as an innocent party. It lists all of the meeting had, and what occurred therein. This account is painfully accurate, and he has little to add. All he wishes for is to get out of that room. 'That all looks accurate enough to me. I am prepared to sign off on this statement, as long as I am – what is the word – indemnified?'

'Yes, that is the word,' nods James. 'And you are indemnified as long as you speak not a word of this to anyone but we the firm's legal representatives. And it goes without saying that you may never contact anyone in the company ever again'.

'Yes, I understand that. I now know where I stand.'

He is given two copies to sign, then one to take away. Abercrombie shakes his hand then opens the door, indicating his release. Stepping outside, the air on the polluted Wells Road tasted positively alpine compared to the suffocation Justin was experiencing inside that claustrophobic room. Shaking, he nevertheless manages to start up the trusty Prius still sitting outside the Bank, and heads towards home.

Justin hardly notices the drive home from Knowle, but somehow makes it to his front door. He slumps on the sofa, his mind a cacophony of contradictory thoughts and feelings. His worries about Magic Carpet, so vivid just hours before, now fade far in the background. He feels now only relief to have gotten out of that ever-shrinking room alive. But he tells himself that he cannot just sit here, wallowing in self-pity. He needs to do something. The gin bottle on the dresser is tempting him, but perhaps not the best answer, with the family due home soon. Ah yes, a private journal entry might be a way to splurge all of this out of his system, without having to tell the dark truth to a single soul. He begins to clatter on his open keyboard.

It is good to be home and alive to tell the tale, but beyond the immediate relief, my gut still wrenches with the thought that the visceral threat from Consignia is far from over. I run over the movie in my head that I might be required to give witness, in a proper witness box; that my reputation will be dragged through the mud, all pretensions for respectability gone, however innocent, how blameless

I might be painted by the prosecution. As my mind spins, I indulge in an orgy of self- excoriation. How did I ever get into this? Why was I so naïve, so reckless, so unthinking of consequences? How come I ever thought I was on the side of right in the first place, and that some sort of divine justice would prevail? Did I really believe that I was doing the right thing, that I was championing the underdog? Why did I ever trust Richard, whom I may never see again? Do I trust people too much, taken in by an instinct to rescue them? Was I as impeccable in all of this that has occurred as I would like to believe; could I truly paint myself as the victim? Or was I as bad as the rest of them: or if not as bad, then just someone just like them trying to do the best that I can to ensure my own survival? Was I allowing my wish to provide for my family, to prove myself professionally, to supersede all rational judgment, all-natural caution? Was it an ego thing, wanting to prove myself in this grown-up commercial world? It seems to me it was a mix of all of those things, a skein of wool that I was unlikely to untangle for quite some time.

Am I truly out of the woods? Well possibly so, but will this sword of Damocles hang over my head for the rest of my life, forever haunting me? I shudder, involuntarily, at the memory of being trapped in that godforsaken room. I recoil at the prospect of the police hammering at my front door, my home violated, the family seeing my shame, and demanding explanations. The cold realisation dawns that I could have been stripped of everything, my dignity, my practice, forever. In fact, that worst fear may still well be realised.

I am so glad that Joy and the children have not yet returned, a small compensation at a time when all seems to be happening at break-neck speed. I need time to compose myself; to somehow halt my brain spinning; to give me time to rehearse how I might account for my baleful day. But when I run through the story I might tell Joy, and rehearse my not even plausible self- justifications, I feel that there is too much woe to recount, too much badness to share, to not devastate the happiness she must be feeling after a celebratory day out with the children.

Perhaps I just need to swallow this awfulness, to keep it all inside while it settles somewhere: to rest in that place where some account emerges that is less damning than the naked truth. The voice of denial says keep the lid on all of this, to the point where it all goes away, and no one will be any the wiser. Unlikely, but good to let this thought of escape run for a while. Perhaps - just as Joy kept her disciplinary threat from me - I need to just swallow this for a while and eat my guilt and remorse alone. But she will ask about my day. Well, I can talk some of Magic Carpet – but I do not need to talk about Consignia. Hey, she does not even know that they were in touch with me today, so she would be none the wiser. I think I might meditate, but the brain is in too much turmoil. Who can I turn to in my misery? Ring the Samaritans? Or even chat to Bert? Better call Bert. I could try his number, but I know he is busy on the golf course, and I have bothered him enough already today. Hey, but this writing thing has worked. Writing all of this down has not solved anything, but it has helped me sort out my options, few as they are. I feel better for writing it down. I also feel exhausted, quite spent.

Closing the lid of his laptop, he reaches for the gin bottle he denied himself earlier, and pours out a large one, his thoughts and fears dissolving slowly. Having exhausted all of the worst possibilities, and even written them down, he promptly falls asleep on sofa.

He is awakened by the clamour of the children, who shove him along the sofa to tell him all about the movie they had just seen. In fact, not just tell him all, but to rejoice in re-enacting their favourite scenes, saying what fun it was. And, they say, that even better, after the movie they were able to build their own pizzas at the speciality Italian place, Giuliani's, at the Mall.

Amelia senses that her father may be feeling left out of all of this excitement. 'But we missed you, Daddy! Why weren't you with us? How were things at the smelly old Ponzi factory, which you obviously prefer to us?'

Justin is happy to get back the Ponzi riff. Anything to lighten the dire reality of his work life. 'You know it is not like that. I would love to have been with you. But Daddy did have a scary moment at work. He had an encounter with the Queen of the Ponzi's, just as frightening in her own way as any of the characters in this movie you have just watched.'

Adam is impressed by this turn of events. 'What? You met with the Queen Ponzi. What was she like?'

'Well, children I hate to say it, but she was really, really mean. I think she might have been a baby-eater.'

Amelia fears for her father, as well she might, but not for reasons Ponzi related. 'Dad, did the bad, bad Ponzi witch put a spell on you? I bet she did!'

Justin rubs his chin, as if in deep thought, 'you could well be right. I do believe she has those special powers.'

Adam feels the need for a literary reference. 'Daddy, has the Ponzi factory become like Mordor. Is it all dark and cold and slimy?'

'Oh yes, what an exact image. It truly has become Mordor-like.'

Adam has a clear idea of where his father might fit in the story. 'And are you like Gollum the keeper of the Ponzi Ring?'

Justin reaches for his most sonorous tone. 'Yes, quite. Your father is the keeper of the Ring of Truth. The truth that none other in the Ponzi kingdom wishes to hear, for fear it might bring the whole of Mordor tumbling down.'

'We will be hobbits and save you Daddy!' squeals Amelia, for there is nothing she likes better than riding to the rescue. 'Yes, we will, because we have a plan and we have good angels on our side.'

'Well, that is so good to know,' says Justin, smiling at her kindness. 'The sooner the recovery and rescue hobbits arrive, the better.'

Amelia rushes to insert a happy ending to her story before her brother has time to introduce a darker outcome. 'Oh, they will Daddy, they will. The hobbits will come in massive numbers, just like in the movie. The good creatures always win out in the end.'

If only it were that easy, thinks Justin. He tries to riposte her wit, to keep this riff going, but his heart is not in it. Joy, sensing he is down, pauses from fiddling with dishes in the kitchen and dispatches the children upstairs, where they continue to live out the movie in real-time. Noticing that the gin has been sampled at this unusual hour of the day, she asks, solicitously, 'Would you like a refill, while you tell me of your day?'

He says, 'No to the refill, much as I want one, but yes to the sharing of the day. But never mind my gin-soaked miseries. I want to put on record what a fine job you have are doing with the kids, and how much they are enjoying it.'

She nods at this acknowledgement, casting her mind back over the hectic week just gone. 'It has been a pleasure, but exhausting. I mean it has been a different version of exhaustion from work, and far more satisfying, but exhausting all the same. You know, it has been lovely to spend a slug of time with them. But I cannot quite believe, don't really want to believe, that I have to go back to Magic Carpet again, so soon. But a crust must be earned, a deep-stuffed pizza crust. A Ponzi crust even. Never mind, to help relieve the dual pressures of work and family, I have made a plan for kids to go to summer camp next week.'

'Great idea. But can we afford that?'

She shows some irritation that Justin should be challenging her spending choices, when it is she who is the principal wage earner. At least for now.

'Probably not, but that is my decision. The money will work itself out. And it does mean that we could have some evening time alone together. Perhaps we could even go to a movie that does not involve monsters? Then the week after that, your shift with Magic Carpet should be over, and you can collect your ill-gotten gains - then it will be your turn to take the strain with the children for a while.'

'Yes, that sounds like a good plan,' agrees Justin, while not wanting reminded of his impending return to his interview room.

'Good plan though that may be, but it does not sound as though it is uplifting you much. Has Dolores been getting you down?' She asks, tenderly. It touches Justin to hear her tone, while knowing he must lie, or at least conceal, the source of his most recent humiliation from her. However, eager to jump on the topic of Draconian Dolores as the least worst conversational option, he grasps at this opening gambit and says, 'yes, as predicted, Dolores – the One who Must be Obeyed – has been on my case, thoroughly, comprehensively, no stone left unturned; then every remaining stone to be picked up to bombard me with. But hey, I live to fight another day, or at least until Monday.

When she will no doubt be lying in wait - to creep out of her murky lair to gleefully persecute me again.'

Joy recognises this scene all too well. 'You are growing to learn that all managers at Magic Carpet go on specialist sadism training. Some reluctantly. Others, like Dolores, have the personality to enjoy and even revel in the powers bestowed upon them to inflict pain. But it sounds like you survived the stoning?'

Striking a cautionary note, he says, doubtfully, 'Well, I do not think that I am out of the dark woods enclosing Mordor just yet. But only one more week of that before the shackles are removed. Hurrah.'

'Yes, let us hope that we both get through next week unscathed, wishes Joy. 'My turn for a gin now. Fancy some telly?'

While half watching some celebrities being interviewed on the edge of a red sofa, happily promoting their latest books and films, Justin drifts once more into his cave of inner self-torture, while glad not to had to have shared the fuller details of the worst day of his life with his wife.

The rest of the weekend passes in a blur. There are mercifully no more mystery phone calls beckoning Justin to his doom, though he tightens with fear each time the phone rings. They take the children to the Clifton Down to watch balloons soaring high into the heavens with a liberating roar of flame. Justin is happy for his fears to take flight with them, until he notices that Consignia sponsor one of the balloons, while another bears the logo of Magic Carpet. He asks himself if it is possible to experience human exhilaration nowadays, without the hand of the corporates being involved? Must every human impulse to express freedom, to seek escape, be monetised and branded?

Fearful that from their positioning high in the sky, those corporate behemoths are watching his every move – probably everyone's every move – Justin suggests that they head off to the Floating Harbour, then take a ferry down the river to Portishead, to seek a view of the open channel out to sea.

The ferry trip proves an excellent diversion, but an inner cloud still hangs over him, wrecking his sleep and peace of mind. On Sunday morning the parents dispatch their children off to their camp in the Forest of Dean in their jolly, rocking minibus, happily waving them off from the front door.

Sitting in the now miraculously silent kitchen, Joy says, 'Yesterday was a lovely day out. And while I know you have been valiantly jolly for the kid's sake – I sense that you have been far away, elsewhere, with something on your mind that you are not telling me about. Can you speak about it now?'

Justin had feared this moment coming, this moment of reckoning. Does he now find some diversionary tactic, or does he reveal all? Knowing the truth cannot be postponed forever, and with the children away, he decides, on the spur of the moment, to confess all regarding the events of Friday afternoon in the solicitor's office, and to trust that Joy will be merciful.

His story comes out slowly at first, but then all in a rush. She listens intently, absorbing the full implications of what she is hearing. She is appalled to hear of the closed room, but glad to know that her husband escaped, Houdini-like, even if his integrity had been compromised. She expresses surprise, but is glad too, that Bert had come up trumps. In fact, the memory of her escapist ride with Bert in the Healey causes her to smile, innerly imagining Bert coming across full of inventive confidence in a crisis. It was what he was born for.

'So, these coaching supervisors can come in useful after all, for all sorts of nefarious purposes,' reflects Joy. 'Well I say that. I would doubt that Brenda would have been any use at all in the middle of a crisis. In fact, I am sure she would have called the police. You know if you do go to prison, I could always take Bert up on his offer of a date. Only joking.'

Ignoring the Brenda reference, and the Bert wind-up, Justin tells Joy how violated, how criminalised he feels, stripped of respectability, at least in his own eyes, forever. He feels condemned to perpetual disgrace. He apologises to her from the heart, expressing penitence that he should be exposing his family, their good name, and future prosperity, to such avoidable dangers. She is thoughtful. Then, choosing her words carefully, says, 'I should be beating you with this cushion at this stage. I do despair that yet again you have landed yourself in an unholy mess. And I think you now know that you should never have been seduced into complicity by Richard. But what is done is done. The toothpaste is now out of the tube, and cannot be squeezed back in. Not without gooey mess sticking everywhere. There is something I need to say, in mitigation.'

'Go on,' encourages Justin, curious to know what she might be on the verge of spilling out.

Joy pauses, then continues, 'I cannot pontificate from too high a height, given the risks I have run at Magic Carpet, for no really good reason, and with the threats now hanging over me as well as a result. I am in deep water as well as you, and of my own making. We are both outlaws on the run, Butch and Sundance gazing over the ravine at the unreachable torrent raging below. So, tell me. You have clearly been agonising over this since Friday, from all angles. What is the worst that can happen?'

Justin needs no prompting to run over the disaster scenario that he has been unwillingly rehearsing all weekend. 'Hmmm.... that I am dragged into court, my name hits the press, my coaching career besmirched, even if I am presented as the innocent party. No smoke without fire and all that. In fact, the worst is that I, somehow, inadvertently spill the beans to a third party, and then I am hit with colossal damages that we could never repay. At which point I go to prison, and we all starve.'

Joy knows all too well Justin's capacity to confess all, to whomever might listen, engaging a reflex that seems well beyond his control to avoid. 'In which case we need to make sure that you never, ever, spill a single bean, not while you walk this earth, even when the temptation is strong to confess to someone, anyone, of your actions, even when you are old and grey. Agreed? I know only too well your compulsion to blurt the truth, often at the worst possible moment. It is almost like some kind of death wish. Like you did with those Carpet supervisors last week, at God alone knows what subsequent cost.'

'Ouch,' squeaks Justin, acknowledging the baleful truth in all of this. 'Yes, I do solemnly swear to silence for ever more, even to the grave.' His only solace in this is that, for now, Joy does not know of the mortal threat he is under from Dolores.

'And what is the best case?' asks Joy, quietly reaching for a straw to cling to.

Justin is thoughtful, glad of his recent journal entry by way of rehearsal. 'The best case is that this storm is over. That they have simply put the frighteners on me, and I will never hear from them again. That is the best case that I run. All that happens then is that I have lost a dodgy piece of work, at an early point, without getting drawn deeper into the mire. In some senses, this was a lucky escape. How is that for a retrospective justification?'

Joy sucks on her teeth, then pronounces, 'I actually think that it has a ring of truth in it. You know, these corporates have their own well-worn tactics for sorting out their own staff without resort to court. They have certainly sorted out you out all right, knowing you will never bother them again. Job done. Then they turn on their own, altogether bigger fish to fry, such as Richard and his mutinous posse. I would be surprised if you ever hear from them again. In fact, from what you say, I am not sure they had much to go on, in your case, anyway, but they have silenced and side-lined you forever, at little cost and in short shrift, which I guess was their main aim.'

'I do hope you are right. And thank you so much for your support, and for your listening,' smiles Justin, from the heart.

'Indeed. Look, let us put this to one side for the time being. "Cheer up, it may never happen," as they say. Let us do something quite different, while we have this freedom from the kids to enjoy. I know! Let's head down the Old Duke to listen to some jazz. Trigger good memories of your father in his hay-day. The Severn Jazzmen men are clearly a living example of survival against all odds. Come on, it is time for the # 1 bus again, Sunday Service.'

The jazz serves them well by way of immersion in something ancient and enduring, as does a late lunch on the river at the Glass Boat. They drift through the evening in sporadic discussion of the events of the week, before calling it a day and climbing upstairs to bed, though Justin is unable to sleep. His mind swings between relief at his release from the Consignia attack, and anxiety as to what Dolores might deliver up to him tomorrow at the call-centre. He knows the USB is out of the picture, but yet, but yet… He tosses and turns, disturbing

Joy in the process. She strokes his arm, saying, 'do try and get some sleep, Justin. It will all work out. We have been so much of late and lived to tell the tale. The main thing is that you are out of full-time jobs that were stultifying your spirit, and there is nothing now that can stand in our way, given the strength we have found in our shared sense of purpose. Trust me on this, Rake… and get back to sleep.'

*If you enjoyed this novel, then the adventures of Justin and Joy Drake continue in the sequel, Rakes Resurgent (ISBN 29742949R00125), available in Amazon Kindle in either eBook or paperback. Happy onward reading. Should you feel so inclined, then I would really appreciate you leaving any review or comments you may have, no matter how short, on https://www.amazon.co.uk/Nest-Rakes-Daniel-Doherty-ebook/dp/B07T8PY59K/ref=sr_1_*

Printed in Great Britain
by Amazon

32968656R00170